D0818378

FORBIDDEN FEELINGS

She backed away from him, confused by the powerful emotions he aroused in her. He made her feel things she had never felt before, things she couldn't put a name to.

"We can't do this," she said.

"I know."

"My grandmother would never approve. And Charlie—" She shook her head. "It just won't work."

"I know," he said again.

But when he reached for her a second time, she didn't object.

Her lips were soft, pliant, indescribably sweet. He cupped the back of her head in one hand, his fingers delving into her hair. The heat and softness of her breasts pressing against his chest stirred his desire. Strange, he thought, that of all the beautiful, well-dressed women he had met back East, it was a little country girl in a blue gingham dress who fired his imagination and filled him with the most incredible longing he'd ever known.

Madeline Baker

Reckless Embrace

LEISURE BOOKS NEW YORK CITY

A LEISURE BOOK®

October 2002

Published by

Dorchester Publishing Co., Inc.
276 Fifth Avenue
New York, NY 10001

ISBN 0-8439-5080-3

The name "Leisure Books" and the stylized "L" with design are trademarks of Dorchester Publishing Co., Inc.

Printed in the United States of America.

Visit us on the web at www.dorchesterpub.com.

My thanks to Kim Ivora,
who took the journey with me
from the beginning to the end
and encouraged me along the way.

Reckless Embrace

Chapter One

Bear Valley
Summer 1908

I sat in the shade of the front porch watching my seven-year-old son, Daniel Blue Hawk, put a pretty little black-and-white Appaloosa filly through its paces while my husband looked on. He was a handsome boy, my Daniel, with his father's thick black hair and my gray eyes. He had inherited the same natural affinity for horses that was so strong in his father and older brothers, and seemed to be inherent in all Cheyenne males. Like his two older brothers, Blue Hawk had a strong sense of pride in his Indian heritage and because of that, he preferred we call him by his Indian name.

Shadow had promised the filly to Blue Hawk, and

1

my son spent most of his waking hours working with the little mare. He had named her Patches and she followed him around like a puppy. Blue Hawk could hardly wait for the day when the filly would be old enough for him to ride for more than a few minutes at a time. Surprisingly, Blue Hawk liked writing almost as much as riding, and when he wasn't outside with the filly, he was usually in his room making up stories about brave knights and fire-breathing dragons.

As much as I enjoyed watching my son, my gaze kept straying to his father. Two Hawks Flying, known as Shadow to his loved ones, was easily the most handsome man I had ever known. Though Shadow was no longer a young warrior, he was still tall and straight, and strong enough to out-wrestle our two grown sons. Though he had long ago traded his breechclout and feathers for Levi's and a Stetson, he steadfastly refused to wear shoes or boots. His feet were encased in a pair of moccasins I had recently made for him.

Shadow. My whole life was filled with memories of Shadow. I remembered the first time I had seen him. I was nine years old; he was twelve, handsome and arrogant even then. In time, we became friends. He taught me how to hunt and fish and how to skin a deer. They were not pursuits I had cared for, but Shadow thought that girl things were foolish and a waste of time, and he refused to do anything he considered silly or undignified, which was just about everything I wanted to do.

I recalled the day of my sixteenth birthday. It was a turning point in our lives and our relationship. I had not seen Shadow for three years or so, not since he had gone away to concentrate on becoming a warrior, which was the goal of all Cheyenne males.

We met by the river that day, and Shadow was even more handsome than I recalled. He wore only moccasins and the briefest of deerskin clouts, and I had not been able to take my eyes off him. His legs were long and well muscled from years of riding bareback; his belly was hard and flat, ridged with muscle. Two livid scars marred his chest, proof that he had participated in the sacred Medicine Lodge ceremony of his people. A third scar zigzagged down his right shoulder. Like a bird hypnotized by a snake, I was unable to tear my gaze away. I could only stare at him, awed by his proud carriage, completely mesmerized by his appearance. He had truly become a warrior. There was no doubt of that.

We had not said much that day, nor had we spent a great deal of time together, yet I had known that our lives would be intertwined from that day forward. And I had never regretted a day of it. In spite of all the hardship and turmoil we had faced during the early part of our lives together, I would have done it all again. I had a wonderful husband and four children who loved me, and I counted myself a lucky woman.

From time to time I glanced down the road leading up to the house. Our second son, Samuel Black Owl, was due home from the East any day now. We had only seen Blackie once since he'd gone away to college to study veterinary medicine just over three years ago. It had been many years since I had been to the East. It was a place that held few happy memories for me. But we had enjoyed our stay with

Blackie, though it had been shorter than I would have liked.

I had been counting the days ever since then until Blackie would be home once more. I was glad that the rest of my family lived nearby. Our oldest son, True Hawk, and his wife, Victoria, had four sons and two daughters. Hawk had been elected sheriff two years ago when Bill Lancaster retired. Considering that there was still a lot of prejudice in the area against Indians, I considered Hawk's election, if you'll excuse the expression, quite a coup. He had hired Joe Finch as his deputy.

Mary was our second child and our only daughter. She lived with her husband, Cloud Walker, on a horse ranch with their six sons. Mary and Victoria were both pregnant again. After six sons, Mary was hoping for a daughter.

Blue Hawk was our youngest, and spoiled by one and all.

I smiled, thinking of my children and grandchildren. They were all healthy, all beautiful, and all bore the unmistakable stamp of Shadow's Cheyenne blood.

Blue Hawk rode the mare around the corral one last time, then dismounted. He spoke to his father, nodded solemnly as he listened to his father's reply, and then led the filly out of the corral toward the barn.

Shadow stared after Blue Hawk for a few moments, then turned and walked toward me. Once again, every other thought fled my mind as I watched him. He moved effortlessly, like a cougar stalking its prey, the habits of a lifetime ingrained too deeply to change now.

The sunlight moved over him like a lover's caress, casting blue highlights in his waist-length hair, which was still thick and as black as a raven's wing. On this day, he was shirtless. His skin was the color of warm copper. The scars on his chest and shoulder had faded to faint silvery lines that were barely visible now.

"Hannah." He lifted one brow, a half smile playing over his lips as he climbed the stairs, his movements slow and sensual.

I stood and moved into his embrace, my fingertips moving over the powerful muscles in his arms, sliding up to measure the width of his shoulders.

"Do you like what you see, woman?" he asked, a faint note of supremely male arrogance evident in his voice.

"I always have," I replied tartly. And he knew it.

Going up on my tiptoes, I kissed him, then rested my head on his shoulder, happy to spend a few quiet moments in his arms.

And that was how Blackie found us when he rode up a few minutes later.

"I guess some things never change," he drawled.

Startled, I looked up at the sound of the familiar deep male voice. "Blackie!" I exclaimed, and fairly flew down the steps. "You're early. We were supposed to meet you tomorrow morning."

"I know. I got lucky and caught an earlier train."

Dismounting, he wrapped his arms around me. For a moment, I stood there, blinking back my tears, marveling at how much he had filled out since I saw him last. Giving him a squeeze, I backed up a little so I could get a good look at him.

He was tall, Blackie was, taller, even, than his

father. And just as handsome. His hair, still worn long, was tied back at the nape of his neck. His skin was a shade lighter than Shadow's, his eyes a brown so dark as to be almost black. He had broad shoulders, a trim waist, and long, long legs.

I felt the tears trickle down my cheeks as my son turned to embrace his father. They were so alike, it was hard to believe I had once agonized over whether or not Shadow was Blackie's father. I recalled the day Blackie was born.

I had been alone in the house when my labor began. After several hours had passed, I knew something was wrong. No matter how hard I pushed, I could not expel him from my womb. Lying there, I imagined Death all around me. I saw Him watching me through the window, lurking in the corners, waiting, and I was certain I was going to die. And then Shadow came home. Shadow, the other half of my heart, the other half of my soul. His voice stilled my fears and he delivered our son as competently as any doctor could have done. Our eyes met as Shadow held our son in his arms. Unspoken between us hung the question of who was the father, Shadow or Joshua Berdeen. At the time, there had been no way to be certain. But seeing Blackie and Shadow together now, there could be no doubt that Shadow was indeed Blackie's father. Joshua Berdeen could never have sired this son of mine.

I met Shadow's gaze. Was he also remembering the day Blackie had been born? Did he also remember the words he had spoken? I heard them now as clearly as I had heard them that day twenty-three years ago. *It does not matter who fathered the child,*

Shadow had said as he placed the infant in my arms. *From this day forward, he will be my son, and I will be his father.*

Other images flashed through my mind: Blackie learning how to ride a horse, his little legs clinging to the sides of one of our old mares, his chubby little hands grasping the reins as Shadow led the mare around the corral; Shadow teaching our son to hunt, to fish, to read the signs of the seasons, to speak Cheyenne. Blackie had been two years old the day he brought home the first in a long line of injured birds and animals. He had brought a sparrow home that day. Together, we had splinted its broken wing. Blackie had fed it and cared for it and been overjoyed when the bird was able to fly away.

I remembered when Blackie had had diphtheria, and how close we had come to losing him. I had prayed as never before, begging the Lord to spare my child. Shadow added his prayers to mine. Even now, I could see him clearly in my mind's eye, standing outside our house, naked save for a loincloth and moccasins. A single white eagle feather was tied in his hair. There were streaks of black paint on his face and chest. His arms, bronze and thick with muscle, were lifted toward the sky in supplication. A small fire burned at his feet, and as I watched, he sprinkled a handful of sacred yellow pollen into the flames, and then raised his arms over his head once again. I knew he was praying to Man Above in the old and ancient way, and I felt a shiver run down my spine as he called upon the gods of the Cheyenne. His voice, deep and filled with pleading, drifted through the half-open window.

Hear me, Man Above, accept my offering and heal my son. He sprinkled another handful of pollen into the fire, and this time the flames exploded upward like many colored tongues licking at the sky. And then with great deliberation, Shadow took a knife and raked the blade across his chest. A thin ribbon of red oozed from the shallow gash in his flesh.

Hear me, Man Above, he cried again. *Accept my pain and heal my son.*

A wordless cry erupted from Shadow's lips as he again raised his arms toward heaven, and at that moment, the sun climbed over the distant mountains, splashing the clear skies with all the colors of the rainbow.

Blackie's fever began to drop that very day, and by the following afternoon it was almost normal.

And now our son was home again, a man grown.

Blue Hawk came running out of the barn, yelling his brother's name at the top of his lungs.

"Blackie! Blackie!"

"There you are, little brother," Blackie said and lifting Blue Hawk off his feet, he swung him around in a circle.

Blue Hawk's laughter mingled with Blackie's, bringing joy to my heart.

Closing my eyes, I offered a quick prayer of thanks to all the gods, both red and white, for bringing my son safely home.

Chapter Two

Blackie stood with his arms folded across the top rail of the corral. He let out a deep sigh as he gazed into the darkness. It seemed strange to be home again after so long, strange to see so much empty land. The sky seemed bigger here than in the city, the stars brighter, the night quieter.

There had been some changes at home while he'd been away. There was a new icebox in the kitchen, a new bread toaster, even a fancy new stove. A grandfather clock stood in the entry, chiming the hour, the half, and the quarter. His mother had a new Singer sewing machine; there were new curtains in the parlor.

One thing hadn't changed, and that was his parents' obvious affection for one another. He grinned, thinking how right it seemed to come home and find them in each other's arms. As a kid, the affection they had expressed so openly and so often had embarrassed him, but he realized now that the love his parents shared was a rare and wonderful thing, found by only a lucky few. Theirs was a love story that had lasted more than forty years, a devotion so strong it had endured war, separation, and heartache.

Blackie's smile faded. His folks looked older. His mother's hair, always a dark red, had strands of gray in it now. There was no gray in his father's hair, but the years were beginning to show in other ways. Blackie turned his thoughts away, not wanting to think of his parents growing older, of a time when they wouldn't be there. They had always been so vital and full of life. He could not imagine them any other way. Growing up, he had listened in awe to the stories they told. His father had fought at the Little Big Horn and later, when other chiefs surrendered, he had continued to fight, riding the war trail as a renegade. And his mother had ridden at her husband's side. They had known Crazy Horse and Gall and even ridden the war trail with Geronimo. His brother, Hawk, had known Sitting Bull. If only he, himself, had been born sooner, Blackie mused. To be a warrior, to ride into battle, to seek a vision; these were things he had coveted his whole life.

He wondered how Hawk and Mary were doing. His brother and sister had both written to him while he was away, as had Cloud Walker and Victoria. His parents had written too, of course. From time to time he had received mail from his nieces and nephews—a few hastily scribbled lines from the ones old enough to write, colorful pictures from the younger ones, usually with a note of explanation written by Victoria or Mary so he would know that the picture drawn by Cole was a horse, and the red blob drawn by Jared was a picture of his new puppy. He was anxious to see them all, adults and children alike.

Blackie sighed again, wondering if he would ever find a woman to settle down with. Back east, he had met a number of attractive young women. Many had been attracted to him because he was different. They had been fascinated by his dark skin and waist-length hair, by the fact that he was a half-breed and therefore forbidden. And even more fascinated that his father had once been a warrior of some renown. Yes, he had met a lot of women—young, old, pretty, not so pretty—but none had held his interest. And once the novelty of his being an Indian had worn off, he hadn't held their interest either, especially when they learned he was planning to go back home, to a little town none of them had ever heard of. City girls born and raised, they were horrified at the idea of leaving the comforts and society of the East for the "Wild West," and while the West wasn't nearly as wild as it had once been, it was still untamed and primitive by eastern standards.

One of the horses left the others to come and stand at the fence. The colt had been born shortly before Blackie left for the East. "Hi, fella." Blackie scratched the young stallion between the ears. "The old man break you to ride yet?"

"Not yet."

Blackie shook his head as his father materialized out of the darkness. Even after all these years, his father moved soundlessly through the night.

His father tugged on a lock of his hair. "If you were a white man, I would have had your scalp."

Blackie nodded ruefully. If there was one thing he regretted, it was that he had never known what it was like to live in the old way, that he had never had the opportunity to seek a vision.

"It is good to have you home again," Shadow said, moving up beside him.

"It's good to be back."

"Your mother was afraid you might like the city and decide to stay."

"She should know me better than that," Blackie said. "I couldn't stay there. It was too big, too crowded, all those buildings, and people everywhere." He shook his head. "And I would have missed you and *nahkoa*. And the rest of the family."

Shadow grunted softly. "What will you do now?"

"I thought I'd go into town Monday morning and look for a place to set up my office." Blackie shrugged. "I know what you're thinking. You're wondering if any of the valley people will trust me with their animals, but I don't think it will be a problem. I helped Chester Cole and no one seemed to mind." He turned around, leaning his back against the corral. "How is Chester?"

"He retired three months ago and went back east."

"I'm sorry to hear that," Blackie said. He had often accompanied the veterinarian on his rounds, eager to learn everything he could.

"The townspeople may be slow to accept you on your own," Shadow said. "But perhaps not. They trust Hawk to keep the peace, to protect their lives and their property."

"So maybe they'll trust me to look after their horses and cattle?"

"Maybe." Shadow gave his son an affectionate slap on the shoulder. "Only time will tell."

Chapter Three

Sunday afternoon the family gathered to welcome
Blackie home. Sitting at the foot of the dinner table
with Mary's two-year-old son, Jared, on my lap, I let
my gaze settle briefly on each face.

Shadow sat at the head of the table. Our oldest
son, Hawk, sat to his father's right, his badge of office winking in the candlelight. Victoria sat at the
other end of the table. She was a lovely young
woman, with auburn hair and sky blue eyes. Five
of their six children sat between them. The ten-year-
old twins, Jacob and Jason, were as alike as two
peas in a pod. They sat closest to their father.
Amanda Marie, age eight, Aaron, age six, and Cole,
age four, sat with their heads close together, un-
doubtedly planning mischief. Victoria held her
year-old daughter, Samantha, on her lap.

Blackie sat at Shadow's left. My gaze lingered on my son's face. How handsome he was, and how I had missed him.

Mary was seated at Blackie's left. At twenty-nine, she was a beautiful young woman. Her hair was dark brown, her eyes a quiet shade of gray. My Mary. Sweet and even-tempered, cheerful and fun-loving, she had never caused us a moment's trouble. I had named her after my mother, who had been the sweetest, kindest woman I had ever known. I had never known my mother to raise her voice in anger or to say an unkind word, and Mary was just like her. She held her ten-month-old son, Cody, on her lap.

Cloud Walker sat to my right. He was a handsome man, with long black hair, deep-set black eyes, and a faint scar on his left cheek. Their other four sons, Adam, Joel, Linus, and Patrick, ages eight, seven, five, and three respectively, sat between their parents. Blue Hawk sat to my left. It still amazed me that I could have a son the same age as some of my grandchildren. Blue Hawk had truly been a surprise, but a welcome one, once I got over the shock of my pregnancy.

Conversation hummed around the table, punctuated by the merry sound of my grandchildren's laughter.

Looking up, I caught Shadow's eye. He smiled at me, and I knew what he was thinking. Long ago, he'd had a vision wherein he had been promised that our family would have long life and happiness. That vision had been fulfilled, I thought, as I glanced around the table once again. Who would ever have thought that a skinny nine-year-old white girl and a proud twelve-year-old Cheyenne boy would find happiness in such abundance, or grow up to rear such a fine family? I thought of all the challenges we had faced, of those long-ago days when I had ridden the war path at Shadow's side, when death had lurked around every bend in the trail, when we had been hunted like wild animals. I had known Crazy Horse and Sitting Bull, shared in the victory over Custer at the Little Big Horn. Even after all these years, I sometimes heard the men in town discussing that battle, speculating on a hundred what-ifs . . . What would have happened if Custer hadn't split his forces? What if he hadn't left the Gattling guns behind . . . what if he had listened to his scouts when they warned him that there were thousands of Indians in the valley, what if he had followed his orders and waited for Terry and Gibbon? What if, what if . . .

Shadow, Hawk, and I had been at the reservation the day Sitting Bull was killed. Hawk had been wounded, and it had been left to Shadow to cut the bullet out of our son's side. Once again, Shadow had lifted his voice in mighty prayer to *Maheo*, the Great Spirit of the Cheyenne. I could still see him, standing with his arms raised and his head lifted toward the sky, the prairie stretching endlessly behind him as the first rays of the sun lit the sky. I knew it was Shadow's faith that once again restored one of our children to health. *Maheo* must have loved him very much, I thought now.

As young boys, my sons had been eager to hear their father's war stories. They had listened proudly as he told of riding against Custer, of fighting alongside Geronimo. But there was another story we had never told, one that we never spoke of. Long ago, Shadow had been captured by two despicable white men who had locked him in a cage and displayed him like some wild animal. They had billed him as "Two Hawks Flying, the last fighting warrior on the Plains." It was a part of his life we never discussed with our sons, a part of his life we never spoke of.

"So." Hawk leaned back in his chair, his hands folded over his chest as he regarded Blackie. "What are you gonna do now, little brother?"

Blackie lifted one brow. "Little?"

Hawk grimaced at the reminder that Blackie now stood fully two inches taller than he did.

Blackie grinned. "I spent three years learning how to be a vet," he said. "And that's what I aim to do." He had hoped to go to Harvard or the Veterinary College in Pennsylvania, but students had to meet rigorous entrance standards, and Blackie simply hadn't been qualified, nor did he have the necessary tuition. He had gone to a smaller school that had been founded in 1894 and offered a first-rate education for those who couldn't meet Harvard's strict admission guidelines. It wasn't until this year, 1908, that the U.S. Secretary of Agriculture had established guidelines for veterinary schools. I knew Blackie wondered how he would have made out if those guidelines had been set earlier.

Hawk nodded. "Well, we could use a new vet, now that old man Cole went back east. There's an empty building over on First Street that might suit your needs."

"Thanks," Blackie said. "I'll look into it tomorrow.

I have to go into town anyway to return that hired nag."

"Isn't it amazing how the town has grown?" Mary asked.

"I didn't notice," Blackie said. "I was in a hurry to get home."

"Well, you won't believe your eyes," Mary said. "Of course, it can't compare to New York or Boston."

"Or even Steel's Crossing," Victoria remarked. "Have you seen that new dress shop? They have the most beautiful blue dress in the window. It came all the way from Paris!"

Hawk rolled his eyes. "Paris," he muttered under his breath, and I knew this wasn't the first time Victoria had mentioned that dress. I also knew that, sooner or later, Hawk would buy it for her. Victoria had come from a wealthy family, and Hawk had always done everything he could to make sure she didn't want for anything.

"Are we going to Steel's Crossing?" Jacob asked excitedly. "They have a nickelodeon there."

"Never mind," Hawk said. "I'm not spending five cents on some moving picture."

"Have you seen one, Uncle Blackie?" Jason asked.

Blackie nodded. "Pretty exciting stuff." He looked at Hawk and grinned. "If your old man won't take you, I will."

The twins fairly jumped up and down in their seats.

"When?" Jacob asked. "When can we go?"

"Well," Blackie hedged, "not until I get settled."

"You promise?" Jason asked.

18

"I promise."

"Can I go, too?" Adam piped up, not wanting to be left out.

"Well, sure."

"And me?" Amanda Marie asked, followed by a chorus of "And me, and me," from Aaron, Cole, Joel, Linus, and Patrick. Even two-year-old Jared chimed in.

Hawk and Cloud Walker laughed out loud at the look of horror spreading over Blackie's face at the thought of playing chaperone to ten of his nieces and nephews at one time. Laughter rippled down the table as the rest of us joined in.

"You put your foot in it that time," Hawk said.

Blackie nodded.

And then Victoria came to his rescue. "I'm sure Hawk will be happy to go with you," she said, slanting a glance at her husband.

"Me? Now wait just a minute. How'd I get into the act?"

"And I'm sure Cloud Walker will go, too," Mary added sweetly.

Hawk and Cloud Walker looked at each other and shrugged helplessly.

Blackie leaned back in his chair, grinning, and I wondered if he had known all along that neither Victoria nor Mary would think of letting a bachelor take their kids to Steel's Crossing by himself.

After dinner, the men and the children went outside while Mary, Victoria, and I cleared the table and did the dishes.

"Blackie looks good, doesn't he?" Mary remarked.

"I'll say," Victoria agreed. "He was always cute,

19

but now . . ." She fanned herself with her hand. "My oh my!"

"He'll be beating the girls off with a stick," Mary predicted.

"I think he'll be too busy setting up his business to worry about girls for a while," I said. "Anyway, he's only twenty-three."

"And how old were you when you ran off with my father?" Mary asked, reaching for a dish towel.

"Never mind," I said, refusing to be drawn into that old argument. "That was different. Besides, women mature sooner than men."

Victoria and Mary looked at each other and then at me, and we all laughed.

"I can't imagine our father as ever being imma-ture," Mary remarked.

"I don't think he ever was," I replied, remember-ing the first time I had seen him. Even at twelve, he had been solemn, older and wiser than his years.

We finished up the dishes, and Mary and Victoria and I went outside to join the rest of the family. Shadow was sitting on the grass, with Blackie, Hawk, and the children sitting in a circle around him, all very quiet as they listened to the story Shadow was telling.

Quietly, Mary and Victoria went to sit with their husbands, and I found a place between Blackie and Joel.

"Far to the north," Shadow was saying, "there is a place where there are always clouds. The sun can-not make his way through the clouds, so it is always cold and dark in this place. There is a being there who is called *Hoimaha*. It is *Hoimaha* who brings winter to the earth. He comes from the north cloaked in a white cloud. When he draws near to the Sun, he says, 'Back away now, I am coming. I am coming.' And as he walks across the land, he brings cold and snow with him.

"The sun goes away for a time, but in the spring, he tells *Hoimaha* to go back to his own place, and to take the cold with him, so that warmth can again cover the earth, calling the grass and other growing things from their winter sleep.

"And so it goes, summer and winter, part of the great circle of life."

The children clapped their hands as Shadow finished his tale. "Tell us another," they begged.

"Just one more," Shadow said. "Did you know that when *Heammawihio* first made people, there was no death in the world?"

"No death?" Adam asked skeptically.

Shadow nodded. "So it was, in the old days. When people died, they were dead for only four nights, and then they lived again. But *Heammawihio* soon discovered that this was not a good thing. Knowing a man would live again made him foolish. Knowing they would live again made them too brave, and they made war too often. *Heammawihio* was saddened by the constant shedding of blood, and so he decreed that people would no longer live again after four days. This gave the people more respect, not only for their own lives, but for the lives of others."

The younger children clapped again, but I noticed the older ones looked thoughtful.

Amid the flurry of farewells, I kissed my grandchildren good-bye, hugged my children and their spouses, then stood on the porch, Shadow's arm around my shoulders, as we watched them depart.

How quiet the house seemed when they were gone, and how happy I was to have Blackie back home.

"Come," Shadow said, taking me by the hand, "let us go for a walk."

It was a wonderful night for a walk. A bright yellow moon lit our way. A summer breeze sang through the leaves. Crickets and frogs played a lively serenade. Away off in the distance, a coyote howled its lonely lament.

I knew without being told that we were headed for the old river crossing where Shadow and I had so often met when we were young.

Our tree was still standing, though it was old and bent now by time's passing. How many times had I come here to meet Shadow in secret? It was here that I had shamelessly seduced him when I was sixteen.

My pulse quickened as he took me in his arms. Once, I had feared that the flame between us might burn less brightly as we grew older, but no more. In my eyes, he would always be the brave warrior I had fallen in love with. His gaze met mine, and then he lowered his head and kissed me, and I was young again, in love for the first time, willing to turn my back on all I knew, all that I was familiar with, to be with the man now holding me so tightly.

As always, there was magic in his kiss, in the heat that flowed between us. Slowly, we sank to the ground, still locked in each other's arms. I slid my hands under his shirt and ran my palms over his back and shoulders, loving the touch of his skin, the muscles that flexed and bunched at my touch.

I sighed and closed my eyes as he caressed me, his breath warm against my neck as he whispered Cheyenne love words in my ear.

I laughed softly when his hand slid under my skirt, gasped when his fingertips stroked the inside of my thigh. "Shadow, what are you doing?"

He grinned at me, his teeth very white in the moonlight. "What do you think?"

"Not here!" I protested.

"Why not here?" His hand moved a little higher on my thigh. "It will not be the first time."

"But . . . I'm a grandmother! Grandmothers don't hike up their skirts in the grass."

"I do not see a grandmother," Shadow said, his voice husky with desire. "I see a girl of sixteen swimming in the river and drying herself in the sun, a girl with hair like fire and eyes the soft gray of a dove's wing."

His words brought tears to my eyes. I remembered that day so clearly. It had been my birthday and I had ridden my old mare Nellie down to the river to go for a swim. Shadow had found me there. It was the first time I had seen him in over three years.

"You remember that day, Hannah?"

"How could I forget?" I punched him on the shoulder. "You should have been ashamed of yourself, spying on me while I swam."

"No man alive could have resisted the temptation."

I wished now that I was that girl of sixteen again, that my body was young and slim, my breasts high and full, that there were no lines at my mouth and my eyes, no gray in my hair. But Shadow did not seem to mind. With the single-mindedness that was so much a part of him, he removed my dress and my undergarments, my shoes and my stockings, and then he spread my dress over the damp grass and laid me on it.

I watched, my heart racing with anticipation, as he shrugged out of his shirt and trousers and moccasins, and in my mind's eye I saw him as he had been on that day so long ago, tall and strong with the vigor of youth.

He came to me, his dark eyes filled with love and desire. I welcomed him as I always had, my hands moving restlessly over his heated skin, sliding up and down his arms, loving the way his muscles quivered at my touch. His body was a welcome weight on mine, and as our bodies fell into a familiar rhythm, the years fell away and I was a young woman again, safe in the arms of the only man I had ever truly loved.

Chapter Four

Blackie rode into town just before eleven o'clock on Monday morning. Mounted on one of his father's horses and leading the horse he had hired from Crocker's Livery the day before, he rode down Front Street.

He left the hired horse at the livery, then rode on down the street. It hadn't changed much in his absence, though the newspaper office was wearing a new coat of paint and boasted a fancy new sign that read:

Bear Valley Clarion,
Established 1886.
Clancy Archibald Turner,
Editor and Publisher

The *Clarion* had started out as a nameless single sheet that had come out once a week and carried local news and recipes. Now it came out daily and carried news from as far away as San Francisco, New York, and London.

He noticed that two rooms had been added to the schoolhouse; he could hear the students in one class reciting their letters as he passed by. The old church was still nestled in a grove of aspens at the far end of town, looking like a daisy in a field of green grass.

He passed the bank and the telegraph office, heard the ring of the blacksmith's hammer as he neared the smithy. The shop had once belonged to Victoria's father. Now it was owned by Jed Crowley, Jr.

Tippitt's General Store looked like it was thriving. Once owned by George and Ruth Tippitt, it had originally been their barn. George Tippitt had died in the diphtheria epidemic back in the fall of 1899. A few years later, his wife had left the valley and gone back to Rhode Island to live with her daughter. Fred and Myrtle Brown's son, Jeremy, had bought the store and the house behind it, which had also belonged to the Tippitts. Jeremy hadn't changed the name of the store, but he had replaced the old sign with a new one. He had put in new windows, and a new door, too. Mary had written that Jeremy had remodeled the inside of the building as well.

Riding on, Blackie passed the soda shop, Myer's Millinery, and Brewster's Pharmacy.

Passing by the barbershop, Blackie saw there was a man in the chair, reading a copy of the *Police*

Gazette while old Oscar Tewksbury cut his hair. The barber shop was a favorite gathering place for a lot of the men in town, a retreat where they could talk about stock prices and brag or complain about the way Roosevelt was running the country while they waited for a shave.

He waved to Hawk, who was heading across the street toward the sheriff's office, which was located on the corner of Front and Cross streets.

"Hey, little brother," Hawk called good-naturedly. "Stay out of trouble, hear?"

Shaking his head, Blackie rode on.

Bear Valley might be growing, but it was still little more than a speck on a map, if it was even on a map. The sign at the edge of town proclaimed the population was 1,073, hardly noteworthy compared to New York's more than seven million people. There were no motor cars or trolley cars in Bear Valley, no telephones. Most of the ranches were located a day's ride from town; a few of the larger cattle ranches were even farther out. He noticed a lot of new houses had been built in his absence. When he was a boy, he had known most of the people in town, but no more. Most of the people he saw on the street were strangers to him.

Steel's Crossing, the nearest town within 150 miles, was more modernized. Homes had telephones and indoor plumbing; there were modern restaurants, numerous department stores, and fancy dress shops like the one Victoria had mentioned the night before. He had even seen a couple of automobiles when he had stopped there on his way home, but nothing as fancy as the Great Arrow, which sold for the outrageously unbelievable price of forty-five-hundred dollars. Blackie had ridden in a car once, a brand-new Packard with polished brass trim. The car had been owned by the father of a girl he had dated a few times.

He grunted softly, wondering how long it would take for Bear Valley to catch up with the rest of the country. The Wright Brothers had finally convinced people that flight was possible, and men all across the country were building strange-looking flying machines, determined to outdo them. Before leaving New York, Blackie had read an article in the paper that quoted Wilbur Wright as opining that the "age of flight had come at last." Even the government was showing some interest. The army had purchased a dirigible, but no one but its inventor, T. S. Baldwin, had been able to fly it, so the contraption had never been used.

Turning right on Cross, he was surprised by the number of new businesses he saw: Lark's Music Store, Ronda's Dress Shoppe, Price's Saloon, O'Toole's Irish Pub, Feehan's Mercantile, Lucinda's Dry Goods. There was a new restaurant—Maud's Diner. And a new hotel. The Cosmopolitan was three stories high, something previously unheard of in Bear Valley. The balcony and shutters were painted bright green. A couple of men sat in the rocking chairs out front. One of them was thumbing through a well-read copy of the *National Geographic*.

The other man leaned forward, his eyes narrowing. "Blackie, is that you?"

"Hey, Mr. Crowley." Blackie reined his horse to a halt, glad to see a familiar face.

"Well, well," Crowley said, slapping his thigh, "you've come home at last."

"Yessir. How's the family?"

Jed Crowley grinned broadly. "Growing bigger every day."

Blackie grinned. Mary Crowley was perpetually pregnant. Blackie had lost count of their kids and grandkids.

"How was life back there in the big city?" Crowley asked. "Did you see the elephant?"

"Yes, sir, I surely did," Blackie replied, laughing. "Seeing the elephant" was an old western term that meant a young man had gone out to see the world and gain some experience. "Tell Mrs. Crowley and the family hello for me."

"I surely will," Jed replied.

Riding on, Blackie turned down First Street. He passed Compton's Law Office, Kruger's Feed and Tack, Ludlow's Funeral Parlor, McMillan's New York Footwear Shop, and a dentist's office that promised painless extractions.

He reined his horse to a halt when he reached his destination. The building located in the middle of the block looked as if it had been empty for quite a while. The lots on both sides were empty, overgrown with grass and weeds. Looking farther down the street beyond the building, he noted there were two new churches, a white frame Lutheran Church and, across from it, a small Catholic church with stained-glass windows.

Clucking to his horse, Blackie rode around the property. If he remembered correctly, the place had been a restaurant some years back. The windows were boarded up now, there were cobwebs hanging from the eaves, and the paint was peeling. But it was a good-sized building, with a large fenced yard in the rear. From his vantage point in the saddle, he could see over the fence. There were a couple of smaller buildings behind the main one, as well as a run-down corral. Riding around to the front, he spied a sign on the door that said anyone interested in the building should see Joey McBride at Feehan's Mercantile.

The town must be growing, he mused, if it could support two general stores. Lifting the reins, Blackie rode back down Cross Street toward Feehan's. The sign read:

FEEHAN'S MERCANTILE
Big Mike Feehan, Proprietor
Best Prices This Side of the Mississippi
Closed Sundays

Dismounting, Blackie dropped the reins over the hitch rack, stepped up on the boardwalk, and entered the building.

Since it was a weekday, the store wasn't too crowded. Bins on the left held a variety of staples; canned goods were stacked on the shelves over the bins. A wood stove at the rear of the building provided heat in the winter. There were some glass-fronted cabinets on the right; large wicker baskets held bushels of apples, potatoes, and other produce.

Blackie glanced at the prices listed on the wall: oranges, twenty cents a dozen; lemons, fifteen cents a dozen; dried apricots, ten cents a pound; eggs, twenty-eight cents a dozen; Swiss cheese, twenty-five cents a pound; milk, eight cents a quart; sugar, six cents a pound; Palmolive soap, ten cents a cake; bread, five cents a loaf. Looked like prices had gone up a mite while he'd been away, he mused.

A man who looked like he should have been wielding a blacksmith's hammer instead of running a general store stood behind the front counter. He had short brown hair and a thick mustache. His white shirt was stretched tight over massive arms. A shiny black string tie was knotted at his throat. A white apron the size of one of Hannah's bed sheets covered the man's chest. Big Mike Feehan, Blackie assumed.

"Can I help you?" The man's voice was as big as the rest of him. His gaze moved over Blackie from head to foot, his brown eyes taking in every detail.

"I'm looking for Joey McBride."

The man's gaze grew wary. "You got business with Joey?" he asked suspiciously.

"I'm interested in that vacant building over on First," Blackie said.

Feehan jerked his thumb toward a door in the rear of the store. "Joey's in the back room checking some inventory."

"Thanks."

Moving past Feehan, Blackie opened the door and stepped into the storeroom. It was a large rectangular room. Shelves crammed with canned goods, boxes, and tins lined all four walls. Wooden crates were stacked in the corners. An oil lamp hung suspended from a chain in the ceiling.

Peering into the shadows at the far end of the room, Blackie saw a young man standing on the top rung of a ladder. The kid, slender as a reed, wore a floppy brimmed felt hat, a red plaid shirt, and a pair of faded Levi's.

"Are you Joey McBride?" Blackie asked, moving up behind the ladder.

Startled, the boy started to turn. He lost his balance, shrieked as he made a mad grab for the side of the ladder, and missed. His hat went flying and the can he had been holding plummeted downward, barely missing Blackie's head before it hit the floor with a resounding thud. Arms flailing, the boy slid down the ladder.

Lunging forward, Blackie caught the boy before he hit the ground. "That was a close call," Blackie muttered. "You should be more careful up there."

"I was being careful," the boy retorted. "And I wouldn't have fallen if you hadn't startled me!"

Blackie stared at the kid cradled in his arms. "You're Joey McBride?"

"That's right. Who the hell are you?"

Two things struck Blackie simultaneously: Joey McBride had the longest eyelashes and the most beautiful hazel eyes he had ever seen, and Joey McBride wasn't a boy.

Joey wriggled in his arms. "Put me down."

"You . . . you're a girl." Stunned, Blackie set the girl on her feet. She had dark brown hair, long dark lashes, and a curvy figure that even the loose-fitting flannel shirt couldn't hide. He guessed her to be about seventeen.

She glared at him, her hands fisted on her hips. "Of course I'm a girl. What did you think I was? And what's the big idea, sneaking up on me like that?"

"I'm sorry"—Blackie stared at her, speechless, before his manners took hold—"Miss McBride."

She arched a brow at him. "You didn't tell me who you are."

"Blackie Kincaid." Since his father didn't have a last name, Blackie and his brothers and sister used their mother's maiden name.

Joey frowned at him. "Kincaid?" Her eyes narrowed. "Are you related to that Indian who raises horses south of town?"

Blackie nodded curtly, a muscle working in his jaw. Even though the Custer massacre had taken place more than thirty years ago, there were still a lot of old hurts and prejudices. He had encountered them here at home, as well as back east. It was hard to believe that after all this time, men were still arguing over the battle at the Little Big Horn. But maybe it wasn't so surprising after all. It seemed that some wounds never healed. In the South they were still re-fighting the Civil War. But this girl was too young to have any memories of an Indian war that had ended long before she had been born.

Joey blew a wayward lock of hair out of her eyes. "Why were you looking for me?"

"I'd like to buy that building over on First Street."

Her eyebrows shot up. "Really? Why?"

"Does that matter? You have a building for sale and I want to buy it."

She lifted her chin and narrowed her eyes. "It's my building. I guess that gives me the right to know what you're going to do with it."

Blackie drew in a deep breath, annoyed by her impudence. "Do you want to talk business or not?"

Her gaze met his for a long moment, and then she nodded.

"How much do you want for it?"

"It's not for sale," she said. "Just for rent."

"Fine," he said impatiently. "How much is it?"

"You still haven't told me what you're going to use it for."

"I'm stockpiling guns and ammunition. Gonna start a revolution down in Mexico."

She stared at him, wide-eyed and openmouthed.

"I'm kidding," he said quickly. "I want to open a veterinary hospital. Is that all right with you?"

"Yes, I suppose so."

"How much is it?"

She hesitated a moment, making him wonder if she was reconsidering renting him the building or thinking about raising the price. "Eleven dollars a month."

Blackie nodded. The price was a little high for a vacant building, but he could afford it. He had managed to save some money while he was back east. He had worked nights and gone to school days and grabbed a few hours sleep whenever he could.

"Can we go take a look at the inside?"

"I can't leave right now," she exclaimed. "I'm working."

"Oh, right. Well, if the inside's what I'm looking for, I'd like to lease the place for a year."

"A year!" Her smile was huge. "That's wonderful!"

"Can you meet me there at noon tomorrow? That'll give me time to go to the bank."

"Noon." She nodded exuberantly. "I'll be there."

"See you then," he said, and left the storeroom.

Leaving the mercantile, Blackie paused on the boardwalk a moment, then headed for the saloon across the street. O'Toole's was quiet this time of day. A couple of old-timers sat at a back table, playing blackjack. Four men stood at the bar, a whiskey bottle between them. He didn't recognize any of them, though the youngest one, who couldn't have been more than sixteen or seventeen, looked vaguely familiar.

Taking a place at the far end of the bar, Blackie ordered a beer. Leaning back, one boot heel hooked over the rail, he thought about the building he hoped to lease. The outside needed a coat of paint and it looked like there was a hole in the roof of the shed. No doubt the inside wasn't in much better shape. He supposed he would have to ask Joey McBride's permission before he did any major renovating or remodeling. Things would be a lot easier if she would just sell him the building outright.

He realized suddenly that the four men at the bar had stopped talking and were now studying him curiously.

One of them turned to face him. The man was short and stocky, with greasy blond hair and little pig eyes. "You're an Injun, ain't ya?" he asked insolently.

Blackie stood up straighter. "That's right."

Pig Eyes grimaced. "I thought so." He looked at the bartender. "Ain't there some kinda law against servin' likker to redskins?"

The bartender shrugged. "If there is, I haven't heard of it."

"Well, if there ain't, there oughtta be," one of the man's companions said. He was of medium height and built like a bear, with a thick neck and hunched shoulders. A thin scar ran from his hairline to his jaw. He had hard brown eyes that looked at Blackie without blinking.

"Yeah," said the third. He was tall and hard-muscled, with bulky arms and a pockmarked face. He wore a battered cavalry hat. "My old man rode with the Seventh. He was killed by a dirty redskin at the Little Big Horn." Anger radiated from this one like heat from a flash fire.

The fourth man had short dark brown hair and hazel eyes. Younger than the others, he didn't say anything, just stood there, tall and silent, nervously toying with a gold pocket watch. Blackie stared at him a moment, wondering why he looked familiar.

Blackie pushed away from the bar, his adrenaline pumping. He recognized the looks on the faces of the four men all too clearly. They were all a little drunk and spoiling for a fight. Any fight.

The bartender realized it too. "You men, I don't want any brawling in here. If you've got a beef with this man, take it outside."

The two men playing blackjack had turned away from their game, more interested in the scene unfolding at the bar than their cards.

Clenching his hands into fists, Blackie took a deep breath. He hadn't been in a fight since he was sixteen, but it looked like that was about to change. He just hoped they didn't expect him to take them all on at once.

"You heard the man," Pig Eyes said, jerking his head toward the door. "Let's go."

"Maybe he ain't got the guts to fight," Scarface said disdainfully. "Never was a redskin who'd fight out in the open. Bunch of sneaky bastards." He drew a small nickel-plated pistol from inside his jacket and leveled it at Blackie. "Let's go."

"Here, now," the bartender said. "There's no call for any gun play."

"Mind your own business," the man in the cavalry hat snarled.

A hush fell over the room.

Scarface made a motion with his gun. "Let's go."

Knowing he'd get no help from anyone in the saloon, Blackie walked slowly toward the door, his mind racing, his palms damp.

Once outside, Pig Eyes gave him a shove, directing him to move into the alley that ran between O'Toole's and the building next door.

Muttering an oath, Blackie did as he was told, his gaze moving back and forth. Damn, where was Hawk when he needed him? The man with the gun took a place near the head of the alley.

"So," Pig Eyes said, "what tribe you from?"

Blackie lifted his head and squared his shoulders. "I'm Cheyenne."

Pig Eyes spat on the ground. "The Cheyenne were at the Little Big Horn, along with the Sioux, ain't that right, Caffrey?" He glanced over his shoulder at the man wearing the cavalry hat.

Caffrey nodded. "They got their licks in, Sal, sure enough. And now it's my turn." Eyes filled with malice, he took a step forward. "This is for my old man," he said, and drove his fist into Blackie's face.

Blackie reeled backward, brought up short by the building behind him. The air whooshed out of his lungs, his vision blurring. With a shake of his head, he cleared his vision in time to see Caffrey swinging at him again. He ducked under the man's fist and drove his own fist into Caffrey's belly. It was like hitting a block of granite. The man grinned at him and then the fight began in earnest.

They traded blows for what seemed like forever before Blackie got in a lucky punch that drove Caffrey to his knees. Before he could finish the man off, Sal and his silent companion moved in. Blackie fought back as best he could, was even gaining ground, until the fourth man came up behind him and grabbed him by the arms.

Blackie glared at his attackers, wondering if they intended to kill him. And then Caffrey staggered to his feet. He wiped the back of his hand across his nose and mouth, stared at the blood. And then, with a feral smile, he drew a long, wicked-looking knife from the sheath on his belt, and Blackie didn't have to wonder anymore.

Chapter Five

I was sitting in the living room, sewing a quilt for Mary Crowley's baby, when Shadow ran into the house. One look at his face and I knew something was terribly wrong. I rose without conscious thought, the quilt falling to the floor unnoticed.

"What is it?" I asked anxiously.

"Blackie's been hurt," he said tersely and went outside again.

I didn't ask questions, though a dozen rose in my mind. *Please don't let it be serious. Please let him be all right.* The words repeated themselves in my mind as I went into the kitchen, filled a pan with water, and put it on the stove to heat. I turned back the blankets on Blackie's bed and found some clean cloths for bandages, should they be necessary.

Moments later, Shadow and Hawk entered the house, carrying Blackie between them. I swallowed the cry that rose in my throat as they laid him gently on the bed. He had been badly beaten. His right eye was swollen and black, there were cuts on his cheeks, his lip was split, the knuckles on both hands were red and smeared with blood, not all of it his own. Blood stained the front of his shirt.

I looked up and met Shadow's eyes. "What happened?"

It was Hawk who answered. "As near as I can tell, he ran afoul of some drifters over at O'Toole's. They were still sore about the Little Big Horn."

He didn't need to say any more than that. I was well acquainted with prejudice in all its hideous forms.

"The bartender over at O'Toole's tipped me off," Hawk said. "Dammit, I wish he'd found me sooner."

"You got there before it was too late; that's all that matters. Hawk, go get the pan of water on the stove. Shadow, help me get him out of his clothes."

Blackie moaned softly as I cut away his shirt and tossed it aside. Shadow pulled off Blackie's boots, unfastened his belt, and eased his trousers down over his hips. I placed a towel under Blackie, dipped a cloth into the pan of water Hawk had brought in, and then began to wash the blood from the wound in Blackie's side. It was a knife wound; I had seen enough of them to know. The gash was long, just deep enough that it was going to need stitching, and as I cleaned it, I silently thanked God that the blade hadn't gone any deeper, that it hadn't pierced any vital organs.

Blackie groaned softly as the warm water touched him. "*Nahkoa?*"

"I'm here. Your father too. Lie still now."

Blackie reached for his father's hand. I noticed in a distant corner of my mind that Blackie's hand was as large as his father's.

"You'll be all right, little brother," Hawk said, his voice thick, his eyes dark with rage. "Don't worry, I'll find the bastards who did this."

We'd had no doctor in Bear Valley since old Doc Henderson passed away a year ago, so it was left to me to stitch the wound. Hawk offered Blackie a drink of whiskey from a bottle we kept on hand for guests. None of the men in my family had a head for strong liquor. Blackie took a long swallow, and then another.

I disinfected the wound, then sterilized a needle and thread with whiskey, remembering another time, long ago, when I had watched my mother stitch a knife wound in Shadow's leg. He still had the scar; it ran from his thigh to his ankle. I had held Shadow's hand while my mother's needle darted in and out of his flesh, taking neat, even stitches. Great drops of sweat had beaded his forehead and I had wiped them away, wondering how he endured such pain without making a sound.

Now, stitching the wound in my son's side, I wondered anew at the bravery of the men in my family. Sweat trickled down Blackie's face and dampened his chest, but he never made a sound as I sewed up the ugly wound.

I wiped the perspiration from his face and chest, bandaged the laceration, drew the covers over him, and then kissed his cheek. "Sleep now," I murmured.

Picking up Blackie's bloody shirt and trousers, I followed Hawk and Shadow out of the room and closed the door behind me.

In the living room, Shadow turned to face Hawk. "Do you know who did this thing?"

"I got a description of the men responsible from the bartender at O'Toole's."

"Where are they now, the men who did this?" Shadow asked.

I looked at Shadow, a sinking feeling in the pit of my stomach. I knew that tone, that voice. It was the voice of Two Hawks Flying, the last fighting warrior on the Plains. I had heard it countless times when we rode the war trail. It was a voice that didn't know the meaning of surrender. I knew that Shadow intended to go after the men who had beaten our son, and that nothing I could say would stop him.

"Damn cowards" Hawk said, his voice filled with scorn. "They took off like a bunch of scared rabbits when I showed up."

Shadow nodded. "Which way did they go?"

"They hit their saddles running and headed north on the old road toward Steel's Crossing. There's still a couple hours of daylight left. I'll be going after them as soon as I leave here. I'll have to stop by the house first to let Victoria know I'm leaving."

"I will go with you," Shadow said.

Hawk nodded, a faint smile tugging at his lips. "I figured you would. I'll meet you in front of the jail in an hour."

"Where are you going, *neyho*?" Blue Hawk asked,

coming into the room. He glanced from his father to Hawk and back again. "Can I go?"

"Not this time, *naha*," Shadow said. He looked at Hawk. "In an hour."

"See you then," Hawk said, and left the house.

Blue Hawk tugged on my hand. "What's going on? Where's *neyho* going? Why can't I go?"

"Blackie's been hurt," I explained. "Hawk and your father are going to go and find the men who did it."

"I want to go," Blue Hawk said. "Blackie is my brother too!"

"You cannot go this time," Shadow said. He placed his hands on Blue Hawk's shoulders. "I need you to stay home and look after your mother and brother. Can you saddle Red Wind for me?"

Blue Hawk nodded, pleased that his father had asked for his help. "I'll put some grain in your saddlebags too," he said, and ran out of the house.

"Shadow." He turned to face me. I had so many memories of telling him good-bye. There had been so many times in years long past when I had watched him ride away, not knowing if I would ever see him again. "Be careful."

He smiled faintly as he drew me into his arms. "Do not worry, Hannah. Do I not always return?"

"Yes, but . . ."

He placed one finger over my mouth. "Do not worry, woman."

"I can't help it," I wailed. "I've worried whenever you left me, whether it was for a day or an hour."

He looked surprised.

"Didn't you know?" I asked.

43

"The woman of Two Hawks Flying hid her fears well."

"I'm not that woman anymore." I slid my arms around his waist and held him tight. He was more precious to me now than ever before. We had weathered so much together, I couldn't imagine my life without him.

Shadow kissed me deeply, then put me away from him. "We will need food for the journey," he said. "Will you pack me some while I get my weapons?"

I nodded.

A short time later, he was ready to go. I noted the eagle feather tied in his hair, the knife in a beaded sheath on his belt, the rifle in one hand. As we stepped out onto the porch, Blue Hawk came up leading his father's horse. Shadow had named the stallion Red Wind in honor of a horse he'd had years before. Red Wind was a beautiful animal, one we had bred several times. I did not miss the fact that, today, Blue Hawk had tied up the stallion's tail for war after the manner of the Cheyenne.

Shadow noticed it, too. "You have done well," he said, ruffling our son's hair. "Take good care of your mother."

"I will," my son replied solemnly.

Shadow embraced Blue Hawk, then turned to me.

I put my arms around my husband and hugged him tightly. "Be careful."

He nodded and then, lowering his head, he kissed me. I clung to him, keenly aware that he was riding into danger, that he could be hurt or killed.

He gave my shoulder a reassuring squeeze, then

turned and slipped his rifle into the boot on the saddle. One more quick kiss and then he swung onto Red Wind's back and took up the reins. His gaze rested on Blue Hawk and me for a moment and then he was riding away, his back straight, the sunlight dancing on his long black hair. He was a warrior again, riding off to avenge wrongs that had been done to his family.

I stared after him, remembering all the other times when he had ridden off to war and I had stayed behind.

"Come back to me," I whispered. "Please come back to me."

Blue Hawk took my hand in his. "Don't worry, *nahkoa*," he said, smiling up at me. "He'll be all right. He'll find those bad men and beat them up good."

I forced a smile. "Of course he will."

I sat at Blackie's side all that day and into the night, making sure he drank plenty of water, giving him aspirin for the pain and to bring down the fever that burned through him.

I only left his room twice—once to fix Blue Hawk's dinner and again to tuck him into bed.

Blackie tossed and turned until his fever broke sometime near dawn, and then he lapsed into a deep sleep. I thanked God that he had not been killed, that his wounds were not more serious.

Not wanting to go to my lonely bed, I fell asleep in the rocking chair beside his bed.

I was cleaning up the kitchen after lunch the following afternoon when Joey McBride knocked on the back door. I was surprised to see her. She was an odd girl. As far as I could recall, I had never seen her in a dress except in church. Today, she was wearing a pair of faded Levi's, a dark blue shirt, and scuffed boots. She wore a battered hat over her dark brown hair, which fell down her back in a long braid. As near as I could recollect, she was nineteen, but she looked much younger. She had hazel eyes, clear skin, a generous mouth, and a fine straight nose.

"Joey, what a . . . a nice surprise. Won't you come in?"

She shook her head vigorously.

"Is there something you need?" I asked.

"I was supposed to meet Blackie at noon, but he didn't show up," she explained. "He said he wanted to rent Gram's building over on First. I just wondered if he was still interested."

"I'm sure he is," I replied, "but he ran into some trouble yesterday, and he won't be up and around for a couple of days."

"Oh, I'm sorry to hear that." She glanced around the kitchen as if she had never seen one before. I didn't know very much about the McBrides, other than that they were poor. Joey lived with her grandmother, who was an invalid, and her younger brother, who was, by all accounts, pretty shiftless. Charlie McBride didn't care much for work. From what I'd heard, he spent most of his time at O'Toole's Saloon, drinking and playing cards. I felt sorry for Joey. Her mother had run off with another man when Joey was eight or nine. Her father had been killed when he fell off a bridge he was working on. Joey had just turned seventeen at the time. A few months later she had moved here to take care of her grandmother. Joey McBride hadn't had an easy life, and it showed in her eyes.

"Would you like to see Blackie?" I asked. "I think he's awake."

She shook her head again. "No. Just tell him to come and see me when he can."

"I will."

She shifted from one foot to the other, then turned and left the house.

I stared after her for a few minutes, then went in to check on Blackie. He looked even worse today than he had yesterday. His face was covered with bruises, one eye was swollen shut, his lower lip was twice its normal size.

"Joey McBride was just here," I said.

He grunted softly.

"She wanted to know if you were still interested in renting that vacant building over on First."

Blackie nodded. "I talked to her about it yesterday."

"She said for you to come see her when you felt up to it."

He nodded again.

I sat down in the rocker beside Blackie's bed. "She's a singular girl."

"I don't remember seeing her in town before."

"She came here to look after her grandmother shortly after you left for college." Maureen McBride had come to Bear Valley several years ago and opened a small restaurant, but she had been forced to stop working when her arthritis got so bad she couldn't stay on her feet. She had hired some smooth-talking man to run the business for her. The man had turned out to be a crook who had robbed her blind and then left the valley. A short time later, Maureen had been confined to a wheelchair. Her health had declined steadily after that. When it got to the point where she couldn't take care of herself any more, she sent for Joey and her brother to come out and look after her.

"I learned the other day that Mrs. McBride's husband was a sergeant in the cavalry," I remarked, thinking out loud. "He fought with General Crook. He was killed in the battle at the Rosebud."

Blackie grunted softly. His next question told me that he hadn't really been listening to what I was saying. "Where's my father?"

It was a question I didn't want to answer, but I couldn't refuse, and I couldn't lie to him. "He went with Hawk to find the men who did this to you. They left yesterday afternoon."

Grimacing, Blackie struggled to sit up. "I should have been the one to go," he said with as much determination as he could muster.

"Don't be silly. You won't be able to ride for several days."

"I'm going."

"You are not." I gained my feet as he slid his legs over the edge of the bed. "You get right back under those covers, young man!"

"This is my fight, not theirs."

I looked at the bruises on his face. His left eye was still swollen, the black fading to a bilious shade of green. "You're in no condition to fight anyone."

Clad in nothing but the bottom half of a pair of long johns, Blackie stood up, towering over me. He wasn't my little boy anymore, I thought sadly, but a man fully grown and in charge of his own life.

Even though he was now taller than his father, he was still my baby, my little boy, and every protective instinct I possessed rose up within me as I stared at the bandage wrapped around his middle.

"Please, Blackie, let your father and Hawk take care of it."

He shook his head, every bit as stubborn as the man who had sired him. "I'm going, *nahkoa.*"

Since I couldn't spank him and I couldn't lock him in his room, there was nothing to do but help him get ready. I put up some food for his journey, then went outside and saddled one of the horses.

Blackie entered the barn a short time later. Fear sat like a lump of ice in the pit of my stomach as I watched him slide a rifle into the saddle boot.

I saw him take a deep breath as he put one foot in the stirrup. It was all I could do to stifle my urge to help him mount. He managed it on his own, but I could see what it cost him by the tight lines around his mouth.

"Be careful," I said, handing him the reins. "Your father was meeting Hawk at the jail. They left late yesterday afternoon. Hawk said the men left town heading north."

Blackie nodded.

I knew Blackie wouldn't have any trouble following their tracks. Shadow had taught all his sons how to follow trail sign, how to find food and water, how to navigate the vast prairie using the sun or the stars as their guides. My only hope was that Hawk and Shadow would have captured the men responsible and be on their way back home by the time Blackie caught up with them.

I clasped my hands to my breast as I watched my

son ride out of the yard, wishing there was some way to stop him. Once again a prayer rose in my heart.

Please, Lord, please bring them all back to me.

Chapter Six

Shadow reined his horse to a halt. Dismounting, he squatted down on his heels, his eyes narrowed. The trail they had been following for the last three days had grown faint and difficult to see in the fading light.

He gestured at the ground. "They have split up. Three of them have turned south. I think the fourth may be circling back toward town."

Dismounting, Hawk hunkered down on his heels beside his father. "We'll go after the three. Maybe they'll tell us who the fourth man is."

Shadow grunted softly as he gained his feet. They would tell him what he wanted to know, one way or the other.

He walked a few yards ahead. Using the toe of his moccasin, he scattered a pile of horse manure.

Squatting on his heels, he picked up a chunk and sifted it through his fingers, noting the color and texture.

"How far ahead are they?" Hawk asked.

"Maybe two hours." Shadow wiped his hand on a patch of grass, then rose to his feet. "They are not riding fast. I do not think they know they are being followed." Shadow studied the tracks a moment longer, then swung onto the back of his horse. "We will catch them tomorrow."

They rode until dark, watered their horses at a shallow stream, and then rode another mile before making camp.

Shadow looked after the horses while Hawk gathered wood for a fire. Rummaging around in the sack of food Hannah had packed, Shadow removed some canned meat and peaches, a hunk of yellow cheese, and several slices of bread. And cookies.

Shadow smiled, remembering the first time he had eaten a cookie. It had been the day he first met Hannah. He had frightened her by riding up behind her. Once she got over her fear, she had accused him of sneaking around on her property. He had told her haughtily that it was not her property, and that she was the one who was trespassing.

"I am not!" she retorted.

"Warriors do not argue with little girls," he replied, his voice thick with scorn.

"You're no warrior!" she said, stung by his disdain. "You're just a little boy!" And then, apparently feeling contrite, she offered him a cookie.

He grinned, remembering how he had taken it from her hand and sniffed it, then popped it into his mouth. She'd had ten oatmeal cookies left from the dozen her mother had sent her off with that day, and he had wolfed them down in no time at all, then licked the crumbs from his fingers. They had spent that summer together. He hadn't told anyone of his friendship with the skinny little red-haired girl. He had taught her to read trail sign and how to find her way home at night by using the stars as a guide. He had taught her how to skin a deer and tan the hide. With the coming of winter, he had gone south with his people, but he hadn't forgotten Hannah. Had he known, even then, that he would spend the rest of his life with her?

Shadow and Hawk bedded down after dinner, intending to get an early start in the morning. Lying there, gazing up at the stars, Shadow found himself thinking of the past, remembering the days when he had been a young warrior, when the buffalo had roamed the plains as far as the eye could see. He missed those days, when the Cheyenne had been wild and free.

Like all Cheyenne males, he had been taught from childhood that war was the noblest pursuit, the only one for a man to follow. He had been taught that no other pleasure could equal the thrill of battle, that to be brave was the worthiest attribute a man could possess. Among Cheyenne warriors, the bravest feat of all was to ride into battle, count coup on a living enemy, and ride away again, leaving the enemy alive. Once, when the Cheyenne were making war on the Ute, Shadow's father, Black Owl, had ridden out in front of his people. Alone, armed with only a coup stick, he had ridden through the enemy line, counted coup on one of the Ute warriors, then turned and ridden back to his own people. It was a story Shadow had heard countless times when he was a young boy. Dying in battle was not to be feared. A man who died in battle was spared the miseries and frailties of old age. Sometimes, when a man was very sick or he had lost the will to live, he would tell his friends that he was going to give his body to the enemy. He would then ride into battle unarmed, counting coup on as many of the enemy as he could before they struck him down.

Lost in the past, Shadow recalled the four days he had spent seeking a vision when he was a young man. It had been on the fourth day that his vision came. Fearing that no vision would be granted him, he had raised his arms above his head and lifted his voice toward the heavens.

"Hear me, Man Above, father of all life! Hear me, and grant me a vision, lest I perish!"

For the space of three heartbeats a great stillness hung over the hilltop, as if the earth was holding its breath. Then a wild rushing noise filled his ears, and as he stared upward at the sun, it seemed suddenly to be falling toward him. In terror, he pressed himself against the damp ground, fearing certain destruction. Suddenly, the sun split in half and out of the middle flew two red-tailed hawks. In perfect unison, they soared through the air, wheeling and diving, moving with timeless grace until they hovered above his head.

"Be brave," the male hawk cried in a loud voice. *"Be brave, and I will always be with you. You shall be swift as the hawk, wise as the owl."*

"Be strong," the female admonished in a loud

voice. "Be strong, and I will always be with you. You shall be smart as the hawk, mighty as the eagle."

With a rush of powerful wings, the two hawks soared upward and disappeared into the sun.

From that day forward, he would be known as Two Hawks Flying.

His spirit guides had come to him again during the medicine lodge. Once again he had lifted his voice to the heavens, and his answer had come in a rush of mighty wings as two red-tailed hawks swept out of the bright blaze of the sun. Side by side, wings touching, they had hovered near his head.

"Be brave," the male hawk cried. "Be brave, and you shall be a mighty war leader among the People."

"Be strong," the female hawk cried. "Be strong, and everything you desire shall be yours."

He recalled the days when he had ridden the war trail, the battle at the Little Big Horn, the great war chiefs he had known, men like Crazy Horse and Gall, Sitting Bull and Geronimo, and others who had ridden beside him—Laughing Wolf and Calf Running and Black Elk.

And he remembered the humiliation of being held captive and put on display by a pair of unscrupulous white men. It had been Barney McCall's idea to put Shadow on display. As if to atone for his lack of physical beauty, McCall had been endowed with a rich, commanding voice. Stewart had been a tall handsome man. Dressed up in fancy buckskins, Stewart had preened onstage while Barney recounted in vivid detail how his partner, world-famous buffalo hunter, trapper, Indian fighter, and army scout, had, single-handedly and at great personal risk, captured Two Hawks Flying, the last fighting chief on the plains.

McCall and Stewart had hired a third man, Rudy, who had stood in the wings, covering Shadow with a rifle to make sure he didn't try to escape. Barney's spiel had all been a pack of lies from start to finish, but the whites in the east had swallowed it horn, hide, and all. Shadow remembered the beating Stewart had given him when he refused to perform a war dance on stage. He remembered how they had stabbed him and left him for dead, and he re-membered hunting them down, the sweet satisfac-tion of dipping his hands in their blood.

It was good to be on the hunt again, he mused. But he was a civilized man now. When they found the men they were tracking, Hawk would arrest them and they would take them back to town to stand trial.

Putting the past behind him, Shadow closed his eyes and thought about Hannah. Even after all these years, he missed her when they were apart.

Blackie stared up at the stars. He was bone weary and his injured side hurt like hell, but he couldn't have stayed home. Even though he knew the chance of catching up with the others was slim, given their headstart, he'd had to try. Like he had told his mother, it was his fight.

He'd had no trouble picking up the tracks left by his father and Hawk.

Yesterday, he had ridden until he couldn't see the trail anymore, and then he had bedded down in a shallow draw, thinking he should have listened to his mother. She had been right, as always. He was in no condition for a long hard ride. He had hauled himself into the saddle again at first light, grateful that he was riding one of his father's horses. They were known throughout the territory for their speed and endurance. With any luck at all, he would catch up with his father and Hawk before they found the four men they were chasing.

He was drifting off to sleep when Joey McBride's image rose up in his mind—long dark brown hair, pretty skin, a full mouth. Hazel eyes . . .

Blackie sat up, cursing as the sudden movement sent slivers of pain through his side. Now he knew why one of those men had looked familiar. His hair and eyes had been the same color as Joey McBride's.

Thursday morning bloomed bright and clear. After a quick cup of coffee, Shadow and Hawk were on the trail again.

Hawk had to admire his father's stamina. Riding all day, sleeping on the hard ground, eating camp grub, none of it seemed to faze him. Hawk shook his head ruefully, wondering if he'd have his father's strength and endurance when he was Shadow's age.

It was still early morning when Shadow reined his horse to a halt. Hawk drew up alongside him.

"There," Shadow said, pointing to a faint puff of smoke drifting on the wind.

Hawk nodded. He could smell coffee and figured the men they were tracking had no idea they were being followed or they wouldn't have lit a fire. Drawing his Colt, he checked his ammunition.

Shadow pulled his rifle from the saddle boot.

Hawk glanced at his father. "I want to take them in alive, if possible."

"That will be up to them."

In spite of the heat of the day, Hawk felt a sudden chill. Though Shadow had lived among the whites for many years, he was still a Cheyenne warrior. Once, he had been the most feared warrior on the plains. He had fought against Custer; he had led a small band of renegade warriors who refused to surrender.

Dismounting, Hawk tied his horse to a tree and waited while Shadow did the same. He hoped like hell the men they were tracking wouldn't put up a fight.

Nodding at his father, he moved to the left, using all the cover he could find.

Shadow watched his son until he was out of sight, then circled around the other way.

The three men were hunkered down on the ground, sipping coffee. They were as the bartender at O'Toole's had described them to Hawk: a tall man with an old cavalry hat shading his pock-marked face, a stocky man with greasy blond hair and close-set eyes, and a scar-faced man of medium height.

Shadow waited until he saw Hawk slip into place behind the men. At his son's signal, he jacked a round into the breech of his rifle and stepped into view.

"Throw up your hands!" Hawk said.

Startled by Shadow's appearance and the voice coming from behind them, the three men sprang to their feet. The blond howled as hot coffee splashed over his hands and arms. The man wearing the cavalry hat started to reach for his revolver, but one look at Shadow's unblinking black eyes changed his mind and he raised his hands over his head. The scar-faced man stood there, unmoving, a surprised expression on his face.

"Keep 'em covered," Hawk said. "I'll get their guns."

Shadow watched the three men. They stood there, every muscle tense. The blonde's gaze darted back and forth between Shadow and Hawk.

"Go on," Shadow said. "Try it."

"You'd love an excuse to cut me down, wouldn't you, you dirty redskin?"

Shadow nodded slowly. Last night, he had been resigned to taking the men back to town for trial, but now, his blood running hot with the memory of what these men had done to Blackie, he would have welcomed any excuse to avenge his son.

Apparently the blond-haired man knew it too.

In minutes, Hawk had disarmed the three men and cuffed their hands behind their backs.

Shadow blew out a breath of relief and disappointment. It seemed the white man's law would prevail after all.

Remembering what his father had taught him, Blackie traveled quickly but carefully, making use of whatever cover he could find as he followed Shadow's trail.

He caught sight of the rider approaching him before the other man saw him. Taking cover behind a clump of sage, Blackie sucked in a breath as he recognized the kid who had been in the saloon with the other three hard cases. Blackie frowned, surprised that the kid was riding back toward Bear Valley. He had assumed the four men were drifting together. He grunted softly, wondering if this kid was one of his neighbors.

As soon as the boy came within hailing range, Blackie drew his rifle and fired a shot a yard or so in front of the boy's mount. The gelding reared, and the rider slid over its haunches to land on his backside in the dirt.

"Keep those hands up where I can see 'em!" Blackie called, and when the kid started to rise, Blackie fired another shot.

This time the kid froze, his hands raised over his head.

Dismounting, Blackie approached him warily.

"Who the hell are . . . ?" The boy's voice trailed off as recognition flickered in the depths of his eyes.

"Lie facedown," Blackie ordered. "And spread your arms and legs."

"You gonna shoot me in the back, redskin?"

"Do what I said."

With a grimace, the kid rolled over onto his stomach.

Blackie searched him quickly and thoroughly, relieving the boy of the knife he found under his vest. He wasn't packing a gun except for an old rifle in a saddle boot. Catching up the kid's horse, he cut a foot or so off of one rein.

"Hey, what do you think you're doing?" the kid exclaimed.

"Sit up and put your hands behind you."

Muttering under his breath, the kid did as he was told, and Blackie quickly lashed his hands together.

Slipping the boy's knife into the waistband of his

trousers, Blackie took a step back. "Get up."

The kid rose clumsily to his feet. He glared at Blackie. "Now what?"

"Where are your friends?"

The kid shrugged. "How the hell should I know? What are you gonna do with me?"

"Maybe give you a dose of what you gave me."

The kid lifted his head, his chin jutting out defiantly. "Go ahead."

Shaking his head at the kid's bravado, Blackie pulled the kid's rifle from the boot. He removed the ammunition, then replaced the rifle in the boot. "Mount up."

"Why?" The kid looked at him suspiciously. "Where are we going?"

"Just do what I said. And don't try anything stupid."

Blackie helped the kid into the saddle, then mounted his own horse. "What's your name, anyway?"

"McBride," the boy answered sullenly. "Charlie McBride."

Blackie swore softly. No wonder the kid looked familiar.

Taking up the reins of McBride's horse, Blackie turned in the direction of his father's trail.

Hawk stood in front of the three white men. His father stood a few feet away and to the side, his rifle cradled negligently in the crook of his arm.

"I want to know the name of the other man who was with you," Hawk said, his gaze moving from the face of one man to the next. "But first, I want yours."

"Go to hell," the scar-faced man said.

"I want to know your name and his," Hawk said patiently, "and we're not leaving here until I have them."

"Guess we'll be here a long time," the scar-faced man retorted. He spat in the dirt.

Hawk uncorked his canteen and took a long swallow. "Take as long as you want, but I think you'll tell me what I want to know."

The man in the cavalry hat snorted loudly. "What makes you think that?"

With a grin, Hawk gestured for his father to come stand beside him. Shadow was his ace in the hole.

The three prisoners exchanged nervous looks as his father strode forward. Shadow handed his rifle to Hawk. He plucked the cavalry hat from the man's head and tossed it aside, then shoved the man belly down on the ground. Straddling the prisoner, Shadow grabbed a fistful of his hair with one hand and yanked his head back; then he drew his knife from the sheath on his belt and laid the edge of the razor-sharp blade against the man's throat.

"My son asked you a question," Shadow said, his voice laced with quiet menace. "Answer him."

"What the hell's he doing?" The short stocky man looked from Shadow to Hawk. "You can't let him do that. You're the law!"

"Can't I?" Hawk nodded at Shadow, who dragged the blade ever so lightly over the man's throat. A fine line of blood appeared in the wake of the blade.

"Dammit," said the man, his eyes wide with fear. "Get him off me!"

"I was wondering," Hawk said, speaking to his father. "Do you still take scalps?"

Shadow nodded, his expression implacable as he jerked the man's head back a little more. "My son asked you a question."

"Go to hell!" The man's voice was defiant, but his face had gone fish-belly white. Sweat dripped from his brow.

Shadow applied a little more pressure to the blade.

"You gonna let him do that?" the stocky man demanded. "Just gonna let him cut us up one at a time?"

"If I have to." Hawk grinned at the three men. "This is my father," he said conversationally. "He used to be known as Two Hawks Flying."

He watched the faces of the three men as the name registered. It was a name they had all heard before, a name that had once been mentioned with the same degree of awe and fear as Crazy Horse and Sitting Bull.

The man with the knife at his throat broke first. "My name's Caffrey, Bob Caffrey," he croaked. He jerked his chin at the scar-faced man. "That there's Gil Hackett, and that's Sal Trijo. The other guy with us was McBride. Charlie McBride."

Hawk and Shadow exchanged glances.

"Where's McBride now?" Hawk asked.

"I don't know!" Caffrey exclaimed. "He doesn't ride with us. I think he lives in town. We played cards together a couple of times, that's all." He swallowed, and the blade cut a little deeper into his skin. "Get him off me, dammit!"

Hawk looked at the other two men. "Either of you

gents know where we can find McBride?"

They both looked at Shadow, at the knife in his hand. Sal Trijo shook his head. "We split up yesterday." He glanced at the thin line of blood welling beneath the blade. "He probably went back to town. That's where he lives."

Hawk nodded. "See how easy that was?"

Shadow cleaned the blade by wiping it against Caffrey's pant leg, then stood and sheathed the knife.

Caffrey scrambled to his feet as best he could with his hands cuffed behind his back. Blood trickled down his neck.

"Charlie McBride," Hawk remarked, shaking his head. "I knew that kid was headed for trouble." The boy needed a father, he thought, someone strong enough to earn his trust and his respect, someone to help him get his life in order before it was too late.

Hawk looked at his father. Someone like Shadow. He remembered the time when his father dug a bullet out of his side, remembered his own pride when his father declared he was brave. He recalled how his father helped him to fulfill his dream of taking part in the medicine lodge. Shadow had gone to the Cheyenne reservation and found a shaman to instruct Hawk, and when the time was right, Shadow danced alongside him, enduring the pain and the power of the medicine lodge ceremony. His father taught him the way to live, and lived the things he taught.

"Come on," he said. "Let's go home."

*　　*　　*

It was just after noon on Friday when Blackie looked up and saw his father and brother riding toward him. They both looked surprised to see him, and even more surprised to see the kid with him.

"Where'd you find him?" Hawk asked.

"What are you doing here?" Shadow asked.

"I ran across him yesterday," Blackie said. He eased out of the saddle, one arm wrapped around his middle. "And I'm here because I have every right to be."

"You should be in bed," Hawk retorted. "You're hurt."

"Would you have stayed behind?" Blackie asked.

Hawk grinned at his younger brother. "No. Come on; we were just about to eat."

"What did your mother say when you left?" Shadow asked.

"She wasn't very happy with me," Blackie admitted. "But she knew I couldn't stay home."

Blackie met his father's gaze and frowned. He knew he looked like he'd been stomped by a loco bronc. "Do you think I should have stayed home, *neyho*?"

Shadow shook his head. "It does not matter what I think. You are a man now, old enough to make your own decisions," he said, and then he smiled. "But I am proud that you are here."

His father's approval made the long ride worth the pain it had cost him.

They rode until dusk, fixed a quick meal, then untied the prisoners one at a time so they could eat.

Blackie watched his father and Hawk carefully. He envied them their quiet confidence. They were men who always seemed to know who they were and what they were about, while he, himself, often felt as if he were drifting somewhere between two worlds. Did they ever feel like that? Was their self-assurance something they had been born with? Or was it, as Blackie suspected, a by-product of the way they had been raised? His father and brother had both sought visions. Both had participated in the medicine lodge. Blackie had a vague recollection of watching, wide-eyed, as an old Cheyenne medicine man pierced his brother's skin and inserted wooden skewers through the flesh over his breasts. Hawk had stood there, tall and proud. He had not cried out. He had not flinched. Blackie had admired his brother's courage and wondered if he would have been as brave. He had watched the medicine man follow the same procedure with his father, and then the skewers had been attached to long strands of rawhide that were attached to the medicine lodge pole. Shadow and Hawk had danced slowly back and forth, their bodies straining against the rawhide thongs. Faces lifted, they had stared up into the sun. From time to time, they had blown on eagle bone whistles. The notes had been high-pitched and long, floating in the air like ghostly cries of pain. Blackie had shuddered each time he heard that sound. Hours had passed. Blackie had fallen asleep, and when he woke, they were still dancing. It was just before sundown when the dancers pulled free. Hawk had fallen to the ground, his eyes glazed with pain, while Shadow had looked on, his dark eyes filled with pride. Blackie had always longed to have his father look at him that way.

Later that night, lying in his blankets, Blackie gazed up at the stars. His ribs hurt with every breath and the wound in his side ached. The skin around his black eye was still swollen and tender to the touch. He searched his mind, looking for something to think about other than the pain of his bruised ribs. Joey McBride's face rose in his mind. There was something about her, he thought, something in her sad eyes that touched a chord within him. He grinned as he remembered her shapely bottom, outlined by a pair of faded blue jeans. How had he ever thought she was a boy?

He would go see her again as soon as they got back to town, let her know he was still interested in renting that old building.

He fell asleep wondering how he could make her smile at him.

Chapter Seven

Monday morning found Joey sitting out on the rickety front porch, chewing on her thumbnail as she wondered where Charlie had gone off to this time. He had been gone almost a week, and while he had been known to take off before, he had never stayed away for more than a day or two. She had asked after him in town, but no one seemed to know where he was, only that he had last been seen in O'Toole's with a couple of drifters.

Joey shook her head ruefully. She knew that Charlie was going to get himself into serious trouble sooner or later. She had done her best to raise him after their father died, but Charlie had always been mule-headed, and he wasn't about to listen to anything she had to say. She was lucky she had managed to convince him to finish school. They had barely been making ends meet when Gram sent for them. Joey's hopes had soared at the thought of moving west, living in a nice house, not having to worry about putting food on the table anymore.

With a sigh, she leaned back in her chair. Those hopes had been dashed the minute she arrived in Bear Valley and saw the shack her grandmother was living in. The only thing her grandmother had of value was the empty building over on First. Joey had suggested selling it, but her grandmother had refused. In spite of everything that had happened, Joey had the feeling that her grandmother felt that selling that building would be like admitting that things would never get any better.

She hoped Blackie Kincaid still wanted to rent it. At least then they would have more money coming in every month. Her job at the mercantile barely covered their expenses, especially now that Charlie had been fired from yet another job.

She let herself think about Blackie Kincaid, something she had tried to avoid doing since she had toppled unceremoniously into his arms. It still piqued her that he had been shocked to learn she was a girl. She glanced down at her cotton shirt and jeans. Maybe she couldn't blame him for mistaking her for a boy, but she only owned one nice dress, and she kept it for church. Anyway, skirts would only get in the way when she was climbing on the ladder or delivering supplies for Mr. Feehan.

She'd had little to do with the Kincaid family. She saw the Kincaid women at church and in town from time to time. They seemed nice enough. At least they always smiled at her and said hello. She was afraid of the Kincaid men, though, especially the father. She had heard all the stories about Two Hawks Flying, how he had fought at the Little Big Horn and then with Geronimo. It didn't take any imagination at all to picture him in paint and feathers, brandishing a war lance. Every time she looked at him, she wondered if he was the one who had killed her grandfather. Hawk looked just as capable of violence as did his father. And though she hated to admit it, she was afraid of Blackie too. He had the same arrogance as his father and brother, the same underlying sense of confidence and strength. She was even more afraid of the way he made her feel, of the things he made her think. He was far too handsome, with his long black hair, coppery skin, and deep dark brown eyes.

She pushed his image from her mind. She didn't want anything to do with him or his family.

Rising, she went into the house and down the narrow hall to her grandmother's room. Gram rarely got out of bed these days.

Joey moved closer to the bed. Her grandmother had beautiful white hair, green eyes, and clear skin. She had no doubt been a beauty in her day. But now there were fine lines of pain around her eyes and mouth. It grieved Joey to know she was always in pain.

"Gram, are you awake?"

Maureen opened her eyes. "You need something, Josephine?"

"No, I just wanted to let you know I'm leaving now. Can I get you anything before I go?"

"No, dear, I'm fine. Amelia's coming by later to look in on me. You go on to work and don't worry. Have you heard from Charlie?"

Joey shook her head. She filled Gram's pitcher with fresh water, brought her a copy of *The Ladies' Home Journal* in case she wanted to read, and an apple in case she got hungry before Mrs. Jackson showed up.

"Thank you, dear."

Joey kissed her grandmother on the cheek. "I'll be home as soon as I can."

Leaving the house, Joey saddled her old mare and rode into town.

She was riding down Main Street when she saw seven riders pull up in front of the sheriff's office. Her eyes widened when she recognized Charlie's buckskin gelding.

Tugging on the reins, she turned her mare down Cross Street, overcome by a sense of foreboding. What had Charlie done now?

"I can handle things okay from here out if you two want to get home," Hawk said, glancing at his father and brother, who were still mounted.

Shadow looked at the four men standing on the boardwalk. "Are you sure?"

"Yeah."

"Do you want us to stop by your place and let Victoria know you're back?" Blackie asked.

"Yeah, thanks. And thanks for your help. Both of you." Hawk slapped his brother on the knee. "You'd better get back in bed. You look all done in."

"I feel that way too," Blackie admitted.

"I'll need you to sign a complaint against these hombres," Hawk said, "but you can do it tomorrow."

Blackie grinned. "Good, 'cause right now I don't think I could lift the pen."

Hawk laughed. "Give *nahkoa* my love, and tell her we'll be out Sunday for dinner, as usual."

"Will do," Blackie said.

Clucking to his horse, Shadow started down the street. Blackie turned to follow his father. It was then that he saw Joey McBride riding toward him. Blackie pulled up on the reins. A moment later, Joey reined her horse to a halt, dismounted, and threw her arms around her brother in a fierce hug.

"Charlie!" she exclaimed. "Oh, Charlie, what have you done now?"

"Nothing, sis," he replied, his tone defiant.

"Nothing!" She drew back to stare at him. "Nothing! They don't arrest you for nothing." She looked at the other three men with disdain. "Is this how I brought you up? To hang around with scum like this? What would Grams say?"

"Scum?" Hackett exclaimed. "You little whore, who you calling scum?"

"Don't you talk to my sister like that!" Charlie said, "or I'll—"

Hackett laughed derisively. "Or you'll what?"

Blackie edged his horse up beside Hackett. "You heard him. Shut up."

Hackett looked up at Blackie and snorted. "Got a thing for scrawny whores, do you?"

"You keep a decent tongue in your mouth around the lady," Blackie said, drawing his knife, "or I'll see that you never use it again."

"That's enough," Hawk said, stepping between the two men. Opening the door to the jail, he motioned for them to go inside.

Joey stepped back as Hawk herded her brother and the other three prisoners inside.

Shadow rode up alongside Blackie. "Are you coming, *naha*?"

"I'll be along after a while," Blackie said, sheathing his knife.

Shadow glanced from Joey to Blackie and back again. With a nod, he urged his horse down the street.

Blackie dismounted carefully, one arm automatically curling around his bruised ribs. His gaze moved over Joey. Today, she was wearing a dark green shirt with the sleeves pushed up, Levi's, and boots. The color of her shirt brought out the green in her eyes. Her hair fell over her shoulder in a long braid. He had a ridiculous urge to undo the braid and run his fingers through her hair.

"What are you doing here?" Joey asked.

"Hawk's my brother."

"Why did he arrest Charlie?"

"For what he did to me."

Joey's eyes widened as she noticed Blackie's bruised face for the first time. "Charlie did that?"

"Not without help."

"Well, he must have had a good reason," she said loyally.

"I'm Indian. He and his friends seemed to think that was reason enough. I guess you agree with them," he said when she didn't say anything.

She crossed her arms over her breasts, her expression defiant. "I didn't say that."

"What *are* you saying?"

"Nothing. Excuse me; I'm going to be late for

73

work, and I need to see if Charlie needs anything before I go."

"Maybe a good lawyer," Blackie muttered.

"A lawyer! But he's just a boy!"

Blackie lifted a hand to his swollen eye. "He doesn't hit like a boy."

"You hate him, don't you?"

Blackie shook his head in disbelief. "You just won't believe he did anything wrong, will you?"

"I can't let him go to jail. It will kill my grandmother."

"I'm sorry, Joey. There's nothing I can do."

She glared at him through eyes brimming with tears, then jerked the door open and went into the jail.

Blackie stared after her. As angry as she made him, he had to admire her loyalty to her no-account brother. He blew out a deep breath. It had been all he could do to keep from taking her into his arms when he saw the tears in her eyes. If he hadn't been afraid of her reaction, he might have tried it. But she looked like the kind of girl to hit first and ask questions later, and he didn't think his ribs could take another beating.

With a shake of his head, he put his foot in the stirrup and then paused, somehow reluctant to leave her.

Tossing his horse's reins over the hitch rack, he followed Joey into the jail.

Hawk was sitting behind his desk. He looked up as Blackie entered. "I thought you were going home."

"I was." Blackie glanced around, looking for

Joey. "But I thought I'd sign that complaint as long as I was here, save myself a trip back to town."

Hawk lifted one brow. "She's in back," he said, jerking his head toward the door that led to the cellblock. "Sit down before you fall down."

"Do I look that bad?"

"I've seen worse. But not standing up."

"Very funny." Blackie lowered himself into the straight-backed chair in front of the desk. "What do I have to sign?"

Hawk slid a sheet of paper across his desk. "This."

"What will happen to her brother?"

Hawk shrugged. "That's not up to me." He held out a pen.

"What happens if I don't sign?"

"You'd damn well better sign it! I didn't go chasing after those guys because I had nothing better to do."

"I can't send her brother to jail. Can't you just hold him a few days? Maybe doing some time behind bars will straighten him out."

"You want me to let those other fellas go too?"

"No."

Hawk swore under his breath. "You're sweet on Joey McBride, aren't you?"

"What?"

"You heard me."

"I'm not sweet on her. Where'd you get an idea like that?"

Looking disgusted, Hawk dropped the pen on the desk. Drops of ink splattered over the desk top. "So your feelings for Joey have nothing to do with this?"

"Of course not. I don't even know the girl."

"So it's just a sudden interest in her brother's welfare that's changed your mind, is that it?"

"No, I just . . ." Blackie paused as the cellblock door swung open and Joey McBride stepped through the doorway.

Her gaze moved from Blackie's face to Hawk's and back again. Blackie felt a rush of heat burn his cheeks. She knew, he thought, knew they had been talking about her. What, if anything, had she heard?

She met his gaze for a long moment, then swept out of the room, her head high and proud.

Blackie watched her walk away, noting the gentle sway of her hips, the way her jeans clung to her backside.

When the door closed behind her, he looked back at his brother to find Hawk watching him, an insufferably knowing grin on his face.

Blackie grabbed the pen. "All right, where do I sign?"

"Down at the bottom," Hawk said, and then chuckled.

"What's so funny?"

"This should be right interesting," Hawk said.

Blackie scowled at his brother. "What in tarnation are you talking about?"

"You and Joey McBride." Hawk laughed out loud. "Ought to be quite a show."

"You're late, Joey," Mike Feehan said, looking up from the papers scattered on the front counter. "Everything okay at home?"

"Yes, fine, Mr. Feehan. I'm sorry."

Big Mike grunted. "There's some boxes in the back that need to be unloaded."

"I'll get right on it," Joey said, and hurried into

the back room, grateful for a chance to be alone with her thoughts, even if those thoughts were of Blackie Kincaid.

She remembered the way he looked at her, though she wasn't sure what it was she had seen in his eyes. Not pity. Not scorn. She was used to those. She had felt his gaze on her back when she left the jail. It had sent a wave of heat rushing through her from head to foot.

He had flustered her so much that she had forgotten to ask him if he was still interested in renting the building. Well, she would just have to see him again, she thought, annoyed that the idea pleased her so much.

She was trying to pry the lid off one of the boxes when she realized she was no longer alone.

"Can you give me a hand here?" she asked, thinking it was Mike.

"I'll try."

She straightened with a jerk at the sound of Blackie's voice. "What are you doing here?"

"I came to talk to you about renting your building. After today, I wasn't sure you'd still let me have it."

"Of course I will," she said coolly. "I said I would, didn't I?"

He moved toward her and she backed up, putting the box between them.

"You said you needed a hand. What's wrong?"

"I can't get the lid off this stupid box."

With a nod, he took the hammer from her hand, eased the claw under the lid, and pried it open. He winced as the movement sent a shaft of pain along his rib cage.

"Thank you," she said. "I'm sorry my brother hurt you."

He handed her the hammer. "Yeah, me too."

"Charlie's really a good boy. He is, really," she insisted when he looked skeptical. "It's just hard on him, not having a father, you know? He won't listen to me. I guess I can't blame him. I'm not much older than he is."

"And a girl, to boot," Blackie mused. He smiled, taking the sting out of his words.

"I hate to think of him in jail."

"Well, don't worry about that. I'm not pressing charges."

She looked up at him, her eyes wide with surprise. "You're not?"

"No, but I told Hawk to keep him locked up for a couple days. It might do him some good to get a taste of what it's like to be in jail."

She put down the hammer and came around the crate. "Thank you." Impulsively, she stood on her tiptoes and kissed him on the cheek, then looked up at him, horrified by what she'd done.

Blackie grinned at her. "Thank you, darlin', but I think we can do better than that," he said, and before she quite realized what he was about, he pulled her into his arms and kissed her full on the mouth.

Lightning streaked through her, making her heart pound like thunder. Her knees went weak, and only his arm around her waist kept her upright. Her eyelids fluttered down, and for one crazy moment, she kissed him back.

She was blushing furiously when he let her go. She stared up at him. He was so tall, so close. She backed away from him, unable to think when he was so near.

"Joey?"

She blinked at him. "How . . . how soon will you be wanting to . . . ?"

He looked at her, one brow arched. "To what?"

"What?" She looked at him blankly for a moment. "Oh. Move into the building. How soon will you want to move in?"

He smiled as if he knew just how his nearness was affecting her. "Right away, if that's all right with you."

"Yes. Sure. Of course," she said, flustered. "But you haven't even seen the inside yet."

"I'm sure it'll be okay. How about meeting me there Wednesday afternoon?"

She nodded. "Wednesday."

"See you then."

Lifting a finger to his hat in a gesture of farewell, he left the room, whistling softly.

Joey stared after him, her heart pounding. Her first kiss. She lifted a hand to her lips, lips that still felt the warmth of his.

She had been afraid of him before, she thought, but not like this.

Chapter Eight

I could tell that something had happened when Blackie got home that afternoon. After assuring me that he was fine, he went to his room to lie down awhile before dinner. That, in itself, told me he was hurting worse than he had let on. But it wasn't just the pain of his injuries that was troubling him, I was sure of that.

I cleaned up the kitchen, folded some laundry, and then went outside to see Shadow. He had said little when he returned from town, only that they had found the men they were looking for, and that Hawk would be by for Sunday dinner, as usual.

Shadow had earned quite a reputation as a horse trainer in the past ten years or so. People came from as far away as Steel's Crossing and beyond to buy our stock, or to breed their mares to one of our stallions, or to have their horses trained by Shadow.

This afternoon, he was working a four-year-old bay gelding that had been badly abused by its previous owner. Shadow had bought the horse at an auction in Steel's Crossing several weeks earlier. The horse had been painfully thin and wild-eyed. Shadow spent the first few days just talking to it, letting the animal grow accustomed to the sound of his voice. He spent hours in the corral, not trying to approach the animal, just letting it get used to his presence and his scent, letting the horse see that it had nothing to fear from him. No one else had been allowed to go near the horse. Shadow fed and watered the gelding, talking to it all the time. When, at last, he had earned the gelding's trust, he started training the horse as though it was a green colt that had never known saddle or bridle before.

Now, he rode the gelding around the corral. Few things in life were more beautiful to me than the sight of my husband astride a horse. Shadow rode fluidly, his body moving in perfect rhythm with his mount. I could detect no movement of Shadow's hands on the reins, nor did I notice any other signals, yet the gelding circled right, then left, spun on its hocks, backed up, moved forward, accelerated from walk to trot to canter and back down again smoothly and effortlessly.

"Bravo!"

Shadow reined the bay to a halt in front of me. I would not have been surprised to see the gelding take a bow.

I stepped up on the bottom rung of the corral and folded my arms on the top rail. "That's amazing. Just amazing."

Shadow grinned at me. He backed the horse up a bit and then, to my delight, the gelding reared, its forelegs pawing the air. I clapped my hands, unable to suppress my delight in what I was seeing. The sound startled the gelding. It came down hard and started bucking.

Shadow clung to the horse's back like a burr to a blanket, a look of pure pleasure on his face as the gelding crow-hopped and sunfished from one end of the corral to the other.

Both man and beast were blowing hard when Shadow again drew the horse to a halt in front of me.

"Looks like he needs a little more work," I said, grinning.

"Or I need a woman who knows when to remain quiet."

"Very funny. You enjoyed that, and you know it. You looked like a kid at Christmas."

He laughed softly as he swung out of the saddle.

I watched Shadow unsaddle the gelding. He spread the saddle and blanket over the top rail, then slipped the hackamore over the horse's head. The gelding tossed its head, shook itself, then lay down and rolled onto its back. The horse rolled from one side to the other, something not every horse could do, then gained its feet and ran around the corral, coming to a sliding stop in front of Shadow. Lowering its head, the horse waited for Shadow to scratch between its ears.

"You do have a way with horses," I mused.

Shadow ducked between the rails to stand beside me. "And with women?"

"Women?" I asked, accenting the plural.

He chuckled. "Woman?"

"That's better."

Arm in arm, we walked away from the house toward the river.

"Do you know what's bothering Blackie?" I asked after a while.

"He has much on his mind," Shadow replied. "The beating he received was unsettling."

I nodded.

"He is thinking of starting his own business," Shadow went on. "No doubt he is also thinking of leaving home and finding a place of his own."

"Leave home! Why would he want to do that?"

"He is a grown man," Shadow said with a shrug. "It is natural for him to want his own lodge."

I knew Shadow was right, but for some reason, it had never occurred to me that Blackie would want to move out of our house. I had assumed he would stay once he returned from New York, at least until he got married.

"You cannot keep him at home forever."

"I know," I said, and I was suddenly glad that we'd had Blue Hawk late in life. I knew a lot of women were anxious for their children to grow up and leave home, but I had never felt that way. I was glad that Mary and Hawk were happily married, that they were raising families of their own, of course, but sometimes I missed having my children about me, missed the sound of their childish laughter, missed the days when I had been the most important person in their lives, the one they turned to for comfort.

Shadow squeezed my hand. "Life goes on," he said quietly. "We cannot stop it."

"I know. But sometimes I wish I could slow it down a little." I let out a sigh. "Funny, when I was little, I never thought I'd be this old."

"You are not old."

"Well, I'm getting there."

We had reached the river crossing. The water was low this time of year. We turned down the narrow path that paralleled the river. The pine tree forest rose on one side. It had been my favorite place to play when I was a young girl. I'd had quite an imagination back then. I pretended the forest was an enchanted fairyland, and I was the fairy queen. The frog on the riverbank was a prince under an evil spell, the raccoon a wicked witch in disguise. The distant mountains were a crystal palace filled with riches beyond compare. That part, at least, had proven to be true. Custer had found gold in the Black Hills, and it had been the beginning of the end for the Indians. But those days were far behind us now.

We walked on until we came to Rabbit's Head Rock. It was an unusual formation, the gray rock shaped like a huge jackrabbit with its ears laid back. As a child, I had been forbidden to go beyond this point. Back then, all the land beyond Rabbit's Head Rock had belonged to the Sioux and Cheyenne.

Shadow gave a tug on my hand. "Look."

I looked where he pointed, felt my eyes fill with tears when I saw it, a dazzling red bloom. It was the same kind of flower that had lured me out onto the prairie when I was nine years old.

"You remember," I said. How many times had I met him here in secret when we were young?

Shadow nodded, then drew me into his arms. "How could I forget?"

It had been here that we had met for the first time, here that I had seduced him. Who could have guessed then the path that we would follow, or that our love would reap such a long-lasting reward?

Shadow gazed down at me, his dark eyes filled with love. "It is a woman," he said. "A woman who troubles our son."

"How do you know that? Did he tell you?"

"No."

"Then how do you know?"

"Because," he said. And then he kissed me, a long sweet kiss that warmed my heart and soul.

"Because?" I repeated.

"He wears the same look I saw in Hawk's eyes when he first spoke of Victoria. The same look I saw in Mary's eyes when she met Cloud Walker for the first time." He smiled down at me. "The same look I saw in your eyes on your sixteenth birthday."

"What woman?" I asked.

Shadow looked at me expectantly.

And then I answered my own question. "Joey McBride."

Chapter Nine

At his mother's insistence, Blackie spent most of Tuesday in bed. He put up a token resistance, but, truth be told, he was glad for a chance to rest after all that had happened. His ribs were sore; the knife wound, though it wasn't deep enough to be serious, was a constant ache in his side. His mother looked in on him from time to time, her expression troubled. He knew she was concerned about his health and his lack of appetite, but he had a feeling there was more to it than that, though he had no idea what else might be worrying her.

Blackie sighed as he stared out the window. Well, he was troubled too, and Joey McBride was the reason. What was there about her that had him all tied up in knots? She wasn't his type at all, he thought, and then grinned. Who was he kidding? He didn't have any idea what his type was. He had only been out with a few girls, and they had all been women he had met when he was back east. None of them really knew him, knew who he was or where he came from. But Joey knew, he thought ruefully, and what she knew she didn't like.

Joey. He would see her tomorrow afternoon.

He stirred restlessly, remembering the last time he had seen her.

Staring out the window, he willed the hours to pass more quickly.

Joey was waiting for him when he arrived at the building on Wednesday afternoon. As usual, she was wearing a pair of faded jeans and a long-sleeved shirt. Her hair was pulled away from her face, held at her nape by a blue ribbon.

Dismounting, Blackie tethered his horse to the fence post. Reaching into his pocket, he handed her the money he had withdrawn from the bank.

"It's all there," he said. "A year's rent. A hundred and thirty-two dollars."

She counted it carefully, then shoved the bills into the pocket of her jeans. "Here's the key," she said. "There's only one, so don't lose it."

Unlocking the door, he stepped inside, and Joey followed him.

"I guess it needs a lot of work," she said, looking around. "I haven't been in here for a while."

"I'm not afraid of a little hard work," Blackie said. "You don't mind if I paint the place, do you?"

"No. It needs it. Gram always hoped this would be a fine restaurant some day, like Sullivan's in Steel's Crossing, but—" She shrugged. "She got sick, and then the man she hired to take over stole her money and left town. I tried to talk her into selling the building, but she won't hear of it." She shook her head, as if shaking off a bad memory. "You can do anything you want to the place, I guess, as long as you don't tear it down."

He laughed at that. "Don't worry."

"Have you always wanted to be a veterinarian?"

"Yeah. I was always bringing hurt and stray animals home when I was a kid. My mother used to say I had a natural talent for healing. I guess maybe I do. I didn't do too well with the book learning in college, but I passed all my tests, especially those in the lab. Is there anything in those old sheds out back?"

"I don't think so."

"Come on, let's go have a look."

The smaller shed was empty. The larger one held an assortment of old garden tools and a big round wooden tub.

"Do you want any of this stuff?" Blackie asked.

"No."

Blackie looked up at the hole in the roof. "I'll have to patch that."

"Why? I mean, what are you gonna keep in here?"

He shrugged. "You never know. I might need a place to quarantine an animal. Always pays to be prepared. I'll have to fix that corral too."

"Maybe I'm charging you too much for this place," Joey muttered, "considering all the work it needs."

"The price is just right," he said, and wished the rent had been more. He had a feeling she needed the money a lot more than he did.

His gaze met hers, and she shifted from one foot to the other. "Well, I guess I'd better get back to work." She stuck out her hand. "Nice doing business with you."

Blackie took her hand in his, his fingers closing over hers. Her skin was warm. He could feel a callus on her palm. She was too pretty to have to work so hard, he thought. Too young to have calluses on her hands.

Joey eased her hand from his. "See ya 'round, I guess."

"Yeah, see ya."

He watched her walk away, his gaze lingering on the curve of her buttocks, the gentle swaying of her hips. He watched her until she was out of sight. Damn, he had it bad, he thought with a wry grin.

He glanced at the old building, picturing the way it would look when it was cleaned up and wearing a new coat of paint. At last, his dream was about to come true.

Blackie was back bright and early the next day. He patched the hole in the roof of the shed, washed down the walls, raked the hard-packed earthen floor, replaced the hinges on the door.

He was fixing the corral gate when he heard footsteps. Glancing over his shoulder, he was surprised to see Joey McBride walking toward him.

"Hi," he said. "What are you doing here?"

She shrugged. "I was on my way to work and I heard hammering." She looked over at the shed. "You've been busy."

"Yeah." She looked prettier every time he saw her, he thought, and wondered how she could look so feminine in a pair of faded Levi's and a flannel shirt.

"Well, I guess I'd better go. Mr. Feehan gets mad when I'm late."

Blackie watched her walk away. And suddenly he didn't want her to go, not yet. "Joey!"

She stopped and turned to face him. "Is something wrong? You haven't changed your mind about the building, have you? I can lower the rent if you've decided it's too high."

"No. What are you doing tomorrow night?"

She looked at him suspiciously. "Nothing; why?"

He took a deep breath. "Would you mind if I came by your place?"

Her eyes widened and she shook her head vigorously. "Oh, I don't think that's a good idea."

"Probably not." It had been a ridiculous idea. Joey's grandmother would never allow him in the house. He thought for a moment. "Maybe you could come out to our place for dinner? I could come by and pick you up at about . . ."

"No!" she said quickly. "I'll meet you there. Tomorrow night. After dinner."

"All right. I'll see you about . . . seven?"

Joey stood in front of the cracked mirror in her bedroom, frowning at her reflection. Why had she said she would go to his house? Blackie lived in a palace compared to the hovel where she lived. And his mother . . . Hannah Kincaid was the prettiest woman Joey had ever known. Just being around Mrs. Kincaid made her feel tongue-tied and inferior. The Kincaids had the biggest spread in the valley, and one of the biggest houses. She remembered the day she had gone to their house. It was the first time she had seen the inside. It was the kind of home she had always dreamed of, with matching furniture that wasn't broken down or threadbare, pretty pictures hanging on the walls, nice rugs on the floor, and best of all, a sense of permanence, of security.

She lifted her chin defiantly. It was no sin to be poor, though it was nothing to be proud of, either. Still, she had an honest job and was doing her best to keep what was left of her family together.

Her family. She thought of Charlie, sitting in a jail cell with those three no-accounts. If not for Blackie, Charlie might be cooling his heels behind bars a lot longer than a couple of days. If only her brother would get himself a decent job instead of spending all his time at the saloon. How could she make him see that he was wasting his life, that they could live so much better if he'd go to work? She knew it weighed as heavy on Gram's mind as on her own that Charlie was always getting into trouble. If only their father had lived. Maybe things would have been different if Charlie had had a father's influence. And maybe not.

With a shake of her head, she straightened her skirt and smoothed a hand over her hair. Her hair was clean and shiny; her dress was freshly pressed, and if it wasn't the latest style, well, that was just too bad. She had earned the money to buy it with her own two hands.

But as she left the house, she couldn't help wishing that she had something new and stylish, something that would make Blackie Kincaid sit up and take notice, though why she should care about his opinion didn't bear thinking about.

She had saddled her horse before getting ready. Now, she tightened the saddle cinch, took up the reins, and climbed into the saddle. The rent she would be getting for the building would greatly increase their income, and for that, she would go calling on the Kincaids.

Blackie grimaced at he stared at his reflection in the mirror. His face was as colorful as one of Cole's drawings. The swelling around his left eye was an ugly green and purple; there was a half-healed cut on his lower lip, a scabbed-over gash on his right cheek.

"Man, you look like you fell headfirst into a bucket of bruises," he muttered sourly.

And he felt like it too. The wound in his side ached with every breath. Damn Charlie McBride and his pals. If it weren't for Joey, he would be happy to see Charlie locked up with the others for a year instead of a couple of days.

Joey. Ever since she had fallen off that ladder and landed in his arms, he hadn't been able to think of anything else. And after he'd kissed her . . . He swore softly. Joey. What kind of name was that for a girl? Hard to believe he had ever thought she looked like a boy, even from the back.

He took a last look at his reflection in the mirror. What did she see when she looked at him? A tall man with long black hair, brown eyes, and copper-hued skin? Or a half-breed? He hadn't been called that very often, but often enough to come to hate the term and the scorn that always accompanied it.

He heard Joey's knock at the door. Taking a deep breath, he left his room.

His mother had already ushered Joey into the parlor and was inviting her to sit down when Blackie entered the room.

"Hi, Joey," he said, smiling at her. "I'm glad you could make it."

Joey mumbled something unintelligible as she sat down and glanced around the room. Blackie's little brother was lying on his belly on the floor, playing with some toy soldiers and Indians. His father was sitting in an easy chair mending a leather bridle. He greeted her with a nod.

Blue Hawk looked up at her and smiled. "Hi, Miss McBride," he said, "I'm playing Little Big Horn." He knocked over several soldiers as he spoke.

"Looks like the Indians are winning again," she said.

Blue Hawk grinned at her as he picked up a tin soldier and an Indian carved from wood. "This is Custer," he said, the tone of his voice clearly betraying his contempt for the general as he held up the soldier. "And this," he said with obvious pride, "is Two Hawks Flying, the last fighting chief on the plains."

Joey glanced at the two figures in the boy's hands. "My grandpa was killed in that battle."

An awkward silence fell over the room.

Blackie tried to think of something to say, something to put everyone at ease, but nothing came to mind. Perhaps inviting her here hadn't been such a good idea after all. The war had been over for years, but old hurts remained on both sides.

Apparently Joey was thinking the same thing. "I

can't stay, really." Rising, she reached into her skirt pocket and withdrew a key, which she offered to Blackie. "I found this at home. I thought maybe you could use it. It goes to that old shed out back."

"Thanks." He took it from her hand and shoved it into his pants pocket. "Don't go," he said quietly. "Not yet. Please."

"I made some cookies this afternoon," Hannah said, speaking to Joey. "Surely you'll stay and have a couple before you go home?"

Blackie smiled at his mother as he said, "No one can resist my mother's cookies."

Joey hesitated a moment and then, apparently deciding it would be rude to refuse, she said, "Thank you, Mrs. Kincaid. Can I help you with anything?"

"No, dear," Hannah said. "It'll just take me a minute."

"You are a guest on your first visit," Shadow told Joey with a wink. Rising, he hung the bridle on a hook next to the front door. "Next time, she will make you wash the dishes."

Joey stared at him for a moment, and then, realizing he was teasing her, she grinned. She hadn't expected Blackie's father to have a sense of humor.

"Sit down," Blackie said. "Make yourself at home."

There were two leather sofas in the room, one on either side of the fireplace. Shadow had taken a seat on one of them. Joey sat down on the other one and Blackie sat beside her.

"How's your brother doing?" Blackie asked.

"He's not very happy about being locked up."

"No, I don't suppose so," Blackie remarked. "But it's only for another day or so."

"Yes."

She was relieved when Mrs. Kincaid returned to the living room.

Hannah placed a tray bearing a plate of oatmeal cookies, a pitcher of lemonade, and five glasses on the large square table between the two couches. Sitting down beside her husband, she poured drinks for everyone and passed around the cookie plate.

They were, as promised, delicious. Joey saw the enigmatic look that passed between Hannah and Shadow when Shadow picked up a cookie. She wondered what it meant.

Joey ate three cookies and drank a glass of lemonade. She would have loved to have had another one if she hadn't been afraid of looking like a glutton.

"Go ahead," Hannah said. "Have another, if you like." She looked at her husband. "Shadow once gobbled down ten at one sitting."

Shadow looked at his wife. Joey did not miss the look that passed between them, a look of such love it made her feel as though she were intruding on a private moment. Taking another cookie from the plate, she looked away.

"One of these days, I'll have to tell you what happened after he ate all those cookies," Blackie told her.

"I'd like that." Wiping her mouth with her napkin, Joey stood up. "I really have to go. Thank you, Mrs. Kincaid, for the refreshments. Good night."

She was leaving the room when she heard

Shadow's voice. "Blackie, see Miss McBride safely home."

Joey paused and turned to look at Blackie's father. "That won't be necessary."

Shadow glanced out the window. "I would not feel right letting you go home alone in the dark."

"I've done it before." The thought of riding through the night with Blackie made her heart pound, whether from apprehension or excitement, she wasn't sure.

"I will not take no for an answer," Shadow said, rising. "If you would rather that Blackie not accompany you, I will go with you."

Blackie stood up. "I'll take her."

She didn't argue. The thought of being alone with Shadow was even more unsettling than being alone with Blackie, although for a completely different reason.

Shadow moved toward the front door. "I will saddle your horse," he told Blackie, and left the house.

Blackie let out a sigh. "I could have done it," he muttered. "I'm not completely helpless."

His mother smiled at him. "He knows that, but you're hurt, remember?"

Joey felt a twinge of guilt, knowing that Blackie wouldn't be hurting if it hadn't been for her brother and his friends.

Shadow returned a few moments later.

She heard Blackie murmur, "Thank you, *neyho*," before he followed her out of the house.

A beautiful black horse with a white blaze was tied to the hitch rack beside her dun-colored mare.

"Hey, Raven." Blackie patted the horse on the neck, then turned to help Joey mount.

She brushed his hand away. "I can do it."

"Suit yourself," he muttered. Taking a deep breath, he picked up the reins and hauled himself into the saddle.

Joey clucked to her mare and rode out of the yard, conscious of Blackie riding beside her.

It was a lovely summer night, warm and clear. Millions of stars twinkled in an indigo sky. A full moon shed its silver light on the landscape. Crickets serenaded the night, falling quiet as they rode by, then filling the air with their night song once again.

Joey tried to think of something to say to break the silence between them, but nothing came to mind. She wondered if Blackie was feeling as tongue-tied as she was, or if he just didn't want to talk to her. It was obvious that he was only with her now at his father's urging. It annoyed her to realize she was glad to have him there beside her, not because it was dark out, but because, whether she wanted to admit it or not, she was attracted to him without knowing why.

She slid a glance at Blackie. Perhaps her attraction to him wasn't all that strange after all, she mused. He was tall and handsome, broad-shouldered and slim-hipped, just like his father. She studied his profile in the moonlight, liking his firm jaw, his straight nose. But, most of all, she liked his eyes. They were deep and dark. And gentle.

All too soon, they reached her house, with never a word spoken between them.

Dismounting, she turned to tell him there was no need for him to do so, but it was too late. He was at her side almost before she was out of the saddle.

When she started to unsaddle her horse, his hand stayed hers. "I'll do it," he said.

"I can do it."

"I know. I'll put her up for you." Taking the reins from her hand, he dropped them over the hitch rack.

"We don't have a barn. Just put her in the corral. There's a rack for the saddle."

"I'll take care of it."

She wasn't used to having a man do things for her. She wasn't sure she liked it, and she wasn't sure how to respond. In the end, she murmured, "Thank you," and headed for the stairs, surprised when he followed her.

He walked her up the steps to the front door, one arm wrapped around his rib cage.

She swallowed, suddenly flustered by his nearness. "Thank you for seeing me home."

He didn't say anything, just looked at her. And then he took her in his arms and kissed her.

At the touch of his lips on hers, her eyelids fluttered down and she leaned into him, curious to see if she had imagined the wonder of his last kiss. Her first kiss. If possible, this one was even better. His lips were warm and firm on hers, the arms that held her strong yet gentle.

When he started to pull away, she moaned in soft protest, and he deepened the kiss, his arms tightening around her. She felt a glow in the deepest part of her, as if she had swallowed a piece of the sun.

When, at last, the kiss ended, she looked up at him, blinking in awe. He didn't look any happier about what was happening between them than she did, even though she wasn't sure exactly what was happening.

She backed away from him, confused by the powerful emotions he aroused in her. He made her feel things she had never felt before, things she couldn't put a name to.

"We can't do this," she said.

"I know."

"My grandmother would never approve. And Charlie—" She shook her head. "It just won't work."

"I know," he said again.

But when he reached for her a second time, she didn't object.

Her lips were soft, pliant, indescribably sweet. He cupped the back of her head with one hand, his fingers delving into her hair. The heat and softness of her breasts pressing against his chest stirred his desire. Strange, he thought, that of all the beautiful, well-dressed women he had met back east, it was a little country girl in a blue gingham dress who fired his imagination and filled him with the most incredible longing he'd ever known.

"Joey." His voice was thick.

"Hmm?"

"Is Joey short for something?"

"Josephine," she replied, her voice low and breathy. "After my other grandmother."

"Joey suits you better," he said, and kissed her again.

She melted in his embrace, her arms twining around his neck, her body pressing intimately against his. It was pleasure beyond compare. It was torture of the worst kind.

Gradually, the sound of a bell ringing penetrated

the haze of passion. Lifting his head, Blackie said, "What's that?"

"My grandmother. She needs me. I've got to go." She smiled shyly. "Good night, Blackie."

"Good night, Joey."

He watched her disappear into the dark house, then led the mare around back. Opening the corral, he led the horse inside, stripped off the rigging, and turned it loose. Dropping the saddle and bridle over the rack, he found himself wondering again what madness had possessed him to kiss Joey McBride not once, not twice, but three times. Even worse, he found himself wondering how soon he could do it again.

Chapter Ten

Blackie was feeling a lot better when he woke on Monday morning. He wasn't surprised when his first conscious thought was of Joey. She had been the last thing on his mind before sleep claimed him the night before. He had helped his father exercise some of the horses on Saturday; had spent Saturday night looking after Blue Hawk while their parents went out for the evening.

He had spent most of Sunday out on the front porch, content to sit in the shade and let his body heal, content to sit and think about Joey. She could be soft and sweet one minute and prickly as a cactus the next. He doubted they could have a future together, yet he couldn't stop thinking about her, couldn't stop remembering how good she had felt in his arms, the touch of her, the taste of her, the warm sweet womanly scent of her hair and skin.

Hawk and Mary and the rest of the family had come to the house after church. He had hardly noticed their arrival, paid little attention to the kids. One by one, Hawk, Victoria, and Cloud Walker had all taken him aside to ask him what was wrong. Mary had taken one look at him and declared it had to be a woman that had him so preoccupied.

How had she known? With a shake of his head, he eased out of bed, washed up, and went into the kitchen.

The room was empty, and he realized he had slept through breakfast. He grinned, surprised that his mother had let him oversleep. But then, maybe it wasn't so surprising after all. She firmly believed that sleep was the best healer.

He made a pot of fresh coffee and put it on the stove, then sat down at the table and munched one of his mother's homemade cinnamon rolls while he waited for the coffee to get hot.

And again, he found himself thinking of Joey. She might dress like a boy most of the time, he thought, but underneath those jeans and that flannel shirt, she was all woman! And damn, but she knew how to kiss. The thought made him smile. And then he frowned. Who the devil had taught her to kiss like that?

He realized, with no small surprise, that he was jealous.

Shaking his head, he rose slowly to his feet and poured himself a cup of coffee. Glancing out of the window, he saw his father working a big bay horse in the corral nearest the house. No one rode the way his father did, he thought proudly, and wished, not for the first time, that he had been born when the Indians still roamed the prairies as a free people. As far back as he could remember, he had yearned to participate in the medicine lodge, seek a vision, go on a buffalo hunt. He had grown up on his father's stories, listening with awe as Shadow spoke of the old days, the old ways. He had heard the longing in his father's voice, the sadness that those days were forever gone. It was a sadness Blackie shared. His father had taught him to ride and to track, to hunt, to skin a deer, to live off the land. Blackie grinned. His father had even shown him how to take a scalp. Of course, in this day and age, Blackie had had little opportunity to practice what he had learned—especially taking a scalp. But he still regretted the fact that he'd never had the chance to seek a vision or hunt the buffalo that had once roamed in vast herds and were now practically extinct.

His father had also taught him something of the Cheyenne religion *Heammawihio*, the Wise One above, was the Supreme Being, the creator of all life. His name was the first invoked in prayer; the first smoke was offered to Him. The Cheyenne believed there was also a god of the Underworld, *Ahk tun o'wihio*. Both *Heammawihio* and *Ahk tun o'wihio* were benevolent beings. There were gods of the four directions as well. When a warrior smoked a pipe, the first six smokes went to these powers. The stem of the pipe was pointed upward first, then down to the earth, and then to the four directions, starting in the east.

Shadow had taught him that *Seyan*, the Place of the Dead, was beyond the place where *Heamma-*

wihio dwelled. All those who died, good or bad, went to live with Him, save for those who had taken their own lives. To reach the Place of the Dead, a man's spirit followed *E kut si him mi yo*, the Hanging Road, which the white man called the Milky Way. There, the spirits of the dead lived as they had lived on earth. It was believed that if you saw your own spirit, or shade, you would soon die.

In the old days, the Indians had feared having their picture taken, believing that when the picture was taken away, their spirit would be taken as well, and that the living person would then die. When mirrors had first been brought to the tribe as trade goods, there had been some who refused to look into them, believing they were seeing their spirit and that bad luck would follow.

His father had taught him that all living things possessed a spirit. Trees, rocks, the mountains, the tall grass, the Cheyenne believed all were alive with a spirit of their own and thus were to be revered. Animals also possessed spirits. No animal was ever to be killed for sport. Life was a circle and man was but a small part of that circle.

It was believed that eagles, ravens, owls, magpies, and hawks possessed powers that could be helpful in time of war. In ancient times, Shadow had told him that wolves and coyotes were never killed, and that women would not handle their skins. The spirit of the deer held much power that could be used for good or evil.

Blackie grinned faintly. His father had told him that white-tailed deer were thought to be powerful helpers in love affairs. Again, he thought of Joey. What would she think of his father's beliefs? Of his own beliefs? His mother believed that *Heamma-wihio* and the white man's God were one and the same. She had no trouble accepting his father's tenets. Blackie and his brothers and sister had been taught the ways of both their parents and been left to decide for themselves which religion they would embrace.

On Sundays, Blackie, Hawk, Mary, and Blue Hawk had sometimes gone to church with their mother and sometimes stayed home to pray and meditate with their father. Mary and Blue Hawk leaned toward their mother's religion. Hawk embraced his father's philosophy, but he went to church with Victoria. Blackie hadn't made a decision one way or the other. Some weeks he went to church with his mother, sometimes he sought out a quiet place at home and communed with the Great Spirit. He wondered if Joey had gone to church yesterday. His mother hadn't mentioned seeing her there.

With a sigh, Blackie finished his coffee and went outside. It was time to stop lamenting what could not be changed and go to work. Time to accept his life as it was. The past was past. He would never be a warrior like Two Hawks Flying. He would never have a vision. Never be the man his father was.

Going to the barn, he saddled the black, slipped the bridle in place, and led the stallion outside.

He stopped when he saw his father walking toward him, leading the bay.

Keeping a firm hold on the reins of the bay, Shadow stopped a few feet in front of Blackie. He studied his son for a moment and then nodded. "You are looking better."

"I feel better. I'm going into town for a while. Tell *nahkoa* for me, will you?"

"Your mother has gone into town also. She was going to mail a letter to Rebecca and then do some shopping."

Blackie nodded. Rebecca was Grandpa Kincaid's widow. After Grandpa died, she had gone back to Philadelphia to stay with her daughter Beth and her family. "I'll look for *nahkoa*. Maybe I can take her to lunch."

"She would like that."

"I should be home before dark," Blackie said. He ran his hand along his horse's neck. Raven had been sired five years earlier by his father's stallion, Red Wind. Blackie had gentled the colt himself, using his father's techniques.

Taking hold of the saddle horn, he put his left foot into the stirrup, took a deep breath, and pulled himself into the saddle.

With a nod at his father, he rode out of the yard.

Dismounting in front of his new office, Blackie took the key from his pocket and climbed the three steps to the porch. He slid the key in the lock, opened the door, and stepped inside. He had only given the place a cursory look the last time he was there. Walking across the floor, he opened the curtains and lifted the shades. Sunlight filtered through the windows, disclosing a large square room he guessed had once been the dining room. The air smelled slightly musty. The floor was made of hardwood; there were windows on three sides. Cobwebs hung from the corners; there was dust on the window sills. His footprints were visible in the dust on the floor.

A swinging door led into what had been the kitchen. There was a long counter against one wall, a large sink, two tall cupboards—one with a door hanging by a single hinge—and a couple of shelves. The wall where the stove had been was black with soot.

Blackie nodded, pleased. This would be his operating room once he got it cleaned up. He would paint the walls white, wax the floors, wash the windows.

He moved back into the main room, which would be the reception area. He would have to buy some furniture—a sofa, some chairs, a couple of tables, lamps. He would need a desk and a chair for himself, a filing cabinet. He would paint the walls in this room a pale green, he thought, or maybe a pale blue. New curtains wouldn't hurt. He would ask his mother for help there.

Running a hand over his jaw, he went outside to check the side yard. There wasn't much there; a wooden chair with a broken leg, a rusty bucket, and a few empty crates and boxes.

Going back to the front of the building, he locked the door, stuck the key in his pocket, and stepped into the saddle.

Going to Feehan's Mercantile, he bought several gallons of white paint for inside and out, a gallon of green paint for the outside trim, a gallon of pale blue for the waiting room, a couple of brushes, and a ladder. He also bought a broom and a dustpan and a couple of buckets. He was waiting for Big Mike to ring up his order when Joey emerged from the back room. As usual, she was dressed in jeans, a shirt, and boots. Her hair hung down her back in a thick braid.

"Hey, Joey," Mike called, "load this stuff into the wagon, will you?" Mike looked at Blackie. "Where do you want it delivered?"

"Joey knows where," Blackie said.

Mike lifted one brow, glanced from Blackie to Joey and back again, and then shrugged.

Blackie paid for his purchases, then picked up the ladder.

"Joey'll take care of that," Mike said.

"I'll just carry it out to the wagon for her," Blackie said.

With a shrug, Mike turned to another customer.

Outside, Blackie dropped the ladder into Feehan's delivery wagon. Joey followed a few minutes later. She carried a can of paint in each hand and had the brushes stuck in the waistband of her jeans.

"Are you trying to get me fired?" she asked.

Blackie shrugged. "I was just trying to help."

"Well, I get paid to help the customers," she said irritably, "not the other way around."

"I'm sorry."

She glared at him, then went back inside to fetch the rest of his supplies. She was still frowning when she untied the reins and climbed up on the wagon seat. Jerking down her hat brim, she clucked to the horse.

With a shake of his head, Blackie mounted his horse and followed the wagon down the street. He had certainly rubbed her the wrong way, he thought. She was as prickly as a hedgehog.

When they reached the building, Blackie dismounted and dropped the reins over the hitching post in front.

He thought about offering to help Joey down from the wagon but thought better of it.

She swung down agilely and moved around to the back of the wagon, where she lowered the tailgate.

"Okay if I carry that ladder inside?" he asked, "Or are you gonna bite my head off again?"

She had the good grace to blush. "I'm sorry about that, but I really need this job. No one else in town would hire me."

With a nod, Blackie picked up the ladder and carried it inside. He put it down as quickly as he could. Though it didn't weigh all that much, it still put a strain on his bruised ribs, and he decided to let her bring in the rest of the stuff.

Joey followed him inside. She put down the cans of paint near the door and dropped the brushes on top of them. It took her two more trips to bring everything inside.

"Thanks, Joey."

She looked up at him, her eyes filled with an emotion he couldn't decipher. "See ya, Blackie."

He stared after her for a moment, bemused, then picked up the broom and began to sweep the floor.

He was cussing the men who had laid into him by the time he was finished. Damn, it hurt to move, even to breathe!

He carried the dustpan out the back door and dumped the contents in the yard, then locked the place up. He was in no fit condition to do any painting. He'd go see what he could find in the way of furniture instead and then call it a day. And maybe, if the opportunity presented itself, he could find an excuse to see Joey McBride again.

Chapter Eleven

I was just leaving McMillan's when I saw Blackie locking up the old McBride building. As he was coming down the steps, he saw me and waved. I watched him walk across the street, noting the careful way he moved and the patchwork quilt of color on his face. I blew out a sigh, thanking God that he hadn't been hurt worse than he was.

"Hi, *nahkoa*," he said. "I was just going to get something to eat and do a little shopping. Wanna come along?"

"Of course," I said. "Shall we walk? Or take the buggy?"

"Let's walk," he said, and I noticed that his arm slid protectively around his rib cage.

"All right, just let me put these in the wagon."

"New shoes?" he asked.

"Yes, for Blue Hawk. Honestly, that boy goes through shoes like they were made of paper instead of leather."

Blackie laughed.

"I never had that problem with you," I said, dropping my package under the buggy's seat. "Of course, I couldn't keep a pair of shoes on you. You took them off the minute my back was turned. Even in church."

"What else did you buy him?"

"Oh, a new book. You know how Blue Hawk loves to read." I thought of the copies of Shakespeare and Dickens that my father had bought years ago. Rebecca had left them with us when she moved back east. When he was older, I would give them to Blue Hawk.

Blackie nodded. "Which book?"

"*The American Boys Handy Book*. They're all the rage, you know. I thumbed through it. It has all kinds of interesting information."

"Such as?"

"Oh, how to make an armed war kite and how to make a boomerang." I smiled at him. "How to skin a bird."

"Did he get the magazines I sent him?"

"Yes." Blackie had sent Blue Hawk a box of dime novels. I wasn't sure I approved of Blue Hawk reading about the exploits of such characters as Fred Fearnot and Bowery Billy, even though these young heroes were pure of heart, ambitious, and brave beyond belief. "He read them until they were dog-eared."

And who could blame him? Another hero of these five-cent novels was Frank Merriwell, who always won the day, whether it was in the boxing ring or on the football field, and who, in true heroic fashion, could outwit any enemy from Chinese bandits to Texas rustlers. Frank loved Mom, home, and apple pie and frowned on bad sports, drinking, bullies, and braggarts.

We walked to Maud's Restaurant. Blackie ordered ham steak, fried potatoes, and coffee. I ordered a bowl of soup and a glass of lemonade.

"So, how's it coming?" I asked after the waitress had taken our order.

"Not bad. The place needs some paint." He looked at me with *that* look, the one I couldn't refuse. "It could use some new curtains, too."

"I guess you want me to make them."

"Hey, that would be great."

"Anything else?"

He shook his head. "Not right now."

"Guess what I heard?"

"What?"

"Jed Junior is thinking about buying an automobile." Jed Junior was the son of Jed and Mary Crowley. The Crowleys had ten children, not counting the three that had died in the same diphtheria epidemic that had almost claimed Blackie's life. Their oldest daughter, Antoinette, had moved to Chicago, where she'd found a job as a stenographer earning fifteen dollars a month. Lucy had gone off to New York to become an actress. The others, except for Jed Junior, still lived at home. Jed lived in a small apartment above the blacksmith shop.

"Noisy contraptions," Blackie said.

Like it or not, automobiles seemed to be here to stay. Back in 1903, someone had actually driven one from San Francisco to New York, averaging an amazing 175 miles a day.

"Who does Jed Junior think he is?" Blackie asked with a rueful shake of his head. "One of the Vanderbilts?"

I grinned. Blackie had sent us copies of Eastern newspapers and magazines from time to time. I had read that Cornelius Vanderbilt had spent five million dollars building a seventy-room Renaissance palace called "The Breakers," and that was the cost before he bought a stick of furniture. In the library, over the fireplace, hung the motto: LITTLE DO I CARE FOR RICHES.

It was hard to imagine anyone having as much money as Cornelius Vanderbilt, or financier J. P. Morgan, or John Jacob Aster, who, at one time, was reported to have owned seventeen automobiles. In the same woman's magazine that had mentioned Vanderbilt's mansion, I had read that one wealthy woman had spent three hundred thousand dollars on dinners and dances. Not to be outdone, Mrs. Cornelius Vanderbilt had imported the entire cast of a New York hit show to perform *The Wild Rose* on her front lawn.

I couldn't imagine having that much money, let alone spending it on anything as frivolous as entertainment. Shadow and I might not have millions of dollars, but we had everything we needed.

"We really do live in a marvelous time," I remarked. "Just think of all the wonderful things that have been invented in the last few years, things we'll have here in the valley one of these days. Telephones. Washing machines and automobiles, electric lights. And look at our town. It's growing bigger every day."

Two years earlier, the Chicago, Milwaukee & St. Paul Railroad had started construction on its Pacific Coast extension. When it was completed, South Dakota would have a transcontinental rail line.

"I'm not sure bigger is better," Blackie said, sounding disgruntled.

I frowned, but refrained from saying anything as the waitress brought our food. Ignoring my lunch, I leaned forward. "What's wrong, *naha*?"

"I wish . . ." He shook his head. "Never mind."

"What do you wish?"

"I wish I'd been born in the old days." He said it as though he were confessing a horrible crime.

"I know, *naha*."

The old days, I thought. And yet, they weren't so distant. The Indians had been subdued, their old life taken from them. And yet life went on. That wily old fox, Geronimo, was still alive, though I was sure he would rather have died in battle long ago. I had read that he appeared at Omaha's International Exposition in 1898 and was at the Pan-American Exposition in Buffalo, New York, back in 1901. Not only that, but he had ridden in Teddy Roosevelt's inaugural parade in 1903, and had been at the 1904 World's Fair in St. Louis. How strange it all must have seemed to him. And how humiliating, to be little more than a novelty. The great Geronimo, reduced to selling photos of himself to tourists.

Remarkably, Wyatt Earp was still alive. And still newsworthy. I read about him in the paper from time to time. In 1885, it was reported that he had given up gunfighting and marshaling and had taken his wife, Josie, to live in San Diego, where he sold real estate and raced horses. Five years later, he had reportedly moved to San Francisco. The last I'd heard, he was in Arizona.

Bat Masterson was still alive, as well. He had given up gunfighting and was now a reporter for a newspaper in New York. It seemed strange to think that these men who had gained such notoriety as gunfighters and gamblers back in the old days of the Wild West were still alive, when so many others had passed on.

I looked at my son again. I understood his longing. The blood of the Cheyenne ran strong in Blackie. Though he had been born long after the People lived wild on the plains, I knew his spirit cried out to his ancestors, knew he longed for the old days, the old ways. I knew that, for years, he had secretly envied Hawk because Hawk had endured the medicine lodge. I remembered the look of uncertainty on Blackie's face when he had watched the old medicine man, Eagle-That-Soars-in-the-Sky, pierce Hawk's chest. I remembered the yearning in his eyes as he watched Hawk dance around the medicine lodge pole.

"Have you ever told your father what you want?"

"No. There didn't seem to be . . ." He paused, his brow furrowing. "How do you know what I want?"

"Blackie, I'm your mother."

"I never could keep a secret from you," he said with a grin, his good mood restored.

"Why don't you ask your father about it? I'm sure if it's at all possible, he can arrange it."

"Do the Cheyenne even practice the medicine lodge anymore?"

"I don't know, but I'm sure your father could arrange for a modified version of one. And I know Hawk and Cloud Walker would help, too. Are you sure about this, Blackie?"

He nodded, and as I looked at my son, I was reminded of the way Shadow had looked so many years ago when he had been a young warrior filled with the fire and determination of youth, when anything was possible and we'd had our whole lives ahead of us.

"Think about it," I said, "and when you feel the time is right, talk to your father."

We spoke then of mundane things, like the upcoming Fourth of July picnic and the fact that Reverend Dunford thought the church needed new pews.

"He could be right," Blackie remarked. "I know my backside hurts like blazes after listening to one of his dreary sermons."

I had to agree. For all that Reverend Dunford was a good man, his preaching was as bland as vanilla pudding. I thought wistfully of Reverend Brighton, who had retired a few years ago. No one had ever slept through one of his sermons. He'd had a voice like thunder, and when he preached hellfire, you paid attention.

We were about to leave when Blackie looked at me, his expression sober.

"What is it?" I asked.

"Do you think you could . . . that is—" He cleared his throat, and I wondered what he was trying so hard to say.

117

"What?"

"Could you see that Joey has a new dress for the Fourth?"

I blinked at my son. Of all the things I had expected him to say, this was far and away the most surprising.

"Yes, of course," I said.

Following Blackie out of the restaurant, I could only shake my head. Shadow had been right again. It was a woman that had Blackie tied in knots, and that woman was indeed Joey McBride.

Chapter Twelve

As anxious as he was to get to work painting his new office, Blackie took it easy for the rest of the week. He spent Tuesday over at Hawk's place, Wednesday helping Daniel build a wooden fort for his soldiers, Thursday at Victoria and Cloud Walker's place getting reacquainted with his nephews, and getting caught up on all the latest gossip in town. He spent Friday sorting through his college texts.

Saturday afternoon he rode into town, ostensibly to look for furniture. Of course, there wasn't much of a selection in the local stores, so he rode over to Feehan's Mercantile, refusing all the while to admit that that had been his destination all along.

Inside, he pulled up a chair to the counter and thumbed through a well-worn copy of the Sears,

Roebuck & Company catalog. You could order just about anything from the wish book, from clocks to Turkish leather couches, from ice cream freezers to coffee grinders, refrigerators and washing machines, phonographs and wagons.

"Finding everything you need?"

He looked up to find Joey reading over his shoulder. "Not yet." He glanced around the store. "Where's Feehan?"

"He went out to lunch."

"Why don't you sit down and help me look?"

She hesitated a moment, then dragged up a chair next to his and sat down. "What are you looking for?"

"A desk, three or four chairs, a table, an icebox."

She turned the page and pointed to a picture of an icebox. "Here's one."

He looked at the price. Eight dollars and ninety-two cents. "All right, put that down."

She found an order form and began to fill it out. He picked out a chair for his desk, three more for the waiting room, a table he could use for operations, and some lamps.

"Anything else?" she asked.

"I don't think so, not right now."

He turned a couple of pages, paused, and looked at Joey, one brow raised.

"Did you find something else?" She glanced at the open page, then felt a rush of heat climb her neck into her cheeks. The ad was for "Dr. Worden's Female Pills," which were reported to contain something called Squaw Vine and promised to bring users "all the help that can be offered." As if that wasn't bad enough, there was an ad next to it for "La Dore's Bust Food." She felt her cheeks grow hotter as she read the ad, which promised to transform a scrawny, flat, and flabby body into one that was plump, full, and well rounded.

Acting as nonchalant as possible, Joey turned the page. "Look at this," she said. "I've always wanted one."

Blackie leaned forward. "A camera?"

Joey nodded.

"Why don't you buy one?"

She tapped her finger on the page. "It costs thirteen dollars and ninety cents," she said. "I can't afford that."

"What are you doing after work tonight?"

She looked at him, her eyes wide, like a deer coming face-to-face with a hunter. He wondered who was more shocked by his question, Joey or himself.

"Why?"

He shrugged. "I thought we could go out to dinner."

"No, I can't."

"All right." It was a crazy idea anyway, he thought, and felt almost relieved that she had said no.

"I have to fix dinner for Charlie and Gram—"

"It's all right," he said. "You don't owe me any explanations."

The bell above the door tinkled. Joey glanced over her shoulder and hastened to her feet when Big Mike entered the store. Without a word, she disappeared into the back room.

Mike glanced at Joey's back, then looked at Blackie. "Everything all right?" he asked. Moving behind the counter, he slipped his big white apron over his head and tied it in place.

"Fine," Blackie said. He pushed the order form across the counter. "Joey was just filling this out for me."

Mike glanced at the form, then pulled a pencil out of his shirt pocket. "I'll total this up and bill you when it arrives."

Blackie nodded. "I want to add one more thing to it, and I need it in time for Joey's birthday. Is that possible?"

"You sweet on that girl?"

Blackie cleared his throat. "Maybe."

"I'm almighty fond of Joey," Big Mike said. "I won't take it kindly if she gets hurt."

"Can I get the camera in time or not?" Blackie asked. He didn't have any intention of discussing his feelings for Joey with Big Mike. Whatever he felt for Joey was his business and no one else's.

Mike rubbed his jaw thoughtfully, then shook his head. "I can't guarantee it'll get here from New York by then, but Hammachers over in Steel's Crossing carries the very same one. I'm going to order some merchandise from them tomorrow. Want me to add this to it?"

"I'd appreciate it, if it's not too much trouble."

"Nothing's too much trouble for Joey. I'll take care of it first thing in the morning."

"Thanks, Mr. Feehan," Blackie said. Whistling softly, he left the store.

Blackie hadn't intended to do any work that day, but he had a sudden need to burn off some energy—he refused to call it anger, even though that was what it was. He knew it was pointless to be angry with Joey because she refused to go out with him. She had her own life, her own responsibilities. But it chapped his hide just the same.

When he reached the site of his new office, he turned the black loose in the yard to graze and then went inside.

Stripping off his shirt, boots, and socks, Blackie opened the can of blue paint, grabbed a brush, and set to work.

In spite of his best intentions, he found himself thinking about Joey. She couldn't go out with him because Charlie was coming home and she had to fix dinner, he thought sourly.

Muttering an oath, he dipped his brush in the paint and slapped it on the wall. Why hadn't she just told him the truth? She couldn't go out with him because her family wouldn't like it. He wondered suddenly if she had told her grandmother who was renting the building.

Dammit, the battle at the Little Big Horn had taken place thirty-two years ago. Why couldn't people just forget it?

He blew out a breath. He was asking the impossible and he knew it. Some feuds lasted hundreds of years. How could he expect people to forget this one? Hell, the War Between the States had been over even longer than the Big Horn battle and people were still carrying grudges. There was one old man in town who still wore his Confederate cap!

Blackie shook his head. If he had as much common sense as he thought he did, he would put Miss Josephine McBride out of his mind and keep her out. The long and the short of it was, her family was never going to accept his family, and that was that.

He worked slowly but steadily, pausing often. When he'd finished three walls, he stood back to admire his handiwork. For someone who had never swung a paintbrush before, he had done a right fine job. And he was going to pay for it tomorrow, he thought. Now that his anger had subsided and he had decided it was for the best all around if he didn't see Joey anymore, he was keenly aware of the ache in his side.

Well, hell, he might as well finish the rest. Tomorrow was Sunday and he could sleep all day.

He tried to keep his mind blank as he painted the fourth wall, but he kept seeing Joey's face. He dipped the brush in the can one last time. Joey. He couldn't seem to get her out of his mind. There was something about her, he thought, something in her eyes that reached deep inside him, something about her smile . . .

"It looks nice."

He paused in mid-stroke at the sound of her voice. Slowly, he lowered the paintbrush and turned to face her. "Shouldn't you be home fixing dinner?"

He regretted the words as soon as he uttered them, but there was no way to call them back.

She looked at him a moment, then turned on her heel and walked out the door.

Cussing under his breath, Blackie dropped the paintbrush and ran after her. "Joey, wait! Dammit, wait a minute!"

He grabbed her arm, wincing as the movement sent pain skittering through his rib cage.

"Let me go!" She swung around to face him, her fists flailing.

He grunted as she struck his injured side. Gritting his teeth, he hung on to her, thinking it was like trying to hold a wildcat. "Ouch, dammit!"

"Let me go!"

"No." He tensed as she drew back her arm. "Try not to hit me in the same eye your brother did, okay?"

She lowered her arm, the fury draining out of her like water over a dam. "Let me go, Blackie. It was a mistake for me to come here. One I won't make again."

"I shouldn't have said what I did. I'm sorry."

She tried to pull her arm free of his hold again. "Let me go."

"Only if you promise not to run away."

"I promise," she said quickly. Too quickly.

"Joey . . ."

She looked up at him, mute. It had been a mistake to come here, she thought, and she had to get away before she made it worse. No good could ever come of this. They were too different. Like had to marry like, Grams always said, if there was to be any lasting happiness. But she couldn't ignore the heat of his hand on her arm, the strength in his fingers, the way he was looking at her, his dark eyes hot.

He gave a gentle tug on her arm, drawing her toward him, and she went without protest, lifting her head as he drew her up against him, closing her eyes as his mouth found hers.

She pressed against him, her body seeking to be closer to his, and he groaned low in his throat, a sound of pleasure and pain all in one. Her hands moved up and down his back, reveling in the warmth of his bare skin.

She tried to tell him that this was wrong, that it would never work, but she couldn't seem to form the words, couldn't think of anything but his tongue teasing hers.

"Joey?"

She looked up at him, dazed by the riot of emotions running rampant within her.

"Meet me later tonight."

"Where?"

"Rabbit's Head Rock," he said. "You know it?"

She nodded.

"Will you meet me there?"

"All right. What time?"

"Ten?"

"No."

"Eleven?"

"All right."

He let her go then, wondering, as he watched her walk away, what they had set in motion.

Joey glanced at the clock. Barely twenty minutes had passed since she last looked at the time. Never had the hours passed so slowly. She had been fidgety all through dinner, so much so that both Grams and Charlie had remarked on it. She had assured both of them that she was fine and blamed her restlessness on the heat. But it was the thought of meeting Blackie that had her so flustered. How could she concentrate on what her brother was saying when all she could think about was the way Blackie had looked without a shirt, his skin glistening with sweat, his long black hair falling like ebony silk over his shoulders? How could she think at all when he kissed her again? The very thought unleashed a thousand butterflies in the pit of her stomach.

And Charlie. Charlie would never understand. He hated Indians, all Indians.

To her relief, Charlie left the house shortly after dinner. At nine, Joey bathed her grandmother, brushed and braided her hair, and helped her into bed, and then she read to her for half an hour.

Going into her bedroom, she picked up her brush and ran it through her hair. "You must be mad," she told herself. "If Grams finds out about this, she'll never forgive you."

And now it was ten-thirty. Laying her brush aside, she tiptoed out of the house and hurried toward the river crossing. The water was low and slow at this time of the year. Barefooted, she waded across to the other side, then hurried through the tall yellow grass.

It was eerie, moving through the tall grass with only the light of the moon to guide her. Rabbit's Head Rock rose up in the distance, shapeless in the dark. The call of a night bird sent a chill down her spine. It hadn't been all that long ago that Indians roamed the prairies. Gramps had been a career army man. From time to time, Grams had told her and Charlie stories that Gramps had told her, stories of Indian raids and bloody massacres. It was easy to imagine Blackie riding a bareback pony, his black hair flowing in the wind, his face streaked with paint, and even easier to imagine his father riding down some helpless soldier, shooting him, taking his scalp. . . .

"Joey, over here."

She jumped as Blackie stepped out from behind the rock. Pressing a hand over her heart, she closed her eyes. "Lord, you scared me."

"Sorry. Did you have any trouble getting away?"

"No."

Taking her by the hand, he led her around the rock to where he had spread a blanket on the ground. He sat down, then offered her his hand. She sat down beside him, suddenly feeling shy.

"I was afraid you wouldn't come," he said.

"I said I would."

"Are you cold?"

"No, why?"

"You're shivering. You're not afraid of me, are you?"

She nodded slowly.

"You are?" he exclaimed, obviously taken aback. "Why?"

She stared at him. What could she say? How could she tell him that he made her feel excited and confused and afraid all at the same time? That he made her heart pound and her knees weak? That just thinking about him made her smile inside and out? That remembering his kisses made her warm and tingly all over? She couldn't tell him that. How could she explain it to him when she didn't understand it herself?

His gaze moved over her, his dark eyes filled with desire. Something deep within her quickened under his regard, almost as if a part of her that had been sleeping had suddenly been awakened. She could feel it stirring, unfolding within her the way a flower unfolded beneath the heat of the sun.

"If you're afraid of me, why did you come here tonight?"

She licked lips gone suddenly dry. "Why did you ask me to meet you?"

His gaze burned into her. "You know why."

Moving slowly so she would not mistake his intent, he slipped his arm around her waist and drew her body to his.

She looked up into his eyes and saw her own fear, her own longing, mirrored there. "This is wrong."

"I know."

"If my brother finds out . . ."

He nodded. "I know."

He lowered his head toward hers, and all thoughts of her grandmother, of Charlie, of right and wrong fled before the knowledge that he was going to kiss her again.

And kiss her he did, as if he had all the time in the world. His lips touched hers, as light as dandelion down. Slowly, gently, his lips moved over hers, learning their shape, their taste. He drew back to look deep into her eyes once more and then he was kissing her again, his tongue stroking her lower lip, slipping inside to duel with her own in an ancient dance of mating.

Her hands slid up and down his arms, exploring the width of his biceps, her fingers squeezing gently, delighting in the hardness she found there. Suddenly brave, she slid her hands around his waist to delve under his shirt. His back was firm, his shoulders broad and solid, his skin warm and smooth beneath her questing fingertips.

He drew her closer, his arms tight around her,

and now they were lying down on the blanket, her length molded to his, her breasts crushed against his chest.

He rose over her, his hair like a black cloud around his face, his eyes burning like lightning. His lower body covered hers. She could feel the heat of him against her, igniting an answering warmth deep inside her.

"Joey." His voice was ragged with need.

She looked up at him, on fire with wanting him but afraid, so afraid. She whispered his name, not knowing if she was asking him to stop or begging him for more.

A wry smile twisted his lips. "Tell me," he said. "Tell me what you want me to do."

"I don't know," she said, even as her body urged her to draw him closer.

Lowering his head, he kissed her one more time, and then he rolled off her and sat up.

"Blackie?"

He stood and offered her his hand.

Confused, she took it and let him pull her to her feet. "Did I do something wrong?"

"No." Picking up the blanket, he draped it over his shoulder, then took her hand in his. "Things are just moving a little too fast. Come on, I'll walk you back."

When he reached home later that night, Blackie was too restless to go into the house and go to bed.

"I should have taken a dip in the river," he muttered. "Maybe that would have cooled me off."

Standing at the corral, with his arms loosely draped over the top rail, he stared at the distant mountains. He had told Joey things were moving too fast, but that had to be the understatement of the century, sort of like comparing a candle's flame to a raging inferno. He hadn't expected her to agree to meet him. Hell, the words had come out of his mouth before he even knew he was thinking them!

He couldn't be falling for Joey McBride. It wouldn't work. Could never work. And yet even as he tried to convince himself all he felt for her was just good old-fashioned lust, he was remembering the way her eyes lit up when she smiled, the husky sound of her voice, the way just looking at her made him feel good all over. He liked her independent spirit, the way she defended her brother even when Charlie was in the wrong.

"Admit it, Kincaid," he muttered. "You're on the edge."

Chapter Thirteen

I stood at the window, watching my son, wondering what was troubling him, though I had a pretty good idea.

Slipping my robe on over my nightgown, I left the house and walked across the yard. "Can't sleep?" I asked.

Blackie glanced at me as I moved up beside him. "You're up late."

"You know me. I can't go to sleep until all my chicks are safely bedded down for the night."

He smiled at me. "I'm not a little boy any longer, *nahkoa*."

"I know. It must be thoughts of a woman that are keeping you from your bed."

"Why would you say that?"

"What else but a woman could have a man talking to himself in the middle of the night?"

"You've got that right," Blackie muttered.

I stood on the bottom rail and crossed my arms over the top one. "Has you tied up in knots, does she?"

"It's never going to work. Her family hates Indians. They'll never accept me, but I can't stop thinking about her."

"It was worse for your father and me," I said, and memories crowded my mind. I remembered the awful tension in the valley the spring of '76, when war between the Indians and the settlers became inevitable.

Shadow had left that year to join his own people, and I had felt bereft even though I knew he felt he had to go. I would never forget the day a band of Sioux Indians attacked us. Years earlier, our homestead had been turned into a sort of combined fort and trading post, the fences replaced by stout walls with lookout towers in the corners. The fortifications came in handy that day, and yet wooden walls were no protection from fire, and before we knew it the Indians were inside the walls.

Our neighbor, Hobie Brown, and four of his sons were there with us. Hobie's wife, Charlotte, and his oldest son, Adam, had been killed in an earlier raid, and Hobie and his remaining sons had spent the winter with us. I thought fondly of David Brown. He had been a sweet, gentle young man. He had asked me to marry him. I had refused, of course, for my heart belonged to Shadow. My father and the Browns fought valiantly the day of the attack, but to no avail. My mother was killed, and I knew it was only a matter of time until the rest of us met the same fate. And then a lone warrior rode into the stockade.

The stranger's face and chest were streaked with broad slashes of vermilion. A single white eagle feather adorned his waist-length black hair. A black wolfskin clout covered his loins; moccasins beaded in red and black hugged his feet. For a moment, he sat unmoving, his narrowed eyes sweeping the yard, the burning barn, and the house in one long glance. He spoke to one of the other Indians, and then he approached the house and called out. "Sam Kincaid can you hear me?"

It had been Shadow, come to bargain for my life. In the end, my father insisted I go with Shadow rather than stay in the fort and be killed. I did not want to leave, but with gentle determination, my father pushed me out the door.

Blinded by my tears, I stumbled out into the yard. I heard Pa close the door behind me, and the sound was like a death knell in my ears. I would have fallen then but for Shadow. Wordlessly, he grabbed me by the arm, steered me toward where Red Wind stood patiently, helped me mount, and I hated him. Hated him because my father and the others were going to be killed and he couldn't do anything about it. Hated him because he was an Indian.

And even as I hated him, I loved him.

Later, when the fort and the sound of gunfire were far behind us, he reined the stallion to a halt near a shallow underground spring. Dismounting, he spread his buffalo robe on the ground and gazed at me speculatively as I slid from Red Wind's back and dropped onto the robe.

"I am sorry, Hannah," he murmured compassion-

ately. And kneeling before me, he held out his arms.

I had known then that I had a decision to make.

I stared hard at Shadow. He had not moved a muscle. He still knelt before me, arms outstretched, face impassive, and for the first time since I had fallen in love with him, I saw him not just as a man but as an Indian. The hideous red paint on his face, the eagle feather in his long black hair, the wolfskin clout he wore all bespoke Cheyenne blood. Cheyenne ways.

How could I spend the rest of my life with this man, this stranger? How could I ever forget that he was Indian, and that it was an Indian who had killed my mother, an Indian who might even now be taking my father's life?

With a sigh, I had gone into Shadow's waiting arms. He held me while I cried bitter tears. I cried until I was empty inside. There were no words spoken between us that night. There was only the silent communication of Shadow's heart speaking to mine, and mine answering. And from that night on Shadow was not an Indian, and I was not white. We were simply a man and a woman desperately in love.

It was a story I had told my children often as they were growing up.

I reminded Blackie of it now, then said, "I know what you're going through, believe me. It might not be easy for either of you, but you weren't responsible for her grandfather's death, any more than Shadow was responsible for the death of my mother."

Blackie nodded. "I'm not sure I love Joey," he said, "but—"

"But she's always in your thoughts. And sometimes she drives you crazy."

He nodded again. "How did you know you loved my father?"

"Believe me," I said, "when it happens, you'll know." Hopping lightly to the ground, I put my hand on Blackie's arm. "Go to bed, *naha*. Things will look better in the morning."

Chapter Fourteen

Blackie had every intention of sleeping late on Sunday morning. He was surprised by how sore he was after painting the day before and sleeping late, reading the latest edition of the *Clarion,* and just relaxing around the house sounded mighty good. Instead, he got up early and went to church with his mother and Blue Hawk. And it wasn't because he wanted to sit through one of Reverend Dunford's desert-dry sermons, or because he felt his soul was in need of spiritual nourishment. It was because he hoped to see Joey there. He knew it, and he had a feeling his mother knew it, too.

As luck would have it, Joey was seated in the pew directly across from him. Blackie managed to sit at the end of the row, near the aisle. Joey looked over at him as he took his seat and the electricity that sparked between them was hot enough, bright enough, to light up the whole valley.

Time and again throughout the sermon, he glanced across the way to find her looking at him. She was wearing the same dress he saw her wear to church every week. It was blue gingham, embroidered with pale blue flowers. The neck was square, the sleeves short and edged with lace. Her hair was brushed back and held away from her face by a pair of tortoiseshell combs. She looked as pretty and fresh as a spring day.

He spent the entire service trying to think of a way to get her alone, at least for a few minutes. Later, after the last hymn had been sung and the last amen had been said, he realized he hadn't heard a single word of the sermon. Heaven help him if Reverend Dunford stopped him on the way out and asked him what he'd thought of it!

Rising, Blackie followed Joey down the center aisle toward the door. He shook the reverend's hand, agreed it was a lovely day, and hurried down the stairs.

Outside, the townsfolk were gathered in small groups. One of the women was showing off her new baby; a couple of the men were standing near Jeremy Brown's rig, admiring his new team. At any other time, Blackie would have been there too, but horses held no interest for him today, not when Joey was nearby.

She didn't live far from town. Had she ridden to church? Or walked?

He saw her talking to one of the Monroe boys, and then she turned and started toward the river crossing. On foot.

Blackie hurried toward his mother. "*Nahkoa*, I'll see you at home," he said, and was gone before she could ask him any questions.

He trailed behind Joey until they were out of sight of the church, and then he ran to catch up with her.

"Joey, wait up."

She turned, her eyebrows lifting in surprise when she saw him running toward her.

"Mornin'." He wrapped one arm around his midsection. Running after her had set his ribs to aching again.

"Morning." She looked up at him, her eyes alight, a shy smile curving her lips.

The sight of her smile slammed into him, and he knew he would have run barefoot over hot coals just to see her look at him like that.

"You look very handsome today," she said.

"And you look beautiful."

She blushed and looked away. "Thank you."

"Can I walk you home?"

"Do you think that's a good idea?"

"I don't know," he said with a shrug, "but I want to."

She smiled up at him. "And I want you to."

He felt like shouting, singing. Instead, he took her by the hand and they walked through the tall grass toward the river crossing.

"Your father never goes to church, does he?" Joey asked after a while.

"No."

"I guess Indians don't believe in God," she said, and then frowned. "But you're Indian, and you go to church."

"My father worships *Maheo* in the way of the Cheyenne."

"Is that the Cheyenne's god?"

Blackie nodded.

"But there's only one God."

"That's what my mother says. She believes they're the same God wearing different names. The Cheyenne are a deeply religious people. They believe all life is sacred, that no life should be taken without cause. They never kill for sport, like some of the men around here do."

"That's not what I heard. Grams says Indians are nothing but savages, that they don't believe in God or religion, that in the old days they killed women and children for the love of it. She said if they weren't all confined to reservations, they'd still be killing and scalping everyone in sight."

"Is that what you believe?"

"I used to," she admitted, "until I met you."

"Joey . . ."

She squeezed his hand. "Don't be mad at me. I don't think I could stand it."

"I'm not mad."

"You can't blame Grams for the way she feels," Joey said defensively. "After all, Indians killed my grandpa."

"They killed my grandmother too, but my mother doesn't hate all Indians because of it."

She came to a stop and turned to face him, her eyes wide. "Indians killed your grandmother? When? Why?"

"Do you want to sit a while?"

"Sure."

They sat down on a deadfall near the river

crossing. Blackie stared at the water tumbling slowly over the rocks. Funny, his mother had been talking about this very thing just last night.

"It happened before the Custer battle," he said. "The tribes were coming together. They knew Custer was coming, and Sitting Bull had sent out a call for all the tribes to join him. A band of Lakota attacked the homestead where my mother lived with her parents. My Grandmother Mary was killed in the battle. My mother would have been killed, too, if my father hadn't come along and taken her away."

"And she went with him? Even though Indians had just killed her mother?"

Blackie nodded. "My folks were very much in love. I guess they always have been."

"Was your grandfather killed, too?"

"No. After everyone else had been killed, my grandfather was so enraged, he burst out of the house, which was on fire, a pistol in each hand. The Sioux pulled back until he was out of ammunition, and then, admiring his bravery, they took him prisoner instead of killing him. He became a slave to a warrior named Standing Elk."

"A slave? I didn't know Indians kept slaves."

"It was pretty common back then. The slaves were usually women from enemy tribes. They usually ended up marrying one of the warriors. Children who were captured were adopted. Men who survived usually joined the tribe. That's what happened with my grandfather. After a while, my grandfather was accepted by the Indians, and when the tribe went to the reservation, my grandfather went with them. He opened a trading post on the reservation and used the money he made to help feed and clothe the Sioux."

"Really? After all they had done to him? That's amazing."

Blackie nodded. "You have no idea. My grandfather was a real Indian hater at one time. But once he got to know them, really know them, all that changed.

"Anyway, about that same time, my father was captured and sent to the reservation, along with my mother and Hawk and Mary. My mother was shocked when she found out that her father was still alive."

"I can imagine!"

"Yeah. I guess they had quite a reunion."

"That's an amazing story. Does your grandfather live around here?"

"No. He passed away a while back."

"Oh, I'm sorry. Your family has been through some hard times, haven't they? I can't imagine what it must have been like to live out here in the old days. All that fighting and killing." She shivered. "It must have been awful."

Blackie shrugged. "I always wished I'd been born sooner. I would have liked to have lived back then."

Joey looked horrified. "Really? Why? Things are so much better now."

"Maybe."

"Maybe?"

"I don't know if I can explain it," he said. "I don't know if I can make you understand, but I feel . . . well, it's like Hawk—he and my father share something that I don't."

"What?"

"The Cheyenne have a special ceremony called the medicine lodge or the sun dance."

"I've never heard of that."

"Well, it's a sacred ceremony. I've always wanted to know if I had the courage to endure it."

"Why do you need courage?"

"It's a ceremony of sacrifice. Before the Custer battle, Sitting Bull offered a hundred pieces of his flesh to the Great Spirit."

Joey's eyes widened. "Offered his flesh? How?"

"He cut the skin from his arms."

"That's awful!"

"There are other forms. Hawk had two skewers embedded in his chest. Rawhide was fastened to the skewers and then attached to the medicine lodge pole. Hawk danced back and forth until he broke free . . ."

"And you're sorry because you never got to do that?"

"It's a brave thing, to offer your pain to *Maheo* in exchange for something you desire."

"And your father did that too?"

"Yes."

Joey sighed. "I guess there are some things about your people I'll never understand."

Blackie nodded and fell silent. Not for the first time, he wondered if the differences between them would prove insurmountable.

"Did you tell your grandmother that I'm the one renting your building?" he asked after a while.

"No."

"Why not?"

"She didn't ask."

"And if she did?"

Joey lifted one shoulder and let it fall. "I don't know. I guess I'll have to tell her, though. Charlie is sure to find out sooner or later."

Blackie snorted softly. "Charlie."

"He's really not such a bad kid," Joey said.

"Uh-huh."

Joey blew out a sigh. "I'm worried about him. He can't keep a job. It seems like all he wants to do is drink over at O'Toole's. And he's always hanging out with one rough crowd or another, like that bunch you got tangled up with. I don't know what to do."

"I'm not so sure you can lay the blame on others."

"What do you mean?"

"He's old enough to know better."

She glared at him. "What do you mean by that?"

"I mean just what I said. You can't keep making excuses for him, Joey. He's old enough to know right from wrong."

"You're right." Tears hovered in the corners of her eyes. "Blackie, what am I going to do?"

Somehow she was in his arms and he was holding her close, one hand lightly patting her back. She smelled of sunshine and soap and starch, and he knew he had never smelled anything more wholesome or more seductive in his whole life.

"I'm sorry." She eased out of his embrace.

"Don't be." He cupped her face in his hands, his thumbs wiping the tears from her cheeks.

And somehow she was in his arms again, her head resting on his shoulder.

"What did Harry Monroe want?"

"He asked me to go to the Fourth of July picnic with him next Saturday."

144

A muscle clenched in his jaw. "What did you tell him?"

"That I didn't think I was going."

He stroked her hair lightly. "I think you should go. With me."

"I wish I could, but—"

"I know. It would upset your grandmother and Charlie."

"I guess I'm just not as brave as your mother," Joey said. "I don't want to cause more trouble at home."

"It's all right. But if you go, we might be able to spend a little time together."

She thought that over for a moment and then said, "All right. I'll be there."

He gave her shoulder a squeeze. He would find a way for them to be alone, one way or another.

"I should be getting home," she remarked.

"I know."

"Grams will be expecting lunch. Charlie too, if he's home."

"They're lucky to have you." He grinned at her. "Are you a good cook?"

"Not bad."

"Maybe you'll cook something for me some time."

"Maybe."

Rising, he offered her his hand. "Come on. I don't want your grandmother's lunch to be late on my account."

He was whistling when he left her a short time later. He hadn't walked her all the way to her door, just to the edge of the McBride property, where he had kissed her, and then kissed her again.

Now, walking back, he thought about how good it felt to be with Joey, how easy she was to talk to, and how easy she was to look at.

"Admit it, Kincaid," he muttered, "you're hooked."

He didn't see Joey for the next couple of days. He paid Blue Hawk to wash the windows and pull the weeds at his new office, and while his little brother did that, Blackie finished painting the inside of the building.

His father stopped by on Wednesday afternoon and repaired the corral in the backyard while Blackie washed down the outside of the building. His mother came over the next day to hang the curtains she had made, and while she was there, she mentioned that she had seen Joey in town and had given her a new dress, as Blackie had requested.

"She didn't want to take it," Hannah said. "That girl's got a streak of pride a mile wide, but I told her I'd had it made for Victoria and that the dressmaker had made a mistake in the size. She wanted to pay for it, of course, but I told her to consider it a birthday present."

Her birthday. He'd forgotten all about it.

"Next Wednesday," Hannah said, her eyes twinkling. "Don't be late for dinner."

"Thanks, *nahkoa*."

He was painting the front of the building on Friday morning when Hawk rode up. Dismounting, Hawk tied his horse to the fence post.

"You missed a spot," he called as he came through the gate.

Blackie grunted. "If you want to help, you could pick up a brush."

"Not me," Hawk said. "I just stopped by to bring you a little something." He handed Blackie a large package wrapped in brown paper, then glanced around the yard. "The place is lookin' good."

"Yeah, but it still needs a lot of work." Blackie unwrapped the package. It was a sign made of solid oak, the letters hand-carved. He read the words out loud. "Doctor Samuel Kincaid, Doctor of Veterinary Medicine."

He stared at it for several moments. Somehow, the sign made his new profession even more real than his diploma. "Thanks, Hawk."

"You're welcome, little brother. When you get this place running, we'll have to have a party to celebrate. I'll talk to Victoria about it. After all, you're the first one in the family to go to college."

"Just don't let her get carried away," Blackie warned. "I remember the going-away party she gave me. She must have invited half the town."

"I'll tell her to keep it down, just the family and a few close friends. We're all expecting big things from you, you know."

Blackie grinned. "That remains to be seen. I may be out of business before I even start."

"I don't think so. Most of the townspeople are pretty tolerant."

"I used to think so too, but now . . ." Blackie rubbed his hand over his ribs, which were still tender. "Now I don't know."

"You're worrying for nothing. Three of those galoots aren't even from around here. As for Charlie, that boy's headed for trouble. And that means trouble for you too, doesn't it?"

"What do you mean?"

"In a word? Joey. We all know you're sweet on her."

"It's that obvious, huh?"

Hawk slapped Blackie on the shoulder. "Only to anyone who isn't blind or dead."

Blackie shrugged and then grinned. "No sense denying it, I guess."

"My deputy took the other three over to Steel's Crossing. They'll be arraigned there. You and *neyho* will have to testify at their trial."

Blackie nodded. It wasn't something he was looking forward to.

"I've got to get back to the office," Hawk said.

Blackie walked his brother to the gate, watched as Hawk swung effortlessly into the saddle of a big bay mare. He tapped a corner of the sign. "Thanks again."

Hawk nodded. "See you Sunday, little brother. Give *nahkoa* my love."

Chapter Fifteen

After Hawk left, Blackie found a prominent place out front to hang his new sign and then rode home to grab something to eat. Later, he took Blue Hawk down to the river crossing and they spent an hour fishing. Blue Hawk let out a shout when he pulled in a catfish that must have weighed five pounds.

When they returned to the house, Blackie hitched the team to the wagon, and Blue Hawk helped him load some of his veterinary supplies into the back.

"You want to come with me to unload this stuff?" Blackie asked.

Blue Hawk shook his head. "*Neyho* said he'd help me work the filly this afternoon."

"All right. Thanks for your help. I'll see you later."

Swinging up onto the wagon seat, Blackie took

up the reins, released the brake, and drove to his office.

He sat out front for a few minutes, staring at the neatly lettered sign.

DOCTOR SAMUEL KINCAID
DOCTOR OF VETERINARY MEDICINE

He'd done it, he thought proudly. He had gone to school. Earned his degree. Now he had an office and a brand-new sign that proclaimed for all to see that he was a veterinarian. He grinned to himself. All he needed now were patients.

Climbing down from the wagon, he went around the back and picked up the large wooden box that held the medicines and supplies he had bought in the East.

Hefting it up on one shoulder, he carried it up the steps, unlocked the door, and stepped inside.

His gaze swept the room. The walls were a soft shade of blue. His diploma hung facing the door. The floors were waxed to a high shine, compliments of his mother. The white curtains she had made hung at the windows. He nodded. The place looked a darn sight better than it had a few weeks earlier. It would look even better when his furniture arrived.

Moving into the back room, he put the box on the counter. The walls here were a pristine white. The sink had been cleaned to within an inch of its life, the counter spotless. Prying the lid off the crate, he spent the next hour sorting through the various bottles, jars, and packets and putting them away. He hung his apron on a hook near the back door, then began sorting through his operating instruments and placing them on the shelf above where his operating table would go.

When he was finished, he stood in the middle of the room and turned in a slow circle, pleased with what he saw. Now if only the people of Bear Valley would give him a chance to put what he had learned into practice.

With a sigh, he went back out into the waiting room, only to come to an abrupt halt when he saw a young boy with a thatch of blond hair and big blue eyes standing near the door, clutching a towel to his chest.

"Hi there," Blackie said. "Can I help you?"

The boy held out the towel, revealing a small brown and white puppy. "Miss McBride said you could fix him."

Closing the distance between them, Blackie knelt in front of the boy. "What's wrong with him?"

"His leg's broke."

"Here, let me have a look."

Blackie took the puppy from the boy. The pup whimpered softly and licked Blackie's hand as he examined the injury. The animal's left front leg was, indeed, broken.

"Can you fix him?" the boy asked, sniffling.

"Sure. Do you want to help me?"

The boy's eyes widened. "Can I?"

"If you're brave enough."

The boy nodded, but his eyes widened even more. "What do I have to do?"

"Just hold him for me while I fix his leg. It's gonna hurt him a little, but he'll feel better if you're with him."

"I'm brave enough."

"Okay . . . what's your name?"

"Jerry. Jerry Rasmussen."

Since his operating table hadn't arrived yet, Blackie spread the towel on the floor and placed the puppy on it. "All right, Jerry. Wait here. I'll be right back."

The boy nodded. Sitting down on the floor, he stroked the puppy's head.

Going into the back room, Blackie collected what he needed, then returned to the waiting room.

Jerry looked up, his expression determined but less than eager. "Will he be all right?"

"Sure. It's not a bad break," Blackie said, kneeling beside the puppy. "How did it happen?"

"He was chasing one of Ma's chickens through the cow pen and one of the cows stepped on him."

"Well, he won't be chasing any chickens for a while. All right, now, hold him still. Be careful he doesn't bite you."

"Aw, he wouldn't do that."

"He might. You ready?"

Jerry nodded.

It wasn't until he'd finished splinting the puppy's leg that Blackie realized Joey was in the room.

Wrapping the puppy in the towel, he handed it to Jerry. "Keep him quiet now, you hear? Try to keep him from chewing on the bandage. If he tears it off, just have your mother wrap it up again. If he gets the splint off, bring him back to see me. Got it?"

Jerry nodded solemnly. "How much do I owe you?"

"No charge for first-time patients," Blackie said,

ruffling the boy's hair. "Just keep him out of the cow pen from now on."

"I will. Thanks, Dr. Kincaid. Thanks a lot!"

Cuddling the puppy to his chest, the boy started toward the door. He paused when he saw Joey. "You were right," he said. "The doctor fixed him up fine."

"I told you he would," Joey replied.

The boy glanced over his shoulder. "Thanks, again, Dr. Kincaid," he said, and then left the office.

Blackie stared after the boy. *Doctor* Kincaid. Damn, but that sounded good.

"You were wonderful with him," Joey said.

Blackie gained his feet, feeling a little self-conscious. "How long have you been standing there?"

"Since you set the puppy's leg. You were so involved in what you were doing, I guess you didn't hear me come in."

"No." His gaze moved over her. She was in jeans and a shirt again, and she looked good enough to eat. "But I'm glad you're here," he said, and took a step toward her.

"I'm glad you could help Jerry," she replied, and took a step toward him.

"My first patient," Blackie said with a wry smile. "Sure hope the next one's got a little money in his jeans."

She smiled at him and he forgot everything else.

The air between them seemed to vibrate with words unsaid, thoughts unspoken.

They looked at each other a moment more, and then, as if on some unseen signal, they moved toward each other, closing the distance between them.

"I missed you," Blackie said, taking her in his arms.

"I missed you."

He drew her closer, his gaze moving to her lips. "Joey . . ."

She slid her arms around his neck and rose on her tiptoes. "Just kiss me," she whispered, her eyelids fluttering down. "Please, just kiss me."

His lips sought hers before she had finished speaking.

She had been waiting for this, hoping for this, for days, she thought. She couldn't eat, couldn't sleep, for thinking of Blackie, wanting to feel his arms around her again, to taste his lips on hers. The same magic she had felt before flowed through her at his touch. Magic, she thought. That was the only word for the way he made her feel, as if she was beautiful, as if he would never let her go.

She slid one hand over his shoulder and down his arm, her fingers curling over the muscle there. She loved his arms, the strength in them. She felt safe when he held her, as if nothing in the world could ever hurt her.

Regretfully, she let him go. "I have to get back to work. I just wanted to run over to make sure Jerry found you."

"I'm glad you did."

"Me too."

"I'll see you at the picnic tomorrow, right?"

"Right. See ya, Blackie."

"See ya."

* * *

The morning of the Fourth of July dawned bright and clear. Blackie thanked his mother yet again for seeing that Joey had a new dress to wear and then left the house, assuring Blue Hawk and his parents that he would see them later.

The annual Fourth of July picnic and dance was the main get-together in Bear Valley. There were dances at Christmas and there was a church social in the spring, but the Fourth was the highlight of the year. There were games for the kids in the morning, and games and contests for the adults too, as well as blue ribbons for the best pie, the best jams and jellies. The men spent a good part of the day arm wrestling or tossing horseshoes. Later, there would be a horse race, which his father or Hawk had won every year for as long as Blackie could remember. After that, Fred Brown, long-time resident of Bear Valley, would auction off the box lunches the women had prepared and decorated. The money earned usually went toward buying new books for the school. After lunch, there would be a pie-eating contest. Then some of the older folks took naps while the younger crowd played baseball. Later, when the sun went down, there would be fireworks and, last of all, dancing under the stars.

Blackie saddled his horse, waved at Blue Hawk, and rode out of the yard.

Joey stood in front of the mirror, admiring her new dress. It was easily the prettiest one she had ever owned. Of course, the Kincaid women could afford to buy expensive clothes. She ran her hands over the front of the dress. The material, of fine-spun cotton, was lavender, with tiny blue and purple flowers. A double row of delicate lace edged the square neck and the short puffy sleeves. One side of the skirt was drawn up and tied with a white bow, revealing a ruffled white lace underskirt. It was a shame Victoria Kincaid would have to do without such a lovely frock, but Victoria had many other dresses. Most likely, she wouldn't miss this one at all.

Joey's smile faded. It had seemed like charity, taking the dress without paying for it. But Mrs. Kincaid had insisted, and it had been so long since Joey had had a new dress, she just couldn't refuse it.

She smiled again, wondering what Blackie would think when he saw her. Hard to believe how much her life had changed since he'd come home. Life didn't seem so dreary anymore, not when each new day held the possibility that she might see Blackie. She hadn't yet told Grams or Charlie that a Kincaid was renting the building. They would find out soon enough, she thought ruefully. She knew they wouldn't like it, but that was just too bad. They needed the money too much to be picky about who paid the rent on the place. If Grams wouldn't sell it, and Charlie wouldn't go to work, well, then, they could just deal with the consequences!

But she wasn't going to think of that now, not when the sun was shining and she was wearing a pretty new dress.

Humming softly, she went into the kitchen to get her box lunch. She had decorated it with Blackie in mind, even though she knew he wouldn't bid on it, not with his family and hers looking on. She told herself it didn't matter who she ate lunch with.

Somehow, she would find a way to spend a few minutes alone with Blackie.

"Joey, you coming or not?"

"Hold your horses, Charlie," she called. Picking up her lunch box, she hurried out of the house.

Charlie and Grams were waiting outside, already in the buckboard. Charlie was tapping the reins against the foot board impatiently. She had to admit, he looked mighty handsome in a new pair of Levi's and a new red-checked shirt. She wondered where he got the money for new clothes.

"Let's go, Josephine," her grandmother said, and then her eyes narrowed. "Is that a new dress, miss?"

"Yes, it is," she said, hoping that neither her brother nor her grandmother would ask where she'd gotten it. Of course, there was no reason why they should. She had a job. And it had been months since she bought anything new.

"Harumph," Maureen said sourly. "Always thinking about yourselves, both of you. I don't suppose it occurred to either of you that I might have liked some new duds myself."

"I'm sorry, Grams," Joey said.

"Yeah," Charlie muttered. "Sorry."

Since there was no room for her up front, Joey walked around the back of the wagon and jumped up on the tailgate.

Charlie clucked to the horse and they were on their way.

Joey looked down at the box lunch in her hands and smiled. Let Grams wail and whine. Let Charlie grumble all he wanted. She didn't care. Soon she would be with Blackie, and that was all that mattered.

Chapter Sixteen

"Hannah, you look as pretty as you did on your sixteenth birthday."

I turned away from the mirror to look into Shadow's smiling eyes. "I thought Cheyenne warriors always told the truth," I said with a teasing grin.

He nodded solemnly. "I have always told you the truth." His gaze moved over me, filled with warmth and love.

My toes curled with pleasure. "And you are as handsome as that young warrior who swept me off my feet."

A faint smile touched his lips at my praise, and then he drew me into his arms and kissed me.

I heard an exaggerated groan and looked around to find Blue Hawk standing in the doorway, a look of long suffering on his face. "Can we go now? I promised Jimmy I'd meet him. We're gonna be partners in the three-legged race."

"I'm ready." I looked at Shadow. "Are you?"

He nodded. "We will continue this later," he said so that only I could hear. And then, louder, "I will go get the wagon. Blue Hawk, come and help me hitch up the team."

Blue Hawk followed Shadow out of the house, I went into the kitchen to get our picnic basket, and we were ready to go. Shadow's horse was tied to the back of the wagon. Red Wind snorted and tossed his head as we drove out of the yard.

The festivities had already started when we reached town. Colorful red, white, and blue bunting hung across Front Street. There were flags flying from all of the buildings. A makeshift stage had been set up in front of the schoolhouse, and rows of wooden chairs were arranged in front of it. Perhaps two dozen people sat there listening to a three-piece band playing a lively polka.

As usual, the saloons were doing a brisk business. A huge sign was strung over the street, announcing that Tippet's was having its yearly Fourth of July sale.

There were several long tables set up in the shade, alongside the schoolhouse. The tables, covered with white cloths, held an assortment of pies, half of which were for the pie-judging contest. The other half were for the pie-eating contest that would be held later in the day.

Several children's games were already in progress. Shadow had no sooner parked our buckboard than Blue Hawk jumped off the back and took off running to find Jimmy Parker.

Hawk and Victoria had arrived first and claimed a place in the shade of a tree near the church. We spread our blanket out alongside theirs. A few minutes later, Mary and Cloud Walker arrived. There was a flurry of hugs and handshakes, and then the older children all ran off to find their friends, leaving the adults to look after Samantha, Cole, Patrick, Jared, Linus, and Cody.

Settling down on the blanket, I let myself be caught up in the laughter of my grandchildren as they scrambled for a place in my lap. Four-year-old Cole insisted on showing me his shiny new top, three-year-old Patrick asked for a story, and two-year-old Jared asked if I had any candy.

"I declare," Mary said with a shake of her head, "that boy would live on candy if I let him."

Shadow sat down beside me with an air of casual equanimity I had always envied and would never obtain. I had never known anyone who moved the way he did, so confident and self-assured, as though everything came easy to him. Part of it was innate, and part of it came from being raised as a Cheyenne warrior, from being taught early in life to rely on one's own self. But it was more than that; Shadow possessed a deep inner sense of peace. He was a man who knew who he was, a man who had fought hard and endured much, who had never backed down from what he believed in. I guess one of the reasons I loved him so much was that I knew I could depend on him to be there no matter what.

I smiled as Shadow reclined. Mary's son, Cody, immediately climbed up on Shadow's chest and began bouncing up and down.

I looked out over the crowd, hoping to spot

Blackie. I saw Nadine and Clancy Turner and Mary
Crowley and a number of other familiar faces, but
not the one I sought.

Blackie wandered around the area near the schoolhouse, his gaze searching the crowd for some sign
of Joey. He stopped for a few minutes to watch Jacob and Jason run in the potato sack race. The boys
had quite a cheering section, with Hawk, Mary,
Cloud Walker, Victoria, and himself all cheering
wildly. He figured his folks must be looking after
the other kids. Jacob and Jason finished in a tie for
second place. Adam and Amanda entered the
three-legged race and came in dead last when
Adam tripped. Blue Hawk and his friend Jimmy ran
in the next heat and came in first. Blackie wasn't
surprised. Blue Hawk had the speed of a jackrabbit
and the heart of a warrior.

Promising Hawk and Mary that he would see
them later, Blackie left the games area and strolled
over to the church, where some of the women were
laying out cakes and pies.

A short distance away, a long table decorated
with red, white and blue bunting held the picnic
boxes that would be auctioned off later that day.

Blackie was about to go look for his folks when
he saw Charlie McBride hop down from the seat of
a rickety old wagon and secure his horse to the
hitching post. A moment later, he felt his breath
catch in his throat when he saw Joey. Dang, he
thought, but she was prettier every time he saw her!

He watched as Charlie lifted a wheelchair from
the wagon bed and settled his grandmother in it.
Joey spread a lightweight blanket over her grand-

mother's lap, then handed her a large fan. Charlie said something to Joey and she replied, her eyes flashing angrily. Charlie shook his head, then stomped off toward Front Street. Joey looked after him a moment, then wheeled her grandmother toward a shady table where a number of elderly women were gathered.

Blackie waited, his heart pounding in anticipation. Surely she didn't plan to spend the day with Mrs. McBride and her friends. But no, Joey was smiling at the other women, patting a hand here, kissing a cheek there, and then she was walking in his direction.

She hadn't seen him yet and he watched her pick her way through the crowd, noting the way the sunlight danced in her hair, the way her skirts swayed with each step, the way she moved, like a wisp of smoke on a soft summer breeze. She laughed as a couple of boys, their faces smeared with chocolate, ran in front of her, and Blackie had a sudden image of Joey holding a child of her own. His child.

The thought made his mouth go dry. And then she was there, within reach, and he stepped out of his hiding place.

"Hi, Joey."

"Blackie!"

She smiled up at him, her eyes sparkling, her voice filled with happiness, and it was all for him.

"You made it," he said, and then shook his head. Of all the dumb things to say. Of course she'd made it. She was here, wasn't she? "What would you like to do?"

"I don't care." She looked up at him. "I'm just

happy to be here." She didn't say the words *with you*, but he heard them just the same.

The look in her eyes made him feel ten feet tall.

"Are you going to ride in the race later?" she asked.

Blackie nodded. "I reckon, though it would save a lot of time if they just gave the trophy to my father."

"Oh? Why?"

"Well, he's won almost every year for as long as I can remember. No one rides like he does, although Hawk comes close."

"Maybe you'll win this year."

"Maybe, but I doubt it. If my father doesn't win, you can bet my brother will."

"Your family is very close, aren't they?"

"Yeah."

"You're lucky," she said wistfully. "Charlie and I used to be close, when we were young, but the last few years, it's like he's someone else, someone I don't even know anymore. I thought coming out here and getting him away from the boys he was hanging around with might change that, but it hasn't." She sighed heavily. "He's just found another bunch of troublemakers to pal around with."

"I guess spending a few days in jail didn't help."

"No." She looked up at him. "Let's not talk about that now. Let's just have a good time."

"All right by me. What would you like to do?"

She shrugged, then tugged on his hand. "Look! It sounds like something's going on over there."

"Arm wrestling," Blackie said. "Do you want to watch?"

"Sure."

Someone had set up a rough plank on top of a beer keg. Jed Junior and Harry Monroe sat on three-legged stools facing each other across the make-shift table, elbows bent, hands locked together.

A circle of men surrounded them, cheering and making wagers on who would win the match.

Muscles straining, faces set with determination, they struggled in a quiet battle of strength and will. Jed Junior won that match, and the three that followed.

"Hey, Blackie," Mike Feehan called. "Give it a try!"

Blackie shook his head. "Not me." The very thought of facing off against Jed Junior made his ribs ache. "Why don't you take him on?"

With a good-natured grin, Mike Feehan took the empty stool across from Jed Junior.

Blackie winked at Joey. "This will be close," he predicted.

And it was. But, in the end, Big Mike Feehan won the match.

Jed Junior shook his head. "Next time I'll take you on first," he said with a wry grin.

Feehan turned to look at Blackie. "Come on, Kincaid, let's see what you're made of."

Blackie wrapped an arm around his middle, wondering if his bruised ribs could take the strain. He was thinking of giving it a try when Joey tapped him on the shoulder.

"Blackie, don't," she said. "You haven't had time to heal up yet."

"I thought . . ." He felt a rush of heat climb up the back of his neck. He wanted to impress her, wanted her to think he was something special.

"Never mind," she said. "You don't have to prove anything to me."

"What's going on here?" Hawk said, coming up behind them.

Joey squeezed Blackie's hand. "Your brother was going to take on Mr. Feehan."

Hawk looked at Blackie and shook his head. "Are you crazy? You want to crack those ribs all over again?"

"How about you, then, Sheriff?" Feehan asked. "You game?"

"Why not?" Hawk cracked his knuckles, stretched his arms, and sat down across from Big Mike.

"Ready?" Feehan asked.

Hawk nodded, and the two men locked hands. They battled back and forth, first one and then the other gaining the upper hand.

"Go, Hawk!"

Blackie glanced over his shoulder at the sound of Victoria's voice. Her face was flushed, her eyes filled with love and excitement as she cheered for her husband. Blackie glanced at Joey, wondering if she would ever look at him like that.

"Come on, Hawk!" Victoria shouted exuberantly. "You can take him. I know you can!"

Blackie would have sworn Hawk didn't have a chance against Feehan, but in the end, his brother won the round.

Victoria ran forward and threw her arms around her husband, almost unseating him. "You did it!" she exclaimed, and kissed his cheek.

"Is that all I get?" Hawk asked with a teasing smile. "A peck on the cheek?"

"Later," she whispered, and then blushed to the roots of her hair.

Amid hoots, hollers, and congratulations, Hawk stood up. Slipping his arm around Victoria's waist, he led her away from the crowd.

Blackie took Joey's hand in his and started to follow Hawk and Victoria when he saw Cloud Walker coming toward him. "Hey, Blackie, your father is looking for you. It is time to get ready for the race."

"Thanks. I'll be right there."

Cloud Walker grinned as he glanced from Blackie to Joey and back again. "Do not be late."

Blackie gave his brother-in-law a look that said mind your own business, then turned to Joey. "Do you want to come with me?"

"I'd like to, but I think I'd better go check on Grams, see if she needs anything."

"All right."

"I'll be there for the race, though."

"See you then."

She nodded, then hurried away.

Blackie stared after her for long seconds, then went to look for his father and Hawk.

"Josephine, land o'goshen, girl, where have you been?"

"Just looking around, Grams. Do you need anything?"

"No, Leona and Ester have been looking after me. Where's Charlie?"

"I don't know. He went to town."

"Went to the saloon, you mean."

Joey glanced at the other women, all of whom

were listening avidly to the conversation.

"The horse race is about to start," she said. "I'm going to go watch. I'll be back when it's over."

"Just you wait a minute, missy. I want to see it too."

Joey felt a sudden heaviness settle over her. "You do?"

"Yes." Maureen smiled at her friends. "I'll be back later."

Leona and Ester and the other old biddies nodded and then put their heads together, talking about Charlie, no doubt, Joey thought irritably as she pushed her grandmother's wheelchair across the grass toward the racecourse.

The starting point was at the back of the schoolhouse. A dozen riders sat their horses. The Kincaid men and Mary's husband stood out like hawks among sparrows. All four of them had removed their shirts. Their skin gleamed like copper in the sunlight. But Joey had eyes only for Blackie. Like his father and brother, he rode bareback. His hair fell down his back like a fall of heavy silk, as black as the horse that pranced beneath him. He was as beautiful as the horse he rode.

He looked in her direction a few moments later. His gaze caught and held hers. Electricity sparked between them, sizzling like summer lightning. She felt it in every fiber of her being.

"Scandalous," her grandmother said, making a *tsk*ing sound.

"What are you talking about?"

"Those Kincaid men," Maureen said, her voice thick with disgust. "Parading around like naked savages. They ought to be ashamed!"

167

Joey choked back the urge to defend Blackie, knowing it would only upset her grandmother more, but it was hard to keep silent.

Glancing down the line of spectators, she saw Blackie's mother and sister standing close together. Hannah Kincaid held a little boy. He was asleep, his head pillowed on his grandmother's shoulder. Mary held her toddler, who was pointing at his father and calling, "*Neyho, neyho.*" A few moments later, Victoria joined them. She was holding a darling little girl with curly black hair and dusky skin. Joey wished that she were a part of the Kincaid family, that she could go stand with Hannah and the others and cheer for Blackie.

The race was about to start. The riders lined up. Joey recognized most of the men as customers she had waited on. There was Jed Junior mounted on a leggy chestnut. Harry Monroe's horse was a short-coupled bay mare. His brother, Richard, rode a nervous dapple gray gelding. Jeremy Brown rode a big brown Thoroughbred. Gene Smythe was mounted on a nervous grulla.

A collective hush fell over the crowd as Clancy Turner raised his pistol overhead, his finger poised on the trigger.

The sound of the gunshot echoed like thunder.

Joey gasped as Shadow's horse reared, forelegs pawing the air. It was an awesome sight. The big red stallion came down running and in no time at all had caught up with the rest of the horses.

It was a long race, the course plotted for speed and endurance. Leaving the schoolyard, the course followed the river for a mile, made a wide turn at the end of town, crossed the river, and followed a narrow path back until it crossed the river again and finished where the race had begun.

Just before the horses went out of sight, Joey saw that Hawk, Blackie, Shadow, and Gene Smythe were in the lead. Cloud Walker was fifth. His horse seemed to be favoring its right foreleg and even as Joey watched, the horse went down. A cry rose from the crowd. Joey held her breath, certain Mary Kincaid's husband was going to be trampled, but he rolled agilely out of the way. Clutching her little boy, Mary ran toward him.

Relieved that he hadn't been hurt, Joey turned her attention back to the race. The riders were out of sight for a few minutes and then burst into view again on the far side of the river.

Shadow was in the lead, closely followed by Blackie and Hawk. The rest of the riders were strung out behind them. Joey took a step forward, hands clasped to her breasts as she watched Blackie. He was leaning forward over his horse's neck, man and animal moving in perfect rhythm, almost as if the two of them were one creature. Hawk rode the same way, but she supposed that wasn't surprising, since Shadow had taught them both. There was a kind of breathtaking beauty in the way the three of them rode. It was a truly beautiful picture—the rolling plains and the winding river, the horses galloping, manes and tails flowing in the wind. The men who rode with such wild abandon were equally breathtaking, their expressions intense yet filled with the joy of the race. She wished she had a way to capture the moment forever.

As they neared the crossing, Blackie's horse pulled into the lead. It was all Joey could do to keep from jumping up and down with excitement. Shadow and Hawk were hard on his heels as they splashed across the river and up the bank.

As they neared the finish line, it was anyone's guess as to who would win. Blackie pulled ahead for a few yards, and then Shadow passed him.

He was going to lose, she thought glumly, but then, that was no surprise. Hadn't he told her that his father won almost every year?

And then, to her surprise, Blackie leaned low over his mount's withers. The big black horse leaped to the fore as, with a wild ululating cry that sent cold shivers down her spine, Blackie crossed the finish line less than two yards ahead of his father. Hawk came in a close third.

Moments later, the rest of the riders crossed the finish line.

Silas Crocker, acting as head judge of the race, stepped forward and presented Blackie with a trophy. Blackie waved it over his head, then swung his leg over his horse's withers and slid to the ground.

Joey watched Hannah Kincaid run up to her son and embrace him, then turn and hug her husband. Victoria ran up to hug Hawk too. Joey wished she could go over and congratulate Blackie on a fine ride. She yearned to hug him, to tell him how proud of him she was. Instead, she remained at her grandmother's side and watched as Blackie's family gathered around him. He said something to his father and the two of them laughed, and then Blackie hugged his father and his brother.

Joey blinked the tears from her eyes as she watched them, wishing again that she belonged to such a warm and loving family. Her grandmother had told her that the Indians were godless savages, that they were incapable of love or tender feelings, but it was obvious that Grams had been wrong. One had only to look at Blackie's family to see how much they loved each other. Hawk was grinning as he lifted his twin sons onto the back of his horse. She watched Cloud Walker come forward to congratulate Blackie. She smiled as Shadow settled three little ones on the back of his horse. What would it be like, to be part of a big family like that? To live in a nice house and never have to worry about money?

"Josephine?" Grams tugged on her hand. "Josephine!"

Startled, she looked down at her grandmother. "Did you say something?"

"Land sakes, girl, where's your mind?"

"I just didn't hear you, that's all."

"I want to go back and sit with Leona and Ester now," Maureen said. "They'll be auctioning off the box lunches soon. That's always good for a laugh or two. I don't know why you never put one up. You're as good a cook as any other girl in the valley."

Joey bit down on her lower lip, wondering if she should tell her grandmother that she had made up a box this year.

"Josephine?"

"I made a lunch this year," she confessed.

"Well, land sakes, you might tell a body these things."

"I'm sorry. I . . . I forgot."

Grams made a *tsk*ing sound. "I swan, girl, sometimes I don't know where your head is."

Joey glanced in Blackie's direction again. He was walking his horse back and forth to cool it out. His little brother and several other children tagged at his heels.

With a sigh, she wheeled her grandmother across the hard-packed earth to where Leona and Ester and the others waited in the shade.

At noon, the auction began. With his dry wit, Fred Brown made a fine auctioneer. As always, he wore a plaid vest and a merry smile.

Feeling a little self-conscious, Blackie stood with the rest of the town's bachelors. He had endured some good-natured ribbing from his brothers and sister when he told them he wouldn't be eating lunch with the family. He hadn't missed the look his parents exchanged, either. As much as he loved his family, there were times, like now, when he wished he had been an only child.

He shifted from one foot to the other, wondering how he was supposed to recognize Joey's lunch, and what he'd do if he bid on the wrong one.

Gene Smythe bid four dollars on a box all done up in pink and yellow ribbons.

Saul Crowley bid five dollars and twenty-five cents on a box decorated with a little wooden bird-cage surrounded by fresh flowers.

Both men looked pleased as punch as they walked off with a lunch tucked under one arm and a beaming young lady on the other.

It occurred to Blackie that the bidding wasn't as random as it appeared, and that the girls had some-how managed to let the men of their choice know which lunch to bid on.

But he'd had no such hint from Joey.

"Well, now, looky here," Fred Brown drawled. He grinned as he held up a large square basket. The top was decorated with a tall stick man with long black hair surrounded by a variety of animals made out of straw and cloth and clay. "I seen lots of unusual decorations in my day, but nothing quite like this. What am I bid?"

Blackie grinned as he raised his hand. All those animals could only be for him. "Five dollars."

"Six."

Blackie glanced over his shoulder to see Harry Monroe pushing his way through the crowd. "Seven."

"Eight," Harry said belligerently.

"Ten."

"Eleven." This from a young man Blackie didn't recognize.

Harry countered with twelve.

"Fifteen," Blackie called.

Harry took a wide-legged stance. "Sixteen."

"Twenty-five dollars," Blackie said.

Gasps and applause rose from the spectators. Twenty-five dollars was a pile of money to spend on a box lunch that likely didn't hold anything fancier than fried chicken and potato salad.

"The bid is twenty-five dollars," Fred called. "Do I hear more?"

There was a lot of conversation and speculation, but no one raised the bid.

"Going once. Going twice. Sold to Blackie Kincaid! Blackie, come on up here and let's see which lady goes with it."

Blackie stepped up on the platform, his heart

hammering as Joey left the crowd to join him on the platform.

There was some scattered applause at first, and then a rousing cheer from Blackie's family as they arrived on the scene.

Joey's face was flushed as he took her by the hand.

"You're not going with him, are you?" Harry Monroe demanded, grabbing her by the arm. "You told me you couldn't make it today."

"I changed my mind."

"Let her go, Harry," Blackie said, aware that they were causing a scene. He could see the apprehensive look on his mother's face, the expectant looks on the faces of those around them. He knew some of the men in the crowd were hoping for a good fight, but he had no intention of giving them one—not today.

"A pretty girl shouldn't have to eat lunch with a dirty half-breed," Harry said, sneering.

Just then Harry's older brother, Cliff, sauntered up, a cigar clenched between his big buck teeth. "What's going on?"

Blackie shook his head. He didn't want a fight, but he'd take them both on if he had to.

"Nothing's going on," Hawk said, coming up behind Harry. The star on his vest gleamed in the sunlight. He rested one hand on the butt of his gun. "My brother just paid twenty-five dollars to have lunch with this pretty little gal. I suggest the two of you let him enjoy it."

Muttering under his breath, Harry released his hold on Joey's arm.

Harry fixed Blackie with a hard look. "This ain't over between us," he warned.

"Just name the day," Blackie said. He looked at Joey and smiled. "Any day except today." Giving Joey's hand a squeeze, he led her away from the crowd.

When he turned onto the path that led into the woods, she knew he intended for them to eat lunch at Rabbit's Head Rock, away from disapproving stares and prying eyes. Already, she thought of it as *their* spot.

"Is this okay?" Blackie asked.

"Perfect."

A blanket was already spread in the shade cast by the rock. Joey sat down, spreading her skirts around her. Blackie sat down across from her and placed the lunch box between them. He tapped the stick man on the head. "Is this supposed to be me?"

"Good likeness, don't you think?"

Blackie stared at the stick figure for several moments, as if giving it serious consideration, and then said, "Well, I'm a little taller."

"And a little fatter," Joey said, giggling.

Blackie patted his stomach. "Not fat enough," he said. "What do you have in that basket?"

"Nothing much," she said. "Just some fried chicken and potato salad and cole slaw, a couple of roast beef sandwiches, some apples, and cookies. Oh, and some cherry pie. And lemonade."

He looked up at her, his eyes dancing with merriment. "You really are going to fatten me up. Were you planning to feed my whole family?"

She smiled up at him, unable to contain her happiness. "No, just you. But, well . . ." She felt herself blushing. "I'm a good cook, and I wanted you to know it."

"Is that right?"

"See for yourself." She lifted the lid from the basket and pulled out two plates, two cups, two napkins, and two forks and laid them out. She piled his plate high and filled his glass before serving herself.

Blackie took a bite of chicken, and then a bite of potato salad. "You're right, you are a good cook," he said, taking another bite of chicken. "Best I've ever tasted."

She basked in his praise. "Really?"

"Really." He finished the chicken and picked up the sandwich, which was thick with rare roast beef and cheese. "Did I tell you how pretty you look today?"

"Do I? Your mother gave me this dress. Do you like it?" She ran a hand over the skirt. "I tried to pay her for it, but she wouldn't let me."

"It looks like it was made for you," Blackie said, grinning. His mother had outdone herself, he thought.

"It does, doesn't it? Congratulations on winning the race."

"Thanks." If he never won another one, it didn't matter. But today he'd had to win, for Joey, and for himself.

"What did you say to your father?"

Blackie grinned. "I told him I never would have beat him if I hadn't been riding a horse he had trained."

Joey laughed softly. "I've never seen a horse race before. It was exciting. But kind of scary. Is Mary's husband all right?"

"Sure, he's fine." Blackie glanced around. "My folks met out here."

"Really?"

"My mother was only nine at the time, and my father was about twelve, I guess. Somehow they got to be friends. They used to meet out here on the sly."

"Sort of like us," Joey remarked.

Blackie nodded.

It seemed very romantic, Joey thought, sort of like Romeo and Juliet, only Hannah's story had ended on a much happier note than Juliet's.

"You have a little potato salad on the corner of your mouth," he said, touching his own to show her where.

Joey reached for her napkin.

"Here," Blackie said, taking the napkin from her hand. "Let me do it."

She leaned forward a little, her eyes widening when he bent his head and licked the bit of mayonnaise from her mouth.

"Yes, siree," he said, "the best I've ever tasted."

She gazed up at him, her heart pounding with happiness. "I think I might have a little here, too," she said, tapping her forefinger against her lower lip.

"I'll take care of it," he said solemnly, and covered her mouth with his.

He kissed her until she was breathless, until her whole body ached with a need she didn't fully understand.

"Dammit, girl," Blackie murmured, his voice ragged, "do you know what you do to me?"

She shook her head. "Blackie . . ."

He kissed her again. "What, honey?"

"I think I'm in love with you."

"Joey!"

"It's all right," she murmured. "I don't expect you to love me back."

He stared down at her, his brow furrowed.

"It's all right, really," she said quickly. "I know I'm not . . ."

"Joey, what do you think is going on here?"

"I . . . that is . . . I'm sure you know a lot of girls. I don't expect you to . . . to . . ." She looked up at him, her cheeks flushed with embarrassment, her eyes bright with unshed tears. "I'm sorry. I never should have said anything."

With a shake of his head, Blackie drew her onto his lap. "Joey." He drew a deep breath, astonished by the tenderness he felt for the girl in his arms. "Ah, Joey, don't you know I'm in love with you too?"

"You are?"

"You sound surprised. Why?"

She rested her head on his shoulder. "I guess I was afraid to hope. Your family is so wonderful, and mine is . . . well . . ."

"Tell me about your family."

She shrugged. "There's nothing much to tell. My mother ran off with another man when I was eight. It broke my father's heart. He started drinking after that; just a little at first. Then he started staying out late at night. Pretty soon he couldn't hold on to a job for more than a few months at a time. We lost our house and had to go live in a rented room." She drew in a deep shuddering breath. "He died three years ago. It was shortly after that when my grandmother wrote and asked us to come and stay with her. I've tried to love her, but she's a bitter woman."

Blackie stroked Joey's back, not knowing what to say.

"I've watched your family," Joey said, sniffing back her tears. "They seem so happy together, and I . . ." Sobbing, she buried her face against his shoulder.

"Joey, what is it? What's wrong?"

She shook her head.

"Joey. Talk to me. Honey, please, let me help."

"I'm just so afraid they won't like me."

"Oh, honey, they're going to love you as much as I do."

She looked up at him through her tears. "Do you really think so?"

"I know so." He cupped her face in his hands and wiped her tears away with his thumbs. "You okay now?"

She nodded. "I didn't mean to cry all over you."

"Any time." He kissed the tip of her nose. "How about a piece of that cherry pie?"

"What the hell's going on here?"

Blackie looked up to find Charlie McBride glowering down at them.

"Charlie!" Joey exclaimed. "What are you doing here?"

"Looking for you. Grams wants to go home."

"Now? But—"

Charlie grabbed her by the arm and hauled her roughly to her feet. "Now. And you—" He jabbed a finger in Blackie's direction. "Stay away from my sister."

Blackie stood up, his hands balled into tight fists.

Joey quickly stepped between Blackie and her brother. The tension between the two of them was palpable. "Stop it, both of you."

"Do you want to go with him?" Blackie asked.

"Yes." She looked up at him, her eyes pleading for him to understand. "Thank you for buying my lunch."

Blackie nodded curtly.

"You heard me, you dirty redskin. Stay away from Joey or I'll finish what Caffrey started."

Blackie fixed Charlie McBride with a cool stare. "Any time," he said. "Any place."

Joey tugged on her brother's hand. "Come on; you wanted to go, so let's go."

"Joey . . ."

"It's all right, Blackie, really. I need to go check on Grams anyway. Thank you for a lovely day."

She turned on Charlie as soon as they were out of Blackie's sight. "How could you embarrass me like that?"

"Embarrass you! How the hell could you go off with that redskin? Dammit, Joey, ain't you got no pride?"

"I like him. A lot."

"No!" Charlie shook his head. "No! I won't have any sister of mine dirtying her hands with the likes of him."

"Listen to me, Charlie McBride, you're not my father or my keeper, and I'll see anyone I want."

"Hah! When Grams finds out, she'll never let you out of the house again!"

"Is that right? And who's gonna put food on the table? You?"

Charlie's expression turned sullen. "If I have to."

Joey snorted disdainfully. "You haven't held on to a job for more than two days in over six months. Who's gonna hire you now? Nobody, that's who."

"I'll get a job," Charlie muttered belligerently. "Wait and see if I don't."

Joey pasted a smile on her face as they neared her grandmother.

"There you are, Josephine. Where've you been?"

"Charlie said you're ready to go home."

Grams nodded. "I need my medicine."

"We'll take you home," Joey said. She sent a last wistful look at the food-laden tables, the decorations, the young people laughing and talking together, and then, with a sigh of resignation, she took hold of the handles of her grandmother's wheelchair and pushed her toward their wagon.

For her, the party was over.

Chapter Seventeen

Chewing on a blade of grass, Blackie sat down on the blanket and stared into the distance. He would have liked nothing better than to put his fist in Charlie's big mouth, and Harry's too, for that matter, but he knew that fighting only would have upset Joey more.

With a sigh, he leaned back against the rock. Joey. She had looked as pretty as a wild rose in that new dress. She had said she loved him. And he had known in that moment that he loved her. The thought had him grinning like a fool. His mother had been right, he thought. When you were in love, you knew it.

Gathering up the blanket and the basket, he walked back to the schoolyard. Victoria and Mary were sitting on a patchwork quilt in the shade. Mary

Join the Historical Romance Book Club and GET 4 FREE* BOOKS NOW!

A $23.96 Value!

Yes! I want to subscribe to the Historical Romance Book Club.

Please send me my **4 FREE* BOOKS.** I have enclosed $2.00 for shipping/handling. Each month I'll receive the four newest Historical Romance selections to preview for 10 days. If I decide to keep them, I will pay the Special Members Only discounted price of just $4.24 each, a total of $16.96, plus $2.00 shipping/handling ($23.55 US in Canada). This is a **SAVINGS OF AT LEAST $5.00** off the bookstore price. There is no minimum number of books I must buy, and I may cancel the program at any time. In any case, the **4 FREE* BOOKS** are mine to keep.

*In Canada, add $5.00 shipping/handling per order for the first shipment. For all future shipments to Canada, the cost of membership is $23.55 US, which includes shipping and handling. (All payments must be made in US dollars.)

NAME: _____

ADDRESS: _____

CITY: _____ **STATE:** _____

COUNTRY: _____ **ZIP:** _____

TELEPHONE: _____

E-MAIL: _____

SIGNATURE: _____

If under 18, Parent or Guardian must sign. Terms, prices, and conditions subject to change. Subscription subject to acceptance. Dorchester Publishing reserves the right to reject any order or cancel any subscription.

had a shawl draped over one shoulder, and he knew she was nursing Cody. Jared, Patrick, and Samantha were napping, sprawled out between their mothers. Victoria was playing checkers with Linus. Nearby, several other women were also reclining in the shade while their children slept. Mrs. Crowley was teaching one of her daughters how to knit.

He didn't see Cloud Walker or Hawk and figured they were looking after the other kids. Hannah and Shadow were also absent.

"Where is everybody?" Blackie asked, sitting down on the edge of the quilt.

"At the baseball game," Victoria answered.

"How was your lunch with Joey?" Mary asked.

"Fine, until her brother showed up."

"Are you sure you want to get involved with that family?" Victoria asked. "Not that Joey isn't a nice girl, but, well . . ." She shrugged. "You know what I mean."

Blackie leaned back on his elbows, feet crossed at the ankles. "I know what you're saying, but . . ."

He shrugged, and Mary and Victoria exchanged knowing looks.

"So," Mary said, "that's the way it is."

" 'Fraid so."

"Does she feel the same?" Victoria asked.

He grinned. " 'Fraid so."

"No sense trying to talk you out of it, then," Mary said with an exaggerated sigh of resignation.

"You think I'm making a mistake?"

"It doesn't matter what *we* think," Mary said. "What do *you* think?"

"I think I just won the game!" Victoria said.

Linus scowled at his aunt. "Good. I was tired of playing anyway."

"Don't be a sore loser," Mary chided, ruffling her son's hair.

Scrambling to his feet, Linus picked up his ball. "Uncle Blackie, will you play catch with me?"

"Sure, hang on a minute." Blackie looked at his sister. "Come on, Mary, what do you think?"

"I think the two of you look good together," his sister replied. "And why should you have an easy time of falling in love?" she said, laughing. "None of the rest of us did."

"That's right," Victoria agreed, packing away the pieces of the game. "My parents disowned me for marrying Hawk, remember?"

"And I was married to another man when I fell in love with Cloud Walker," Mary said.

"It wasn't easy for your parents, either," Victoria added. "At least the Kincaids and the McBrides aren't at war with each other."

"Close enough," Blackie muttered. "I didn't get this black eye running into a door, you know."

"You'll work it out," Mary said confidently. "The Kincaids have a way of coming out on top, no matter what the odds."

Blackie nodded glumly. "I sure hope you're right."

Joey stared into the distance, her jaw set, her hands fisted in her lap while her brother and Grams berated her for spending time with Blackie Kincaid. She was a damn fool. The Kincaids were no good. She was a decent, God-fearing girl. He was nothing but a heathen savage in spite of his city clothes. It hadn't been that long ago that his father was riding the war trail, killing and scalping innocent white people.

She wanted to argue with them. She wanted to remind Charlie and her grandmother that Shadow and Hannah Kincaid had practically settled Bear Valley single-handedly, that Shadow had once saved a little girl's life. Not only that, but Hawk was the sheriff, and Mary and Hannah and Victoria all went to the same church Grams did, but she knew she would just be wasting her breath. Grams would never forget that her husband had been killed by Indians, and she would blame them all for his death until the day she died.

And where Indians were concerned, Charlie was just as narrow-minded and blind as was Grams. She looked up as his voice rose.

". . . not to see that redskin again if I have to lock you in your room and throw away the key."

Joey looked at her brother, unable to believe her ears.

"Is that right?" she retorted angrily. "Well, I'd like to see you try!"

"Don't push me, Josephine McBride," he warned. Rising, he clapped his hat on his head. "You stay clear of that redskin and his family, you hear? You'll be sorry if you don't."

"You listen to your brother," Grams said, shaking her finger in Joey's direction. "He's the man of the house."

Joey made a sound of disdain low in her throat. "Well, why doesn't he act like it, then?" She glared at Charlie. "Why don't you stop spending all your time in saloons and get a job, Mr. Man of the House? Why don't you grow up?"

"Why don't you shut up?" he retorted angrily.

"Why don't you try and make me?"

Too late, she realized she had pushed him too far. Muttering an oath, he slapped her. Joey reeled back, stumbled, and hit her chin on the edge of the doorway. She stared at her brother, unable to believe he had struck her, then turned and ran out of the room.

Reaching her bedroom, she closed and locked the door, then threw herself facedown on the bed. Grams was being mean and Charlie was hateful, and between them they had ruined what had been the best day of her life.

Closing her eyes, she let the tears flow.

The sound of firecrackers roused her. Rising, she went to the window. Night had fallen while she slept. Looking toward town, she saw several skyrockets explode, lighting the sky. It wasn't fair that she should have to miss the fireworks. She had looked forward to seeing them all year.

Another skyrocket exploded. Joey leaned forward to get a better look, then gave a little shriek when she saw a face staring back at her through the window.

Letting out a sigh of relief, she lifted the sash. "Blackie! What are you doing here?"

"I just wanted to make sure you were okay."

She smiled at him, happiness replacing the heaviness in her heart. "I'm fine."

"The dance will be starting in a few minutes," he said. "Will you come with me?"

"I shouldn't . . ."

"It's all right, I understand. I just came here to make sure . . ."

"But I will." Lifting her skirts, she climbed over the sill and into Blackie's arms.

He kissed the tip of her nose, then carried her to where his horse was waiting. He settled her in the saddle, then vaulted up behind her. Taking up the reins, he clucked to his horse, and the stallion moved out at a brisk walk.

Joey leaned back against Blackie, her hand folded over his arm where it circled her waist.

"Did they give you a bad time?" he asked.

She lifted one hand to her cheek. "No. Not really."

They heard the music long before the grange hall came into view. Joey smiled with delight when she saw the colorful paper lanterns that lined the pathway to the building. Couples walked toward the building, smiling and laughing.

In the interim between the baseball game and the dance, the townspeople had gone home to have dinner and change clothes. Now the men wore their good trousers and go-to-meeting shirts; the women were clad in colorful dresses with full skirts.

Blackie reined his horse to a halt near a picket line. Dismounting, he tied the stallion at the end of the line, then lifted Joey from the saddle and took her hand.

Smiling with anticipation, they hurried toward the hall.

It was already crowded. All the windows had been opened, and a soft breeze stirred the red, white, and blue bunting that hung from the rafters.

Long tables laden with punch bowls, pies, cakes, and cookies were situated at both ends of the hall. The musicians stood on a raised dais in one corner playing "Shine On, Harvest Moon." The floor was crowded with couples. A makeshift dance floor made of wooden planks had been set up outside the hall to handle the overflow, and to accommodate those who wanted to waltz under the stars.

Blackie looked at the crowded floor, then looked at Joey. "Why don't we . . ." His voice trailed off. Frowning, he touched her chin with the tips of his fingers. It was red and slightly swollen. "What happened here?"

She winced at his touch and pulled away. "Nothing. I'm fine."

"Nothing? Did someone hit you? Who? Charlie?"

"I . . . it was an accident."

Taking her by the hand, he said, "Let's go outside."

Feeling miserable and ashamed, she followed him.

Once they were alone, he turned her to face him. "What happened, Joey? You can tell me."

"It was nothing, really. Charlie and I were arguing like a couple of kids and things sort of got out of hand, that's all."

Blackie's gaze searched hers. "What were you arguing about?"

She looked away, but not before he'd seen the answer in her eyes.

"It was about me, wasn't it? About us?"

"Yes, but it doesn't matter. It doesn't change anything. I'm a big girl. I don't need their permission."

Drawing her into his arms, he kissed her chin lightly. "I'm sorry, Joey."

She leaned against him, and he welcomed her weight.

"If he ever lays a hand on you again, I'll kill him."

"Blackie, don't say that!"

He stroked her hair, thinking it was a good thing Charlie McBride wasn't there now. He would like nothing better than to give the kid a taste of his own medicine.

He held her for a long moment, then kissed the top of her head. "Would you like to dance?"

Joey nodded, glad for any excuse to be in his arms.

Paper lanterns lit the way to the makeshift dance floor.

"This is much more romantic than inside," Blackie said as he swept her into his arms.

Joey felt a moment of hesitation as he began to twirl her around the floor. She hadn't danced very often and was a little self-conscious at first, but Blackie soon put her at ease. He was light on his feet, easy to follow, and she was soon laughing with delight.

She saw Mary and Cloud Walker and, a moment later, Hawk and Victoria. Mary smiled broadly. Victoria waved. Putting one hand over his heart, Hawk winked at Blackie.

Blackie laughed and twirled her away.

It was a beautiful night, warm and clear. Overhead, the stars twinkled like millions of tiny fireflies around a full butter-yellow moon. Dancing under the stars, she felt like a princess in a fairy tale, and Blackie was her prince. She shied away from casting Grams as the wicked witch but had no trouble imagining Charlie as the villain.

"What are you grinning at?" Blackie asked.

"Nothing," she said, and laughed out loud.

"Tell me."

"I was just thinking of a fairy tale my mother read me, about a poor princess and how a handsome prince rescued her from a life of drudgery."

Bending down, he brushed a kiss across her lips. "I hope I'm the prince," he whispered, and read the answer in her eyes.

There was a pause in the music, and then the strains of a waltz filled the air. With a sigh, Joey rested her head on Blackie's shoulder. It was a magical night, she thought, and for the first time in her life, she felt beautiful, felt as if her whole life was about to change for the better.

Blackie loved her.

And she loved him.

Closing her eyes, she let him whirl her around the floor.

When the music ended, she was surprised to find Blackie's father standing there.

"*Neyho*, you know Joey. Joey, you remember my father?"

"Yes, of course." She gripped Blackie's hand, wondering if his father had come to express his disapproval.

Shadow looked at Blackie as the musicians began to play another waltz. "Do you mind if I dance with Joey?"

Her eyes widened in surprise even as she hoped Blackie would refuse.

"Of course not," he said, and handed her over to his father.

Her heart was pounding like a runaway train as Shadow led her onto the dance floor.

"Relax," he said quietly. "I promise not to scalp you."

She smiled faintly.

He took her in his arms, and for a moment they danced in silence. Gradually, her heart stopped hammering and her breathing returned to normal. He danced remarkably well, she thought with surprise. She had heard the Indians did war dances and rain dances, but she had never heard of them doing the waltz. She supposed Hannah must have taught him.

She looked up, conscious that he was watching her. "Are you having a good time, Miss McBride?" he asked.

"Yes."

"You and Blackie dance well together."

She felt her cheeks grow hot. "Thank you."

"My son is very fond of you." His eyes were black and direct. "Do you feel the same?"

Her heart started beating in double time again. *Here it comes*, she thought. *He's going to tell me to stay away from Blackie.* She lifted her chin defiantly, not wanting him to know how afraid she was. "Yes, I do."

Shadow smiled down at her. She knew then why Hannah had defied her parents to be with this man.

"I think you have the heart of a warrior," he said. "My son has chosen well."

Joey stared up at him, speechless. Nothing he might have said could have touched her more.

191

When the waltz ended, he walked her to the edge of the dance floor, where Blackie was waiting.

Shadow smiled at her as he placed her hand in Blackie's. "Thank you for the dance, Miss McBride."

"Please," she said, "call me Joey. And thank you. For everything."

"What was that all about?" Blackie asked when they were alone.

"I think your father just welcomed me into the family."

Blackie grinned, his expression one of happiness and relief. "That's good to know." His gaze searched hers. "Would you like to be a part of my family, Joey?"

"Are you asking me to marry you, Blackie Kincaid?"

"I reckon I am," he said without hesitation. "Will you marry me, Miss Josephine?"

"Oh, yes," she replied softly. "Yes, yes, yes!"

"Joey!" Unmindful of the crowd, he pulled her into his arms and kissed her.

She was blushing furiously when he released her.

"Come on," he said, taking her by the hand. "Let's go get some punch to celebrate."

Mrs. Crowley beamed at them from behind the table as she handed them each a glass of punch. "Looks like there's going to be a wedding soon." She winked at Blackie. "She'll make a lovely bride."

"How'd you know we're getting married?" Blackie asked.

"Pshaw, I've seen that look Joey's wearing on the faces of my own girls often enough to know what it means."

"Well, keep it quiet, will you?" Blackie asked. "We haven't told anyone yet."

Mrs. Crowley rolled her eyes. "Land sakes, boy, you won't be able to keep a secret like that for long. Not in this town." She shook her head, her expression sobering. "Mercy, what's Maureen going to say?"

"Please don't say anything to Grams," Joey implored. "Or to my brother."

"Not a word," Mrs. Crowley promised. "But I don't know how you'll get rid of those stars in your eyes, child."

They moved away from the punch bowl. "Do you want a piece of cake or some pie?" Blackie asked.

Joey started to say no. The thought of telling her family and the scene that was sure to follow had spoiled her appetite, but then she nodded, determined not to let anything ruin the moment. She would worry about Grams and Charlie later.

Carrying their punch and dessert, they made their way outside. Blackie found a quiet place away from the hall and they sat down.

"How's that pie?" Blackie asked.

"Good. Do you want a taste?"

He nodded, but when she offered him a forkful, he ignored it and licked her lips instead.

"Hmm," he said, "that is good."

Joey laughed softly. "Better than your chocolate cake?"

Blackie took a bite. "See for yourself."

Leaning forward, she licked the frosting off his lips. "I can't decide which is the best," she said. "Maybe I'd better have another taste."

"I think you should," he said, his voice suddenly husky.

They reached for each other, dessert plates tumbling to the ground as Blackie drew her onto his lap, his mouth covering hers in a kiss that was hot and hungry.

The darkness closed in around them, cocooning them in a world of their own. The music from the grange hall faded into the distance and he heard nothing but the pounding of his own heart and the soft moans rising in Joey's throat. Her breasts were warm against his chest; her hands trembled slightly as they delved under his shirt to stroke his back. He groaned as need spiraled through him.

"Joey." He took a deep, calming breath. "Joey, we've got to stop."

They were, he thought, the most difficult words he had ever uttered.

She looked up at him, her eyes huge in the moonlight.

"We'd better get married soon," he said, forcing a light tone into his voice, "before you take advantage of me."

Happiness bubbled up inside Joey and she laughed merrily. It was, she thought, absolutely, positively and without doubt, the very best day of her whole life.

They danced there, alone in the dark, sharing kisses when the music stopped, whispering their hopes and dreams for the future.

When he kissed her good night outside her bedroom window just after midnight, she knew it was a night she would never forget.

Chapter Eighteen

Blue Hawk was asleep in the back of the wagon by the time we got home from the picnic. Shadow carried our son to bed and I tucked him in, and then I followed Shadow outside and into the barn. I sat on a bale of straw while he led the first horse into its stall. My curiosity was killing me and I couldn't keep silent any longer.

"All right, what did you say to Joey?"

He glanced at me over his shoulder. "What do you mean?"

"You know what I mean. She looked scared to death."

Shadow chuckled as he closed the stall door and led Red Wind into the one next to it.

Sometimes he could be the most aggravating man! "Tell me," I insisted.

He closed and latched the door. "I asked her how she felt about Blackie."

"You didn't!" I stared at him in horror. "Oh, I don't believe it. You did! How could you? What did she say?"

"She is as fond of him as he is of her." He grabbed the pitchfork and forked hay for both horses.

"A blind man could see that," I muttered.

"I think we will have another daughter soon."

"Do you think they'll be happy together? As happy as we are?"

"No one is as happy as we are." He put the pitchfork away and then pulled me into his arms, his chin resting on top of my head.

"What's wrong?" I asked.

"Nothing."

"Something's bothering you," I insisted. I'd been married to him long enough to recognize the signs.

"I sense trouble coming."

"What kind of trouble?"

His hands lightly massaged my back, soothing and arousing at the same time. "I do not know."

He brushed his lips across the top of my head, then slid his arm around my waist, and we left the barn. Shadow closed the barn door and we walked up to the house, pausing at the foot of the porch stairs.

It was a beautiful night. I wondered where Blackie was, if he was still with Joey. I had seen the way they looked at each other while they danced, and I knew Shadow was right. There would be another wedding in the family soon.

"What about Joey's family?" I said, frowning. "I'm

sure they won't give Joey their blessing. And that brother of hers . . ."

My voice trailed off as Shadow drew me close and began raining feathery kisses over my face and neck.

"And what about . . . ?" I shivered with delight as his hands moved over me. After all these years, he could still excite me, still make me tremble like a young girl in love for the first time.

"What about what?" he asked. He knew exactly how his touch affected me. I heard the sly amusement in his voice, the faintly smug note of masculine satisfaction.

I faked a huge yawn and pushed him away. "We'll have to talk about it later," I said, one foot on the bottom step. "I'm too tired to talk about it tonight."

"Too tired?" He came up behind me, his body pressing close to mine so that I could feel his arousal.

"Yes, sorry."

His hands folded over my shoulders, holding me in place. His breath was warm against the side of my neck as he kissed me behind my left ear. "Maybe I can change your mind." He drew me back against him so there could be no doubt of what he wanted. Ever so lightly, his tongue outlined my ear, then slid down my neck.

Unable to help myself, I shivered again. A moment later, I was in his arms and he was carrying me into the house, down the hall and into our bedroom.

He pushed the door closed behind him, locking out the rest of the world.

*　　*　　*

I woke abruptly, not knowing what had awakened me, but knowing instantly that I was alone in bed.

I sat up. "Shadow?"

"The barn is on fire."

"What?" I scrambled out of bed and hurried to the window.

A moment later, there was a knock on the door and Blackie burst inside.

"*Neyho*, the barn's . . . !"

"I know. Let us go."

Grabbing my robe, I shrugged it on as I followed them out of the door. I could hear the frightened neighing of the horses trapped inside the barn as soon as we left the house.

Shadow ran toward the barn and flung the big double doors open wide. I felt my heart leap into my throat as he went inside the burning building, with Blackie close on his heels. Knowing it was useless, I grabbed a bucket, filled it in the horse trough, lugged it around the back of the barn, and threw it on the flames. The horses that were in the corrals raced back and forth, their eyes wide, their nostrils flared as the scent of smoke and ash filled the air.

Turning, I almost knocked Blue Hawk off his feet. He too was carrying a bucket. He dumped it on the flames and we ran back toward the trough. Back and forth, back and forth.

It was a waste of water and effort and I knew it, but I couldn't stop.

I saw Shadow and Blackie leading the horses out of the barn. How many were in there? Six? Eight? I couldn't remember. As soon as the ropes were removed from their necks, the horses scattered, disappearing into the darkness, running from the smoke and the flames.

The flames licked at the wood, climbing higher. There was a faint explosion from inside the building and the flames burst higher, fed by the dry wood and the straw in the loft.

In a distant part of my mind, I wondered how many horses were left inside.

"Hannah!"

I heard Shadow cry my name, grunted as he suddenly pushed me to the ground. His hands slapped at my back and legs. "What are you doing?" I exclaimed.

"Your robe is on fire," he replied, and smothered the last of the flames with his bare hands.

"Where's Blue Hawk?" I looked around, suddenly frantic. "Where is he?"

Shadow rose to his feet and helped me up. I glanced around but didn't see Blue Hawk anywhere.

And then I heard Blackie shout his name.

Together, Shadow and I ran to the front of the barn. The whole building was in flames now.

I screamed as I saw Blue Hawk run into the barn. "What he's doing?"

Shadow swore, something he rarely did. "He is going after that Appaloosa filly. He must have heard me tell Blackie we couldn't save her."

"No. No!" I screamed the words as Blackie ran into the barn. When I would have gone after him, Shadow held me back. "Let me go!"

Shadow pulled me into his arms. "No," he said. "I will not lose you too."

I beat against his chest and scratched at his face,

but he wouldn't let me go. Ignoring my cries, he held me in his arms, impervious to my struggles.

There was an ominous roaring sound, a huge crash as the back wall collapsed. I buried my face against Shadow's chest, all the fight gone out of me, my stomach heaving as I imagined my sons caught in the conflagration.

"Hannah! Hannah, look!"

Lifting my head, I saw Blackie race out of the barn scant seconds before the roof caved in. I stared, hardly daring to believe my eyes. He was carrying Blue Hawk over his shoulder and leading the Appaloosa. Blue Hawk's pajama top was tied over the filly's eyes.

No sooner had they emerged from the barn than the whole building collapsed. Sparks filled the air and winked out.

Twisting out of Shadow's arms, I ran toward Blackie, my gaze fixed on the small burden draped over his shoulder, tears streaming down my face. "Is he alive?"

"Yes."

I took Blue Hawk from Blackie's arms. He was unconscious, his hair singed. His pajamas were scorched in a dozen places, his skin blistered from the heat.

"I'll look after the filly," Blackie said. "She's got a couple of bad burns." He glanced back at the barn. "We got all the horses out but one."

Shadow nodded, then followed me into the house.

I carried Blue Hawk into his bedroom, waited as Shadow drew back the tangled covers. Gently, I lowered my son to the bed. His breathing was labored and uneven. I looked up at Shadow and saw my own fears mirrored in the depths of his dark eyes.

I stared down at my son, fear for his life leaving me numb and unable to move. I had treated bullet wounds and knife wounds but never anything like this.

"Hannah."

I looked up at Shadow. "He's going to die, isn't he?"

"I do not know. Undress him. We need to wash him and then treat his wounds."

"How?"

"My people used bear grease for burns."

I nodded and Shadow left the room.

Murmuring a silent prayer, I eased Blue Hawk out of his ruined pajama bottoms. He moaned as I covered him with a sheet and I quickly removed it. Going into the kitchen, I heated a pan of water, found a piece of soft clean white cloth, a bar of mild soap. When the water was warm, I poured it into a bowl and carried everything into the bedroom. Placing the bowl on the table, I soaped the rag and began to wash my son. He cried out as the cloth touched him and I jerked my hand back. His head rolled back and forth on the pillow; his arms and legs twitched convulsively.

I looked up as Shadow entered the room. "I can't do this," I said. It had been one thing to sew up the cut in Blackie's side, but this was my baby. How could I cause him more pain?

"You can, and you will," Shadow said. "You have always done what was necessary."

He placed a clay bowl on the floor and lit the

contents. The smell of sweet sage quickly filled the room. Holding an eagle feather in his hand, he chanted softly, and as he did so, he drew the feather through the smoke so that it wafted over Blue Hawk's body.

Shadow's chanting filled the room, soft, soothing, yet filled with power. Blue Hawk turned toward the sound, his body going still.

I let the sound engulf me, surround me. Drawing on Shadow's strength, I washed the ash and soot from my son's face and body, and as I did so, I remembered again the day he was born. I had struggled too long and too hard to bring him into the world. I could not lose him now.

I dried him carefully, then applied a thin coat of bear grease to the numerous ugly burns and raw places on his face, neck, arms, and legs.

When that was done, I made him a cup of weak tea, held it to his lips while he took a sip. He took a few swallows and then vomited it back up again.

I longed to hold my son in my arms, but I was afraid it would only cause him more pain, so I sat on the edge of the bed, one of his hands in mine, while Shadow continued to chant softly.

A short time later, Blackie entered the room. "Is he all right?"

"We have done all we can," Shadow replied quietly. "It is in *Maheo*'s hands now."

I sat at Blue Hawk's bedside all that night, clinging to his hand, afraid that if I let go, if I left his side for even a moment, if I dared close my eyes, I would lose him forever.

It was the longest night of my life, and Shadow was there beside me, lending me his strength.

Dawn was painting the eastern horizon with bright splashes of lavender and crimson when Shadow left the room.

A short time later, I stood to stretch my legs. Blue Hawk was sleeping soundly. Going to the window, I looked out over the yard. All that was left of our barn was a pile of blackened lumber and ashes. I could see Blackie and Shadow standing near one of the corrals. Three of the horses that had run off the night before stood together in front of the corral. Apparently they'd had enough of freedom. Blackie opened the gate and Shadow walked into the corral. The three mares followed him inside, and Blackie closed and latched the gate. Slipping through the rails, he went inside, and while Shadow spoke to the horses, Blackie checked them over to make sure they were uninjured from the ordeal of the night before.

Shadow spoke to Blackie for a few minutes, then Blackie grabbed a hackamore that was hanging from one of the fence posts. He dropped it over the head of a deep-chested bay, then swung onto the animal's bare back. Shadow opened the gate and left the corral, and Blackie rode out after him. He spoke to his father, then rode out of the yard.

Going into the kitchen, I put a pot of coffee on the stove. I wasn't hungry, but I needed coffee, and I knew Shadow would also welcome a cup.

When the coffee was ready, I poured two cups and went outside in search of Shadow.

I found him behind the house. We had a Cheyenne lodge set up back there under a tall tree. We kept it in memory of the old days. When our children were younger, they liked to sleep out there in the summer.

I found Shadow standing beside the lodge. He had stripped down to his breechclout and stood with his arms raised, his head back. A small fire burned at his feet; a plume of blue-gray smoke spiraled upward toward the sky.

How often had I seen him stand thus, his arms raised in mighty prayer? It amazed me that there were whites, some living here in the valley, who believed that the Indians were heathen savages. True, there had been times when I had seen the dark side of my husband. I recalled a day, long ago, when I had been raped by a soldier. The man had hit me several times when I resisted. I had been pregnant at the time, and it had been fear for my unborn child that ended my struggles. Shadow had appeared out of nowhere like the angel of death, a knife in his hand. Even now, the memory of Stockton's body, torn and bleeding, had the power to turn my stomach.

One other incident stood out in my mind. It had happened while we were riding the war trail. Shadow's men had taken three prisoners. Shadow's warriors had seen their wives killed in cold blood, had seen their old people trampled beneath the iron-shod hooves of cavalry mounts, seen their little ones slaughtered. I knew what his people had suffered at Sand Creek and at the Washita. Hatred had been running hot in our camp that night. Shadow had not participated when his warriors closed in on the white men, but he hadn't tried to stop them either. The lust for blood had been a tangible force. One of the captives had recognized me as a white woman. He had begged me to help him. It had been the worst moment of my life. I had felt Shadow's hand on my shoulder as he told me there was nothing I could do, nor was there any reason for me to stay and watch. But I had refused to leave. I had fought at his side. I had shared his grief when our warriors were killed. I stayed at his side that night and watched it all. And had nightmares for weeks afterward.

In spite of all that had happened in the past, Shadow was one of the most religious men I had ever known. He saw the hand of the Great Spirit in every rock and tree, every flower, every blade of grass.

I felt his inner strength, his power, wash over me, and I added my own prayers to his, pleading with the God of my childhood to spare the life of our son.

Lowering his arms, Shadow sprinkled a pinch of tobacco into the fire, then offered tobacco to the gods of the east, west, north, and south, to Mother Earth, and to the sky above. Chanting softly, he drew his knife and raked the edge of the blade across his chest and down each arm. My stomach clenched as fine lines of red appeared in the wake of the blade.

"Hear me, Man Above, I ask that you bless my son this day. Heal his wounds. Oh, *Maheo*, give me the courage to follow the warrior's path, to accept Your will in all things."

Tears welled in my eyes as I watched him drag the finely honed blade across his chest yet again.

Setting the two coffee cups on the ground, I went to my husband and took the knife from his hand.

He looked at me through eyes dark with grief and fatigue, but he did not protest when I took the knife. Keeping my gaze on his, I made several small cuts in my left forearm. It hurt, but the pain in my arm was nothing compared to the pain in my heart.

I watched small drops of blood ooze from the cuts as I returned the knife to Shadow.

He nodded once, his dark eyes warm with understanding and approval.

We stood there for a long time, each of us praying for a miracle, praying for the courage and the strength to accept God's will for our son.

Chapter Nineteen

Blackie slowed his horse to a walk as he rode into the yard at Hawk's place. It was early, probably too early for anyone to be awake, especially on a sleepy Sunday after the Fourth.

A red-bone hound scrambled out from under the porch, teeth bared, hackles raised.

"Be quiet, Samson, it's just me," Blackie said.

Dismounting, he scratched the dog's ears, then climbed the steps and knocked on the front door. Inside the house, a puppy started yapping. He heard Hawk's voice telling the dog to be quiet. The door eased open a little, and then swung wide.

"Blackie! What are you doing here at this time of the morning?" Hawk blinked the sleep from his eyes. "Is something wrong at home?"

"It's Blue Hawk. He's bad hurt. There was a fire out at our place last night."

"A fire?" Hawk swore softly. "Are *nahkoa* and . . . ?"

"They're fine. The barn was destroyed, but the fire didn't spread to the house."

"What about the stock?"

"We lost one horse." He didn't think he'd ever forget the horrible shriek the mare had made as the back wall collapsed.

Hawk ran a hand through his hair. "Been a hell of a night. Someone broke into Crockers and made off with several head of horses. If this keeps up, I'm gonna have to hire more help. Any idea how the fire started?"

Blackie shrugged. "I think it was set deliberately."

"Why the hell would anyone do that?"

Blackie shifted nervously from one foot to the other. "I'm not sure, but I think the message was for me."

"You? Hell, you've been gone for three years. Who'd have a grudge against you?" Hawk exclaimed, and then he swore softly.

"Yeah," Blackie said heavily. "Charlie McBride."

"I wouldn't have thought he had that much sand. Hell, he's just a kid."

"Maybe so, but I'm the one who brought him in."

Hawk snorted. "And you're the one who got him out. If it wasn't for you, he'd still be cooling his heels in jail." He muttered another oath. "Let me tell Victoria what happened and get dressed, and I'll ride back with you. Have you gone out to Mary's yet?"

"No. I came here first."

"Why don't you ride over and let her know, and I'll meet you at the house?"

"All right."

"Be careful, little brother."

"Yeah, you too."

Blackie stopped at Mary's house to let her know what had happened, and then he rode out to the McBride place, thinking he might get a chance to confront Charlie. Of course, if Charlie had set the fire, he might not be home. The other thing that drew him was the thought that he might catch sight of Joey, though that was unlikely as early as it was. He drew rein out of sight of the house.

He muttered an oath as he glanced around at the house and the front yard. Charlie McBride ought to be horsewhipped for letting the place go like this, he thought. Instead of spending so much time hanging around the saloon, the kid should spend a little time at home, taking care of the place. Besides being old, his grandmother was stuck in a wheelchair. Joey worked eight hours a day to put food on the table. The least the kid could do was keep the place up. Maybe if Charlie put in a hard day's work once in a while, he wouldn't have the time or the energy to go around setting things on fire.

Blackie checked the corral alongside the house, looking for Charlie's roan, but the corral was empty. He was about to look in the backyard when Joey rounded the corner of the house. She held a bowl in one hand and, as he watched, she began tossing chicken feed to the dozen or so hens that were soon clustered around her, clucking and scratching in the dirt.

Dismounting, Blackie tied his horse to a tree and

ran up to the side of the house. Taking cover behind a tree, he called her name.

Joey looked up, her eyes widening in surprise when she saw him. Dumping the rest of the chicken feed on the ground, she hurried toward him.

Reaching out, he took her hand and pulled her behind the tree and into his arms.

Joey smiled up at him. "What are you doing here?" Her smile faded when she saw the look on his face. "Is something wrong?"

As quickly as possible, he told her about the fire.

"That's awful! Poor Blue Hawk. I hope he'll be all right. Is there anything I can do?"

"I don't think so." He hugged her close. "Is Charlie home?"

"No, why?"

"Did he come home last night?"

"I don't think so. He wasn't here when I got in, and I didn't hear him come in later. He might have . . ." Her voice trailed off. "Wait a minute." She drew back, her brow furrowed. "You don't think Charlie had anything to do with that fire, do you?"

Blackie shrugged. He didn't want to alarm her, but the more he thought about it, the more certain he was that Charlie had set the fire.

"You do!" she exclaimed. "You think Charlie set that fire, don't you?"

"I'm sorry, Joey, but you know he's got a grudge against me for bringing him in and keeping him in jail."

"I don't care! He wouldn't do anything like that. He wouldn't! I know he's kind of wild sometimes, and not very responsible, but he wouldn't . . ."

"All right, Joey, forget I asked."

She looked up at him, her gaze searching his. "You don't really think he did it, do you?"

"I'm afraid so. That fire didn't start itself."

She sagged in his embrace. "I tried my best to raise him right," she said, her voice thick with defeat. "If only . . ." She shook her head. "I've got to go. Gram will be expecting breakfast, and I have to get her ready for church."

"I'm sorry, Joey. I hope he's innocent."

"He is," she said without conviction. "I know he is."

Putting one finger beneath her chin, he tilted her head up and kissed her lightly. "See you later."

When he returned home, Blackie found Hawk and his father sifting through the ruins of the barn. Dismounting, he walked closer, his nostrils filling with the scent of smoke and ash and another smell that he recognized as burnt horseflesh. The thought made him sick to his stomach.

He moved up behind Hawk. "Find anything?"

"Not yet."

"How's Blue Hawk doing?"

Hawk shook his head. "Not good."

"I stopped at McBride's," Blackie said. "I asked Joey if Charlie was there. She doesn't think he came home last night."

"Over here," Shadow called.

Blackie looked over at his father and saw him hold up a scorched can of kerosene. The words MILLER'S KEROSENE could be seen in one corner, miraculously untouched by the fire.

"Is it ours?" Blackie asked.

Shadow shook his head. "No. I do not buy this

brand, and I do not keep kerosene in the barn."

Hawk looked at Blackie. "You were right, then. It was set."

Blackie and Hawk stayed where they were while Shadow quartered back and forth, looking for sign.

"Find anything?" Hawk asked when his father returned.

"There is a faint trail of kerosene leading from the edge of the woods up to the door of the barn."

"So," Hawk said, thinking it through in his mind. "He ran a trail of kerosene from the woods into the barn, doused one of the bales of straw against the back wall, then hightailed it back to the woods and put a match to the trail of kerosene. The straw would have gone up in no time at all."

Shadow nodded. "Those are my thoughts, as well."

Blackie frowned. "Why did he leave the can behind?"

"That's a good question," Hawk replied.

Blackie watched as their father scouted the ground a second time. When he reached the place where the corner of the barn had stood, he paused a moment, his gaze sweeping the ground, and then he began to walk toward the woods, being careful where he stepped.

He hadn't gone more than half a dozen yards when he stopped and hunkered down on his heels.

Hawk grunted softly. "He's found something. Come on."

It turned out to be a slight indentation in the dirt.

"What is it?" Hawk asked.

"It is a footprint," Shadow said. He studied it for

several minutes, then stood up and continued walking.

Blackie looked at Hawk. "It doesn't look like any footprint I ever saw."

"Me either."

Blackie and Hawk exchanged glances. If there were any more tracks to be found, their father would find them. And sure enough, he found several more of the scuffed footprints leading away from the tree line, but once they entered the woods, there was no sign to be found.

Doubling back toward the house, Shadow paused once again.

Blackie felt a surge of hope, only to have it wiped out when his father said, "This print belongs to one of our horses."

Blackie frowned. "What are you saying?"

"Whoever burned our barn wrapped cloth over his boots to disguise his footprints. After he set the fire, he rode away on one of our horses."

Hawk swore a short pithy oath. "Do you think he walked here?"

"I do not know." Shadow pointed at the ground. "These other tracks were made by our horses last night when they ran from the fire."

Blackie shook his head. He didn't think even his father would be able to sort out the tracks. The ground was badly chewed up, the hoof prints overlaid with the family's footprints. In some places, where they had spilled water trying to put out the fire, the tracks were little more than a blur.

"I think he knew *neyho* would be able to follow his horse's tracks," Hawk remarked, frowning.

Blackie nodded. Anyone who lived in these parts

would be aware of Shadow's tracking ability.

"The way I see it," Hawk went on, thinking out loud, "there were two of them. They rode up to the far edge of the woods. One guy walked here to set the fire and the other one took his horse and rode back to town. The guy who set the fire took one of our horses because he knew *neyho* would be able to follow his tracks. I'll bet you ten bucks we'll find our missing horse somewhere in town."

"Maybe," Blackie said. "Either that, or they'll just turn it loose and it'll come home on its own."

"Don't worry, little brother," Hawk said. "We'll find out who did this sooner or later."

"Let's hope it's sooner," Blackie said.

They were walking back toward the house when something in the grass caught Blackie's eye. Stooping, he picked it up. It was a gold pocket watch. The back was engraved with the words *To My Husband Ira, with love, Maureen.*

Hawk and Shadow walked back toward him.

"What have you found?" Shadow asked.

Blackie held it out for his father and Hawk to see.

The three men exchanged glances.

"It's Charlie's, no doubt of that," Hawk said. Taking the watch from Blackie, he shoved it in his pocket. "I'll go out and pick him up." He looked at his father. "And then I'll check around in town and see if I can find your missing horse."

A few moments later, Jeremy Brown rode up leading two of their mares.

"What the hell?" Jeremy exclaimed. He shook his head ruefully as he glanced at what was left of the barn. Dismounting, he handed the lead ropes to

Blackie. "I knew something was wrong when I saw your stock in my yard. How'd it start?"

"It was set," Blackie said grimly. Clucking softly, he led the horses over to one of the corrals, opened the gate, and turned them loose inside.

"Set?" Jeremy repeated. "Who would do such a thing?"

Hawk shrugged. "I couldn't say right now, but we've got an idea or two."

Jeremy looked at Shadow. "Let me know when you're ready to rebuild."

Shadow nodded.

"I'd best get back home," Jeremy said.

"Thanks, Jeremy," Blackie said.

With a nod, Jeremy rode out of the yard.

"I'd best be going too," Hawk said. "I'll see you later, little brother."

"Be careful."

"Always."

Hawk had no sooner left than Saul Crowley rode up with another of their horses in tow. A few minutes later, Jimmy Parker's father, Alfred, rode up leading another mare. A foal gamboled at his dam's side.

So, Blackie thought, all the horses that had been in the barn were accounted for, except for the one Charlie McBride had used to ride away from the scene. Leaving his father talking to Saul and Alfred, Blackie went around to the back of the house to check on the little Appy filly that had been injured in the fire.

She whinnied softly as he approached, and he spent several minutes scratching the filly's neck before he examined the burns on her shoulders and flanks. She had lost some hair and some skin, but she wasn't badly hurt. If only his little brother was in as good shape as the filly.

Clenching his hands at his sides, Blackie swore under his breath. Damn Charlie McBride! He hated to think what this would do to Joey and her grandmother. Even worse, he wondered how it would affect his relationship with Joey.

When Blackie got back to the house, Saul and Alfred were gone and his father and mother were in the kitchen. His mother's face was pale; his father was standing at the sink, staring out the window.

Blackie looked from one to the other. "He's worse, isn't he?"

Shadow nodded curtly. "I am going to Steel's Crossing to get the doctor. Stay here and look after your mother and brother until I get back. I do not want them left alone."

"I understand, *neyho*. I'll go saddle your horse," Blackie said and left the room, giving his parents some privacy so they could say good-bye.

Chapter Twenty

Shadow put his hand on my shoulder and gave it a squeeze. Rising, I moved into his arms, blinking back my tears as I did so. Blue Hawk was getting worse, and I feared he might be coming down with pneumonia. His breathing was labored, his face pale. He had no appetite, and he slept most of the time.

I rarely left his side, afraid to leave him alone, afraid if I did that he would slip away from me. I talked to him even when he was asleep, assuring him I was there, telling him that his filly was safe, reminding him of how much we all loved him, urging him to hang on, promising him a trip to Steel's Crossing to see the circus in the fall.

I clung to Shadow when I felt him start to draw away.

"Hannah, I must go."

"I know."

He kissed the top of my head, gave me a hug, and I let him go. "Hurry," I said.

He nodded.

I walked him to the door. Red Wind was saddled and waiting. With a heavy heart, I watched Shadow swing effortlessly into the saddle. He would ride to town, leave his horse at Crocker's, and catch the train to Steel's Crossing. With luck, he would be back tomorrow with the doctor in tow.

I watched Shadow ride away until he was out of sight, and then I went back into the kitchen. As always, even with Blue Hawk and Blackie in the house, it seemed horribly empty without Shadow. He had been a part of my life for so long, it was as though he had taken a part of me with him.

I put our coffee cups in the sink and then went in to sit with Blue Hawk. He stirred when I entered the room.

"*Nahkoa?*"

His voice was weak, so weak.

"I'm here." I moved to the bed and took his hand in mine.

"Will you hold me?"

I bit down on my lip, afraid of hurting him, yet wanting to hold him more than anything. Sitting on the edge of the bed, I lifted him into my arms and rocked him back and forth the way I had when he was a baby.

"Am I going to die?"

"No! No, sweetheart. You'll be up and around in no time at all. You have to be," I said, forcing a smile. "Your filly misses you."

218

"Is she all right?"

"Yes, she's fine. Blackie's looking after her for you."

Blue Hawk yawned, his eyelids fluttering down. "He was brave . . ."

"So were you."

"Tell me a story."

"Which one?"

"How *Heammawihio* created the earth."

I smiled. It had once been Hawk's favorite story too.

"Once upon a time, many, many years ago, water covered the face of the earth. A Person floated on the water. There were no other people on the earth. There was no land, just water and water birds, like ducks and geese and swans.

"The Person called the water birds to him and told them to look for some earth. One by one, the birds dived into the water to try to reach the bottom so they could bring up some earth, but none of them were successful . . ."

"Except the mud hen," Blue Hawk said.

"Yes. She went down very deep and surfaced with a tiny bit of mud in her bill. The Person took the mud and worked the wet earth in his fingers until it was dry, and then he spread little piles of dry earth on the water around him, and the little bits of earth spread out and became dry land.

"After the earth was made, the Person made a man and a woman. He made the man from a rib taken from his own side, and he made the woman from a rib taken from the man. After he created the man and the woman, *Heammawihio* separated them. He put the woman in the north, where it was cold. The woman was given control of *Hoimaha*, the storm. She had gray hair, but she was not old, and she never grew older.

"*Heammawihio* put the man in the south. He was young, and he grew no older. The woman controls the cold and the snow, sickness and death. The man in the south controls the thunder. *Heammawihio* gave the man fire to protect himself from the cold.

"After *Heammawihio* sent the man and the woman away, he was alone again, and so he created other people. These people multiplied and . . ."

I paused so that Blue Hawk could say his favorite part—they became the Cheyenne. When he didn't end the story, I realized that he had fallen asleep.

He was warm, so warm. I could feel him trembling in my arms.

I held him until my arms were numb and my back ached, and then I tucked him under the covers as gently as I could.

I watched him sleep for a time, and then I knelt beside his bed and pleaded with Shadow's god and my own to spare the life of my son.

Chapter Twenty-one

Joey was in the kitchen making lunch when Charlie came in the back door.

"Don't look so surprised," he said, his tone surly. "I live here, remember?"

"I remember. I was beginning to wonder if *you* did. You didn't come home last night."

Charlie sat down at the table, shoulders slouched.

"Well," she asked impatiently. "Where were you?"

He shrugged. "Just out."

"Someone burned down the Kincaids' barn late last night."

"So?" He stared at her, and then his eyes went wide. "You don't think I did it?"

"Of course not. Here." She put a bowl of stew and

a couple of slices of bread in front of him. "Eat it while it's hot."

She fixed a bowl for herself and sat down across from Charlie. She spread her napkin in her lap, and began to butter her bread. "Grams is worried about you."

Charlie grunted. "She's always worrying about something."

"She loves you, Charlie."

"Yeah, I know. Where is she?"

Joey put down the knife. "She left this morning to go play cards with Leona and Ester."

Charlie swallowed a few spoonfuls of soup and gobbled down a piece of bread. "Do you think maybe Feehan could find some work for me?"

"Charlie? Do you mean it?"

He dragged his hand across his mouth. "I've been thinking about it."

Leaning across the table, Joey squeezed his forearm. "I'll ask him first thing tomorrow." She frowned as she heard a knock at the door. "I wonder who that is."

"I'll get it," Charlie said. Dropping his spoon, he pushed away from the table.

Joey smiled as she watched him leave the room. It was all she could do to keep from shouting out loud. Maybe, at long last, her prayers had been answered and Charlie was ready to get a job and settle down. A little extra money would go a long way. They could fix up the house, maybe hire someone to look after Grams during the day.

She frowned as she heard a commotion in the other room. Rising, she went into the parlor, her eyes widening when she saw Charlie struggling with the sheriff.

"I didn't do it!" Charlie exclaimed, a note of panic in his voice. "Dammit, let me go!"

"We found your pocket watch there," Hawk replied curtly. "I need to ask you some questions."

Joey felt a chill run down her spine. Charlie never went anywhere without Grampa McBride's watch.

"No!" Charlie swung at Hawk, his fist glancing off the sheriff's jaw.

Hawk's head snapped back. Lunging forward, he grabbed Charlie by the arm, twisted it behind his back and wrestled him down to the ground.

"We can do this easy, or we can do it hard," Hawk said. "It's up to you."

Charlie bucked beneath the sheriff, yelped with pain as Hawk applied more pressure to his arm.

"Stop that!" Joey shouted. "He didn't do anything!"

"Keep out of this!" Hawk said. He reached for the handcuffs in his back pocket, and as he did so, Charlie managed to break free.

Scrambling to his feet, Charlie bolted for the front door, only to be drawn up short when Hawk grabbed a handful of his shirt and hauled him back.

Charlie whirled around, his fists flailing. "I ain't going back to jail!"

"You are now, you damn fool!" Hawk roared.

There was a ripping sound as Charlie wrenched free of the sheriff's grasp.

Joey watched the two men come together swinging. Turning on her heel, she dashed into the kitchen and grabbed the first thing she saw. Hurrying back into the parlor, she stood on her tiptoes and brought the heavy cast-iron frying pan down on the top of Hawk's head.

With a grunt of mingled surprise and pain, he pitched forward and lay still.

Charlie looked up at her, one arm wrapped around his middle, a huge grin on his face. His eye was turning black; his lower lip was bloody.

Joey looked down at the sheriff, a sick feeling rising in her stomach. "What have I done? Oh, Lord, is he dead?"

Kneeling beside the sheriff, Charlie rolled him onto his back and checked his pulse. "No, he ain't dead. But he's out cold." Laughing, he stood up. "You sure do pack a heck of a wallop for such a little bit of a thing."

Still laughing, Charlie went into the kitchen and began throwing food into a burlap sack.

Joey followed him. "What are you doing?"

"I'm getting the hell out of here while I can."

"No! You can't."

"Like hell. I'm not going back to jail."

"What was your watch doing out at the Kincaid place?"

"How the hell should I know? Trijo won it off me in a card game while we were cooling our heels in jail."

"You gambled with Grandpa's watch? Charlie, how could you!"

"What difference does it make now? I'm leavin'."

"Please, Charlie, don't go. Don't you see? Running away just makes you look guilty." She followed him to the front door. "Charlie, listen to me! You've got to stay and tell the sheriff about Trijo . . ."

"I'll get in touch with you when I can."

She watched in disbelief as he hurried down the porch steps and untied the sheriff's horse.

"No! Oh, Charlie, no, don't!"

He grinned at her. "I ain't never had my hands on a horse as good as this one, and I'm not likely to get one in the future. So long, sis."

Stunned, she watched Charlie secure the burlap sack behind the cantle. Swinging into the saddle, he threw her a salute and rode out of the yard. She watched him until he was out of sight, and then she went back into the house.

The sheriff was still unconscious on the parlor floor. Her first instinct was to try to revive him. Going into the kitchen, she got a dish towel and soaked it in cold water. Returning to the parlor, she knelt beside him. She was about to place the cold cloth on his brow when it occurred to her that the longer the sheriff was unconscious, the more of a head start Charlie would have.

With that in mind, she went back into the kitchen and washed the dishes.

Hawk groaned softly as he opened his eyes. His head was pounding like a Cheyenne war drum. He lifted a hand to the back of his head, surprised that it wasn't twice its normal size. Damn. He had a bump the size of a goose egg.

When he sat up the room spun out of focus, and he closed his eyes. What the hell had happened?

When the dizziness passed, he grabbed hold of the end of the sofa and hauled himself to his feet. For a minute, he didn't know where he was, and then it all came back to him. He was at the McBride place.

He winced as he bent down to retrieve his hat.

A movement out of the corner of his eye caught his attention, and when he turned in that direction, he saw Joey McBride standing in the doorway nervously chewing on her lower lip.

"I take it your brother's long gone," Hawk muttered.

Joey nodded. "Does your head hurt?"

"What do you think?"

"Are you going to arrest me?"

"I sure as hell should," Hawk said sourly. "At least I'd have one of the McBrides behind bars."

Her lower lip quivered. "I'll have to find someone to look after Grams."

Hawk swore softly. "Forget it. I'm not taking you in."

"You're not?" Her eyes grew wide. "Why not?"

"Because my brother would never forgive me, that's why." Settling his hat carefully on his head, Hawk stalked out of the house, only to come to a dead stop when he reached the end of the porch.

He glanced over his shoulder to see Joey watching him. "Where the hell is my horse?" He knew the answer even before she spoke.

"Charlie took it. But he's not the one who burned the barn. He told me so. He told me he lost his watch in a card game."

"Innocent men don't run," Hawk retorted. Muttering an oath, he stomped down the stairs.

Turning right, he headed for the livery, his anger fueling his footsteps.

Several men called greetings as he passed by, but he wasn't in the mood to make small talk. His head throbbed with every step he took. He was madder than a rained-on rooster by the time he reached the livery barn.

Crocker was out front, currying one of his horses.

"Silas, I need a good horse right quick."

Crocker glanced over his shoulder. "Something happen to yours?"

"Yes, something happened to mine, and when I've got time, I'll tell you about it. I need that horse, and I need it now."

"What the hell happened to you?" Crocker asked, getting a good look at Hawk's face.

"Dammit, Silas, you got a horse for me or not?"

"Sure, sure." Crocker tossed the dandy brush aside and went into the barn.

Hawk lifted a hand to his eye, winced, then shook his head. Damn those McBrides, they were nothing but trouble, the whole lot of them!

Crocker emerged ten minutes later leading a big line-back dun. "This is the best horse I've got."

"Thanks." Gritting his teeth, Hawk swung into the saddle.

"How long will you be gone?" Crocker asked.

"As long as it takes to catch me a horse thief."

Chapter Twenty-two

Blackie sat out on the front porch, staring into the darkness. Inside the house, his mother was asleep in the rocking chair beside Blue Hawk's bed. His father would be back sometime tomorrow with the doctor.

Blackie smiled faintly. The doctor from Steel's Crossing would come whether he wanted to or not, Blackie had no doubt of that. His father had a way of convincing people to see things his way.

Blackie's smile faded as his thoughts turned to Joey. He hadn't seen her since early that morning. It seemed like years had passed since then. Damn Charlie McBride! Blackie clenched his fists. His family had always been openminded and understanding, but he didn't know how they would feel about his marrying Joey, not now. And if Blue Hawk died . . . how would his parents feel about Joey and her kinfolks then? He knew his parents wouldn't blame her for Blue Hawk's death. And yet she had raised Charlie. Would they look at her and think of Charlie? Would they look at her and remember the pain her brother had caused?

What was she doing now? What was she thinking now? Had Hawk arrested Charlie? He hated to think of Joey's brother in jail, not because he didn't deserve to be there, but because of what it would do to Joey. She'd had enough misery and unhappiness in her life. She didn't need any more.

He swore under his breath as a new thought occurred to him. He had been so preoccupied with wondering what his family would think, he hadn't stopped to wonder if this would change how Joey felt about marrying him. Would she still want to be part of his family after all this was over? Feuds that had lasted hundreds of years had started over less.

Leaning back, he closed his eyes, wondering again what Joey was doing, what she was thinking.

Joey sat at the rickety table in the kitchen, her hands clenched around a cup filled with coffee that had long since grown cold as she contemplated the events of the day. Even now, she couldn't believe she had hit the sheriff over the head with a frying pan. She was still amazed that he hadn't hauled her off to jail.

She blinked back her tears. Even if Charlie was innocent of setting the fire, he was now guilty of stealing a horse. And from the sheriff, of all people!

She took a sip of coffee, grimacing at the bitter taste of the cold brew. She didn't want to believe

Charlie was guilty, but he hadn't come home Saturday night, and he had refused to tell her where he'd been. Had Charlie started the fire? She hated to think her brother was capable of such a cowardly, despicable thing, that he would stoop to doing something so vile just to get back at Blackie. If Charlie had any sense, he would be grateful to Blackie and his family. If it wasn't for Blackie, Charlie might still be in jail from his last run-in with the law. But somehow Charlie had twisted it all around in his mind, so that everything that had happened to him and his pals had been Blackie's fault.

Leaning back in her chair, she wondered where Charlie had gone, and when, if ever, he would come back. Maybe it would have been better if Blackie had pressed charges against Charlie. Maybe only something as awful as spending time in prison would make Charlie come to his senses. And yet, just before Hawk came to the house, Charlie had been talking about getting a job. Why had this had to happen now?

Joey blew out a sigh, wondering what to tell her grandmother. Grams had been exhausted when she got home that evening. Joey had fixed her grandmother something to eat, and then Grams had gone to bed.

Joey had spent the evening hoping to see Blackie, but that hope had faded as the hours passed by. She had told herself he couldn't get away because he was busy at home, probably helping his father clean up after the fire, but she didn't really believe it. If Blackie had wanted to see her badly enough, he would have found the time. Perhaps, after what Charlie had done, Blackie no longer wanted to marry her, no longer felt she would be welcomed by his family. And the worst of it was, she couldn't blame him, or them.

Feeling as though her heart would break, she put her cup in the sink and went to bed to cry herself to sleep.

Blackie rose early Monday morning. After checking on his mother and Blue Hawk, he went outside to feed the stock. He filled a bucket with fresh water for the dogs, tossed some grain to the chickens, looked in on the cat and her kittens, thinking that he'd take the little calico one up to show Blue Hawk later that day.

After feeding the rest of the stock, he carried a flake of hay around back for the Appy filly. He applied a little more ointment to her burns, pleased to see that she was healing just fine. Most likely, she'd have nothing to show for her brush with the fire but a scar or two on her right flank. It wouldn't keep her from being a good riding horse, but it was going to ruin Blue Hawk's hopes of showing her at the fair in Steel's Crossing next year. Still, his brother and the filly were both lucky to be alive.

He clenched his hands in helpless anger. What sort of man set fire to a barn filled with animals? His anger turned to quiet rage as he thought how close his little brother had come to dying. If he ever got his hands on Charlie McBride, he'd wring his neck!

Blackie was currying one of the horses later that morning when Shadow drove up in a rented carriage. An elderly man sat beside him. Their missing horse was tied to the back of the carriage.

Blackie followed his father and the doctor into the house. His parents hugged one another, and then Shadow introduced the doctor.

Dr. Malcolm Greenberg was about fifty years old. He had brown eyes, a brown beard liberally sprinkled with gray, and a generous paunch. Dressed in a brown suit and brown bowler hat, a pair of spectacles low on his nose, he did not look happy to be there.

Hannah shook the doctor's hand; then she hurried the doctor down the hall into Blue Hawk's room and shut the door.

"I take it he didn't want to come here," Blackie remarked, following his father into the kitchen.

Shadow poured a cup of coffee for himself and another for Blackie, then sat down at the table. "No, he did not."

"But here he is." Blackie sat down. Sipping his coffee, he regarded his father over the rim of his cup. "So, did you bring him at gunpoint, or just threaten to scalp him?"

Shadow grinned faintly. "Under that hat he has no hair to take. Was there any trouble here after I left?"

"No. Everything's been quiet. Where did you find our horse?"

"Jed Junior found her tied up in front of one of the saloons."

"I don't suppose anyone saw who left her there?"

"No."

Blackie glanced down the hallway, wondering how his little brother was doing. He hated waiting, hated not knowing.

The doctor emerged from Blue Hawk's room a

short time later. He looked somewhat taken aback to find Shadow standing in the parlor, waiting for him.

"How is my son?" Shadow asked.

Greenberg held his black bag close to his chest, as though he needed some sort of barrier between himself and Shadow. "Resting comfortably. I've given . . ." He paused, obviously flustered. "I've given your . . . ah, woman instructions on how to care for him."

"The woman is my wife."

"Yes, of course." Greenberg cleared his throat. "I've fulfilled my end of the bargain. I trust you will now fulfill yours."

"I will take you to the train station as soon as I see my son," Shadow said.

"Very well," the doctor said. "I'll wait for you outside."

Blackie followed the doctor out onto the front porch. "How's my brother? Is he gonna be all right?"

"Yes, I believe so. Whoever treated his burns did the right thing. He had a minor infection, but I believe we have it under control now. Your . . . ah . . . mother was afraid he was coming down with pneumonia, but his lungs are clear. Probably just inhaled a bit of smoke in the fire. With medication and proper rest, he should recover nicely. He'll have a few scars on the backs of his legs, but I don't believe he'll have any other lasting effects from his ordeal." The doctor cleared his throat. "That man in there, he's your father?"

Blackie nodded.

"He's quite . . . fierce, isn't he?"

"He can be," Blackie agreed, recalling some of

the stories his mother had told him of the days when his father had ridden the war trail.

The doctor glanced back at the house and lowered his voice. "He wouldn't really have covered me with honey and buried me in an anthill if I had refused to come with him, would he?"

"You must have thought so," Blackie said with a shrug. "You're here."

Greenberg went down the stairs, tossed his bag in the back of the buggy parked in front of the porch, then hauled himself up onto the seat.

Shadow emerged from the house a few minutes later. A smile twitched at the corners of his lips when he saw the doctor sitting in the buggy, his arms tightly folded across his chest.

"Guess he cannot wait to get back to his office," Shadow remarked.

Blackie choked back a laugh. "You should be ashamed of yourself, threatening to bury him in an anthill."

"He told you that?"

"Uh-huh."

"It might have been fun," Shadow mused with a twinkle in his eye. "Though it would have had to be a very large hole."

Descending the steps, he unhitched the horse, then climbed up onto the seat of the buggy. He looked up at Blackie and grinned as Greenberg flinched and scooted over.

Taking up the reins, Shadow released the brake and clucked to the horse.

It was a quiet ride back to town.

Shadow delivered Greenberg to the railroad station. The man climbed out of the buggy with alacrity, grabbed his bag out of the back of the buggy, and hurried into the depot without a backward glance.

With a grin and a shake of his head, Shadow slapped the reins on the horse's rump. He stopped at Crocker's Livery and left the horse and buggy with Bobby Evans, the kid who worked part-time for the livery owner. Crocker, it seemed, was home today with a sudden case of the gout. Evans saddled Red Wind and led him out of the barn. The stallion whinnied a soft welcome as Shadow took the reins and swung into the saddle. He was about to turn for home when he decided to stop by the sheriff's office and bring Hawk up to date on Blue Hawk's condition.

He was turning down Front Street when he saw Hawk riding up to the jail.

They reached the sheriff's office at the same time.

"*Neyho*. Just the man I wanted to see."

Shadow lifted one brow as he got a good look at his son's face.

Hawk lifted a hand to his eye, which was black and swollen. "I went out to the McBride place looking for Charlie yesterday," he explained. "I found him." He shook his head ruefully. "When I tried to take him in so I could question him, he started swinging. While I was trying to subdue him, Joey came up behind me and hit me over the head with a frying pan. She sure packs a wallop for a girl. Knocked me out cold. When I came to, Charlie was gone." He swore softly. "If it wasn't for Blackie, I'd have thrown Joey McBride in jail. To make things worse, that damn kid stole my horse! Anyway, I followed Charlie up into the hills, but I lost his trail in the rocks. I thought maybe you'd be able to pick up where I left off."

Shadow nodded. "I will go with you."

"Thanks." Hawk chuckled softly. "I think I should swear you in as a deputy."

"There is no need. I will go tell your mother I am leaving and pick up my trail gear."

"All right. I need to check in with Finch. And with Victoria. I'll meet you out at the ranch."

With a nod, Shadow wheeled his horse around and rode hard for home.

Blackie was currying Blue Hawk's Appy filly when his father rode into the yard.

Dismounting, Shadow handed Blackie the reins. "I am going with Hawk to look for Charlie. Cool Red Wind out for me, will you? And put some grain in my saddlebags."

"I'll go with you," Blackie said.

"No. Someone must stay here to look after your mother and Blue Hawk."

Blackie swore. Dammit, why did he always have to stay home?

"I am sorry, *naha*, but it is the way it must be."

Blackie couldn't keep the resentment out of his voice when he said, "Sure, I understand."

A short time later, Hawk rode up.

"What the hell happened to you?" Blackie asked.

"That little hellcat of yours happened to me, that's what," Hawk said.

Blackie's eyes widened in disbelief. "Joey did that?"

"Not exactly," Hawk replied, and as succinctly as

possible, he told Blackie what had happened at the McBride house.

Blackie stifled a grin as he imagined Joey whacking Hawk over the head with a frying pan.

Hawk glowered at him. "It's not funny."

Blackie laughed out loud. "Yeah, it is."

Just then, Shadow came down the steps. He had a rifle in one hand, a heavy jacket and a bedroll in the other. "Ready?"

Hawk nodded.

"Stay close to the house," Shadow told Blackie. He slipped his rifle into the saddle boot, tied his jacket behind the cantle.

Blackie nodded. "Don't worry."

He stared after his father and brother as they rode away, his heart heavy with resentment.

The rest of the day passed quickly. Blackie had hoped to find time to ride into town and see Joey, but he never got the chance. Mary and Cloud Walker came over to look in on Blue Hawk. Shortly after they left, Victoria showed up. She was feeling lonely and worried about Hawk. While his mother and sister consoled each other, Blackie entertained the kids. It was after dark when Victoria and her brood left for home.

Blackie stood on the porch after they left, his thoughts turning toward Joey. Tomorrow, he thought, one way or another, he would see her tomorrow.

Blue Hawk seemed better the following morning. After feeding the stock, Blackie took the calico kitten up to the house. The kitten made Blue Hawk smile, and after roaming around the bed, sniffing the pillow and the blankets, the kitten curled up on Blue Hawk's chest and went to sleep.

"Will you tell me a story?" Blue Hawk asked.

"Sure." Blackie sat down in the rocking chair beside the bed. "Which one?"

"The one about Eagle Feather Chief."

"All right," Blackie said, "if I can remember it."

"A long, long time ago," Blue Hawk said. "That's how it starts."

Blackie grinned. "Right. A long, long time ago the Cheyenne warriors didn't know how to use eagle feathers for their war ornaments. One day one of their men climbed a high mountain. He lay there for five days, crying, without food. He hoped some powerful being would see him and come to him, to teach him something great for his people.

"He was glad when he heard a voice say, 'Try to be brave, no matter what comes, even if it might kill you. If you remember these words, you will bring great news to your people, and help them.'

"After a time, seven eagles came down, as if to fly away with him. But he was brave, as he had been told, though he continued to cry and keep his eyes closed. Now the great eagles surrounded him. One of them said, 'Look at me. I am powerful, and I have wonderfully strong feathers. I am greater than all other animals and birds in the world.' This powerful eagle showed the man his wings and his tail, and he spread all his feathers as wide as possible. He showed the man how to make war headdresses and ornaments out of eagle feathers.

" 'Your people must use only eagle feathers. If they do, it will be a great help to them in war and bring them victories,' the eagle said.

"Since there were no loose feathers about, the seven eagles shook themselves, and plenty of feathers fell to the ground. The warrior picked them up and gratefully took them home to his tribe. On that day, eagle feathers were seen for the first time by the Cheyenne, and they knew where they came from.

"The man showed his people how to make war ornaments from the eagle feathers, as he had been told. From that day onward, the man became a great warrior in his tribe, and their leader in war parties. He became so successful, his people named him Chief Eagle Feather, and he wore his eagle feathers war bonnet as he led the Cheyenne with dignity and pride."

"That's a good story," Blue Hawk said. "Someday I will be a brave warrior."

"You're already brave," Blackie said. "Get some rest now. I'm going out to give your filly a little exercise."

"All right," Blue Hawk said, yawning. "Give her a carrot for me."

"I will."

Blackie had just finished exercising the filly when his mother came looking for him. "I need you to go to Feehan's for me," she said. "I want to make dumplings for dinner tonight and I'm out of flour."

He was more than willing to go. Five minutes later, he was riding toward town.

Joey looked up as the door opened. She didn't really expect Blackie to show up at the store, yet every time the door opened, her stomach fluttered with anticipation, and then sank with disappointment.

239

She was stocking a shelf of canned goods when the bell above the door rang again. She didn't bother to look up this time. And then she heard his voice bidding Big Mike a good morning. And still she didn't turn around.

And then she heard his voice behind her.

"Joey?"

She swallowed, took a deep breath, and turned to face him. "Hello, Blackie."

He lifted one brow. "I thought you might be a little happy to see me."

"I am. It's just that I wasn't sure you'd want to see me."

"Why would you think that?"

"You don't know, then?"

He frowned. "Know what? What are you talking about?"

"Never mind."

Conscious of being watched by Big Mike and several customers, Blackie took her by the hand. "Come on," he said, heading for the front door. "We need to talk."

"I can't leave!" she exclaimed, trying to pull her hand from his. "I'm working."

Blackie looked over at Mike Feehan, who was watching the two of them while he rang up an order for Mrs. Crowley.

"I'll have her back as soon as I can, Mr. Feehan," Blackie said, and practically dragged her out the door.

Joey hit him across the back with her free hand. "What do you think you're doing?"

"Taking you somewhere where we can talk." He lifted her onto his horse's back, took up the reins, then swung up behind her. He touched his heels to the horse's flanks, and Raven moved out at a brisk walk.

A few minutes later, he reined the horse to a halt in front of his office. Lifting her from the saddle, he carried her up the steps, unlocked the door, and carried her inside.

"All right," he said, putting her on her feet, "what's bothering you? Why did you think I wouldn't want to see you?"

"I thought Hawk would have told you . . ."

"Oh, that." In spite of himself, Blackie laughed. "Yeah, he told me all about it. Wish I'd been there to see it."

"You're not mad at me, then?"

"Of course not. I can't blame you for defending your brother." He caressed her cheek with his fingertips. "I'd probably have done the same thing."

"Blackie, what are we going to do?"

"I don't know, honey. My father and Hawk are out looking for Charlie right now."

"He didn't do it! I know he didn't. He wouldn't."

"We found his watch near the barn."

"Someone else could have put it there," she said urgently. "Charlie told me that he lost his watch in a card game. Don't you see?"

"Then he shouldn't have run."

"That's what Hawk said. But Charlie was scared of going back to jail. Trijo could have framed him."

"Trijo? What's he got to do with this?"

"He's the man who won Charlie's watch."

Blackie frowned thoughtfully. "Trijo couldn't have set the fire. He's in jail with the other two. And

241

even if he wasn't, why would he try to frame Charlie? I thought they were pals."

"I don't know. I just know Charlie didn't do it."

"Did you tell Hawk about all this?"

"Yes, but he didn't believe me."

"Well, we can't do anything about it until Hawk gets back." Needing to hold her, Blackie slipped his arm around Joey's waist.

"Your parents must hate me now," she murmured.

"I don't reckon your grandmother will be too happy with our family either when Hawk puts Charlie behind bars."

"Do you still love me, Blackie?"

"Of course I do, darlin'."

"But . . ."

"Let's not worry about all that now."

"It seems like everything is against us."

"Quit that. I want you to come out to the house for dinner tonight."

"What will your mother say?"

"I don't know. Will you come?"

"Yes." She looked up at him. "Are you ever going to kiss me?"

"Yes, ma'am," he said. "Right now." And lowering his head, he claimed her lips with his.

Their bodies yearned toward each other as he deepened the kiss. Blackie groaned low in his throat, his desire for her sparking to life, burning away every other thought. He wanted her, he thought, wanted her more than anything he'd ever known, but he couldn't take her here, on a bare wooden floor, couldn't defile her. He loved her too much, respected her too much.

242

With an effort, he put her away from him. "I'd better get you back to work," he said. "And I've got to get home."

She looked at him through eyes hazy with passion. "Now?"

"Right now." He glanced around the room. "I've got a lot of work to do myself," he said, "but it'll have to wait until my father gets home. Come on," he said, taking her by the hand. "I don't want you to get in trouble with Feehan."

Back at the mercantile, Blackie picked up a sack of flour for his mother, gave Joey a quick kiss good-bye, and left the store. He made one more stop before returning home. It didn't take him long to make up his mind. Whistling softy, he bought the ring he wanted, dropped the small square box into his pocket, and headed out the door.

It was midafternoon when he got home. Tying Raven to the hitch rack, he went into the house and dropped the sack of flour on the kitchen table, then went down the hall to Blue Hawk's room. Looking inside, he saw that his mother and Blue Hawk were napping.

Grabbing a couple of apples, Blackie went back outside. He ate one of the apples, fed the core and the second apple to Raven, and then gave the horse a good rubdown. Currying the horse was relaxing, soothing even. When he was finished, he turned Raven loose in one of the corrals.

He stood there a moment, thinking of Joey, and then he took off his hat and shirt, tied his kerchief over his nose, and began cleaning up the debris from the fire. It sickened him to see the remains of

243

the horse, to think how the animal had suffered before it died. Damn Charlie McBride!

He held on to his anger as he dug a hole a good distance away from the house to bury what was left of the horse. What kind of sick mind set fire to a building filled with livestock?

He worked until dusk, and when he finished, he had a sizable part of the area where the barn had stood cleared of debris.

Using his shirt, he wiped the sweat from his face and chest, then, whistling softly, he went into the house to get cleaned up. Joey would be here tonight.

Chapter Twenty-three

"You did what?" I stared at Blackie, unable to believe my ears.

"I invited Joey to dinner."

I shook my head. I didn't want Joey McBride in my house, not now. I knew better than to blame Joey for something that wasn't her fault. It was a lesson I had learned years ago, when the army blamed Shadow's people for killings that had been done by other tribes. I had seen innocent Cheyenne accused of crimes they hadn't committed. I knew it wasn't Joey's fault that her brother had set our barn on fire and I wouldn't hold her responsible, but just having her here would be a constant reminder of how close I had come to losing my baby.

Blue Hawk was getting a little better with each passing day, but he was still in pain. He spent most of his time sleeping, due in part to the pain and in part to the medication the doctor had left for him.

"Nahkoa?"

I looked up, aware that Blackie had spoken.

"Will you make her welcome?" he asked.

Could I refuse to welcome Joey into my home? How serious was the relationship between Joey and Blackie? Could I hurt and embarrass one son because of what had been done to another? What would Shadow say? What would he do?

"Nahkoa?"

"Of course she'll be welcome," I replied, though I wasn't sure either my expression or my tone gave credence to my words.

Blackie nodded. "I'm going out to feed the stock," he said, then turned and left the room.

I stared out the kitchen window, my thoughts in turmoil. The doctor had assured me that Blue Hawk would recover completely, in time. Shadow and Hawk were out hunting Charlie McBride. I found it hard to believe that the McBride boy had burned our barn. I didn't know Charlie very well—hardly at all, in fact—and yet he didn't seem the sort to do such a sneaky, contemptible thing. Most troubling of all, it appeared that Blackie was falling in love with Joey, which, at this particular time, could only complicate things further.

Nevertheless, Joey was coming to dinner.

I was glad now that I had spent the latter part of the afternoon doing the housework I had been neglecting. The floors had been mopped, the furniture dusted. Now, keeping my mind carefully blank, I fixed chicken and dumplings, baked pie, spread one of my good tablecloths over the dining room table, then set it with my best dishes and our good silver.

When everything was ready in the kitchen, I went into my room to change my clothes.

I was in the kitchen when Joey arrived thirty minutes later. Stepping into the parlor, I saw that she wore the dress I had given her to wear on the Fourth. Her hair was clean and shiny, her expression a little withdrawn. I knew it couldn't be any easier for her to be in my house than it was for me to have her there.

I saw the way Blackie's face lit up when he welcomed her, the love in Joey's eyes when he kissed her cheek.

I put a smile on my face. "How are you, Joey?"

"Fine, thank you, Mrs. Kincaid."

"Dinner's just about ready. Why don't you and Blackie sit down?"

"Is there anything I can do to help?" she asked.

"No," I said quickly. Too quickly. I saw Blackie's disappointment and Joey's hurt and felt ashamed of myself. "Maybe you could fill the water glasses," I suggested.

Gratitude flickered in my son's eyes as Joey went into the kitchen.

We sat down to dinner a short time later. The conversation was strained, to say the least. We spoke of the weather, which was cool for this time of year. I asked after Joey's grandmother and learned that Maureen was feeling a little better these days. We avoided the subject of Charlie altogether. As soon as I could, I excused myself, saying I had to fix a plate for Blue Hawk.

* * *

Joey let out a sigh when Mrs. Kincaid left the room. "I shouldn't have come here."

"But I'm glad you did. Come on, let's go outside."

"Let's clear the table first."

"You don't have to do that."

"I know, but I want to."

Once they had the table cleared, Joey insisted on washing the dishes.

"I guess that means I have to dry them," Blackie muttered.

"That would be nice," Joey said. She scraped the plates, then filled the sink with water. "Do you know how?"

"Very funny." Blackie pulled a clean dish towel from the drawer, then leaned one hip against the counter while she put the dirty dishes in the sink.

Joey hummed softly as she began to wash the dishes. It was all too easy to imagine that she was Blackie's wife, that this was their house.

"Your office looks really nice the way you've fixed it up. Your family must be proud of you."

"I reckon. I'm the only one who's gone to college, but—" Blackie shrugged. "I'm really the only one who had the chance."

"You'll be a wonderful vet."

Her praise warmed him as nothing else could. "It's the only thing I've ever wanted to do." He wiped the last dish and put it in the cupboard. Spreading the towel over the back of a chair, he took Joey's hand in his. "Come on."

"Where are we going?"

"You'll see."

He led her out the back door, down a narrow path to where a Cheyenne lodge stood under a tall tree. Untying the flap, he held it back. "Go on inside," he said.

"You're coming, aren't you?"

"Of course." He followed her inside. Pulling a kitchen match from his pocket, he lit the kindling in the firepit located in the middle of the lodge. When it was burning steadily, he added a few small pieces of wood.

Joey glanced around, her eyes wide with curiosity. There was a buffalo robe spread on the floor, hairy side up. Kneeling, she ran her hand over it, surprised that the fur was so soft, the hide so big.

Blackie leaned back against what looked like an armrest made of willow branches. "So, what do you think?"

"It's bigger inside than I would have thought."

"Mary and Hawk and I used to come out here sometimes in the summer, when it was too hot to sleep in the house. We'd roll up the sides to catch whatever breeze came up, and then we'd tell ghost stories. I remember one night Hawk was telling some scary story when *neyho* burst into the lodge. His body was covered with white paint and he had big black circles drawn around his eyes. Scared the hell out of us."

"Who's ney-ho?"

"It means father in Cheyenne."

"Oh." Joey laughed. "I can't imagine your father playing pranks like that."

"Because he's Cheyenne?"

She nodded. "Somehow I never thought of Indians as having a sense of humor, or playing with their children."

"Just going to war and scalping people?" he asked dryly.

"I'm sorry. I didn't mean to hurt your feelings."

He leaned forward and kissed her cheek. "You didn't. But you have to understand that my father's people are no different from yours or anyone else. Most parents love their children and want the best for them. They laugh when they're happy and cry when they're sad. They get hungry and grouchy. Some are kind and some aren't. The only thing most people know about Indians is what they've been told, and most of that isn't true. My father's people fought the army, sure, but it was to protect their land and their families. All the Indians wanted was to live the way they'd always lived. I'm sorry," he said with a wry smile. "I didn't mean to lecture you."

"I don't mind. I need to learn more about your father's people. After all," she said, her cheeks turning pink, "our children will be part Indian."

"So, you haven't changed your mind about marrying me, then?"

"Of course not. You haven't changed your mind, have you?

"Well . . ."

"You have, haven't you?"

"That depends."

"On what?"

"On whether you plan to hit me over the head with a frying pan."

That quickly, despair turned to joy. "Oh, you! You scared me to death."

"Among my father's people, Cheyenne men are expected to court a girl for at least a year, and often longer. When a man is sure the girl he desires will say yes, he sends one of his relatives or an old friend to ask for her hand in marriage. He also sends horses with the messenger. The messenger ties the horses in front of the girl's lodge and then he goes inside and says, 'Blackie wishes your daughter, Joey, for his wife.' "

Joey looked at him, a half-smile playing over her lips. "Are you serious?"

Blackie nodded. "As soon as he says what he came to say, the messenger leaves."

"Doesn't he wait for an answer?"

"No. Sometimes the father decides whether or not he will consent to the marriage. Sometimes he talks it over with his relatives. If the answer they decide on is no, the horses are turned loose and driven back to the young man's lodge. If the answer is yes, the girl's father sends the girl to the lodge of the young man. If the young man offered five horses for the girl, the girl's father sends her to him with six horses or more."

Blackie took a deep breath. "If you were a Cheyenne girl, I would offer many horses for your hand, but all I have is this." Blackie pulled a small square box out of his pocket, lifting the lid to reveal a diamond ring. "Will you marry me, Joey?"

"Oh, Blackie, it's beautiful." She held out her hand. "Will you put it on me?"

He slipped the ring on her finger. "Does this mean you'll marry me?"

"Yes. Oh, yes!" she exclaimed, and threw herself into his arms with such force, he fell backward and she landed on top of him, laughing and kissing him at the same time.

And then he was kissing her in return, his mouth

251

hot and urgent. Her laughter turned to soft sighs of pleasure as his hands moved over her back and slid down her sides, the tips of his fingers ever so lightly brushing against the curve of her breasts.

In a single agile movement, he rolled over so that she was lying beneath him.

"Joey." He gazed into her eyes, then lowered his head and kissed her again.

She wrapped her arms around him, startled by her body's swift response to the weight of his body on hers. She could feel his desire pressing against her and that too aroused her. He loved her. He wanted her. And she wanted him. Oh, how she wanted him! All of him. She arched up toward him, fretting at the layers of clothing that separated her flesh from his.

"Joey." She heard his need in the way he groaned her name. "I want to hold you and kiss you and never let go. I want . . ." He kissed her again, one hand cupping her breast.

"What do you want?" she asked breathlessly.

"It doesn't matter." Reluctantly, he drew away from her. "Come on. I'd better get you home before one of us gets in trouble."

Chapter Twenty-four

Charlie sat cross-legged in front of a stingy campfire, his hands fisted around a tin cup of coffee. What the hell was he doing out here anyway? It had been stupid of him to run away, stupid to steal the sheriff's horse. Joey had been right, as usual. Running just made him look guilty, but he had panicked at the thought of being locked up again. Those few days he had spent in jail with Caffrey and the others had scared him a hell of a lot worse than he would have ever imagined or admitted.

Tomorrow he was going back to town. He would return the sheriff's horse and pray that somehow he could prove his innocence. He hadn't burned the Kincaid's barn. How could they prove he had? Just because they had found his watch there didn't mean he had set the fire.

He nodded. He had been running most of his life. Running from his old man's death, running from authority, from responsibility. It was time he grew up. Time to stop acting like a kid and start acting like a man. He would get this whole sorry mess straightened out somehow, and then he'd find a job and make something out of himself. One thing was certain—he didn't want to end up behind bars like Caffrey and the others.

Feeling better about his future and about himself, he lifted the cup to his lips, then froze as he heard footsteps coming up behind him.

"Keep those hands where I can see 'em," warned a familiar voice.

"Hackett!" Charlie exclaimed. "What the devil are you doing out here? How'd you find me?"

"Just luck," Hackett replied. "We were looking for a place to spend the night and saw your fire. Got any more of that coffee?"

Charlie jerked his chin toward the pot sitting on the edge of the coals. "Sure, help yourself."

Hackett hunkered down beside him as Caffrey and Trijo emerged from the shadows.

Charlie felt a twinge of unease as the three men surrounded him. "How'd you fellas get out of jail?"

"It wasn't too hard," Hackett said. "Caffrey and Trijo were in a cell together. Caffrey pretended to be sick and when the deputy came in to check, Trijo knocked him over the head with a chair."

"Oh," Charlie said. "Well, it's . . . ah, good to see you fellas."

"Uh-huh." Caffrey slid his gun from the holster and aimed it at Charlie. "We ain't too happy with the way things turned out."

"Hey, it wasn't my doing!" Charlie said, his gaze darting from Caffrey's face to Hackett's and back again.

"No?" Caffrey looked at Hackett and Trijo. "I didn't see our friend Charlie, here, in jail with us there in Steel's Crossing, did you?"

Hackett shook his head.

"I looked," Trijo said, his eyes glittering. "He wasn't there."

"I think it was because of his sweet little sister," Caffrey said with a leer. "I saw the way that half-breed kid looked at her." He nodded, as if to confirm his own words. "I think that lawman let old Charlie off so's his brother could get Charlie's little sister in the sack."

Charlie surged to his feet. "Why, you dirty-minded bas . . ."

The words died in Charlie's throat as Caffrey thumbed back the hammer of his Colt.

"We ain't too happy about being arrested," Caffrey said. "So we've decided a little payback is in order."

"So it was you," Charlie said. "You burned the Kincaids' barn. That's how my watch got there."

Caffrey nodded. "We knew you'd want to be in on it."

"It was just a little warning," Hackett said. "First the barn, and then we'll take care of that half-breed bastard who caused all the trouble, and then the sheriff."

"And then the bank," Trijo said, rubbing his hands together.

Feeling sick to his stomach, Charlie shook his

head. Joey had warned him that he was heading for trouble. Looked like she was right again.

"Well, let's ride," Caffrey said. "Trijo wanted to kidnap your sister to draw that 'breed and the sheriff out of town, but I told him we wouldn't have to do nothing like that, not with you on our side."

"You leave my sister out of this."

"I told you he wouldn't go for it," Trijo said. "I told you he ain't one of us."

"Sure I am," Charlie said, a note of desperation in his voice. He looked at Caffrey. "You know I am."

The light of the campfire cast orange shadows on Caffrey's face, giving him a devilish look.

"Bob—" Charlie swallowed the bile rising in his throat. "Didn't I help you whip that half-breed? Bob, listen to me—"

"I'm afraid you're right, Gil," Caffrey said with mock regret. "I'm afraid we can't trust Mr. McBride."

Charlie's gaze darted frantically from one man to the next, searching for some sign of hope, of reprieve. Three pairs of unblinking eyes stared back at him.

He knew, in that moment that seemed to stretch into eternity, that he was a dead man.

In desperation, he made a grab for his rifle. His last conscious thought was that he had let Joey down again.

Chapter Twenty-five

Blackie woke late the next morning. Rising, he pulled on a pair of pants and a shirt, slipped on a pair of moccasins, combed his hair. He found his mother in Blue Hawk's room. He gave his brother a smile, kissed his mother on the cheek, then went into the kitchen and poured himself a cup of coffee. He sipped it slowly, put his cup in the sink, and then went outside to do the morning chores. His father had been talking about hiring help for years, but nothing had ever come of it. Blackie fed the stock, filled the water troughs, looked after the Appy filly's wounds. He cut some firewood, watered his mother's garden. She had already fed the chickens, gathered the eggs, and milked the cows.

Since he wasn't anxious to face her and explain why he had gotten in so late the night before, he continued clearing the pile of rubble left by the fire.

It was midafternoon when Victoria stopped by.

Blackie wiped the sweat from his brow with his kerchief, then went to help her dismount. "Hey, Victoria, what brings you out here?"

"I made some sugar cookies this morning and thought maybe Blue Hawk would like some."

"And?"

"Those men who attacked you? They escaped from jail over in Steel's Crossing. They killed one man and hurt another one pretty bad." She looked at him anxiously. "You don't think they'll come back here, do you?"

"Not if they're smart." Blackie frowned. "How'd you find out about this?"

"Finch told me."

"When did they get away?"

"He wasn't sure. Sometime Thursday night, I think he said."

"Thursday? And he just now found out?"

"The wires have been down. Finch just found out about it this morning. I wish Hawk was here."

"I'm sure he'll be back soon."

"I hope so." She reached into one of the saddlebags and withdrew a round cookie tin. "How's Blue Hawk getting along?"

"He's doing okay."

"I'm glad." She smoothed a hand over her hair. "Be careful, Blackie."

"I will. Listen, are you gonna be here for a while?"

"I don't know, why?"

"I need to go into town and I don't want to leave *nahkoa* alone."

"All right. My kids are over at Mary's. I'll stay until

you get back, but don't be long, you hear?"

"Thanks, Victoria."

Grabbing his shirt, he went to get cleaned up. Thinking about what Victoria had just told him and about what Joey had said yesterday, he wondered if his father and Hawk were following the wrong trail.

Feehan's was doing a brisk business when Blackie entered the store. He found Joey in the back room, unloading a shipment of pots and pans.

He moved up behind her, slid his arms around her waist, and kissed the side of her neck. "How's the future Mrs. Kincaid?"

A soft sigh whispered past her lips as she leaned back against him. "I was just thinking about you."

"Oh? What were thinking?"

"I was wishing you were here." She turned in his arms and smiled up at him. "And here you are."

"I think you might be right about Charlie," Blackie said. "I think he's innocent."

Hope flared in her eyes. "You do? Have you heard something?"

"I saw Victoria. Joe Finch told her those men that Charlie was mixed up with escaped from jail Thursday. That would have given them plenty of time to hop on a train, get back here, set the fire, and leave your brother's watch where we'd be sure to find it."

"I knew he didn't do it!" Throwing her arms around his neck, she kissed him enthusiastically. "Maybe things will work out after all."

"I hope so, darlin'. I just wanted to let you know, and ask you to come to dinner tonight."

"Two nights in a row? Do you think that's a good idea?"

"Darn right. You'll come, won't you?"

"Of course."

He kissed her again, and then, whistling softly, he left the storeroom.

Joey stared at her reflection in the mirror as she ran a brush through her hair. She didn't look any different, she thought, and yet in the last few days, her whole life had turned upside down.

"Mrs. Blackie Kincaid." She whispered the words to her image, feeling a wave of happy excitement wash over her. She was going to marry Blackie. It was incredible but true. She smiled at her reflection. Just thinking about being his wife put color in her cheeks and a glow in her eyes.

Removing her engagement ring from her skirt pocket, she slipped it on, eager for the time when she could wear it for everyone to see. She lifted her hand, turned it this way and that, admiring the way the diamond reflected the light. Butterflies danced in her stomach as she thought of seeing Blackie again, of the kisses they had shared the night before. And soon she would be with him again. With a sigh, she took the ring off and put it back in her pocket. Her grandmother and Charlie would never approve, she thought glumly, but they would have to get used to the idea sooner or later, and if they didn't . . . Joey blew out a sigh. No sense in worrying about that now.

She took one last look in the mirror, then went into the parlor to tell her grandmother she was leaving.

Maureen looked up from the book in her lap, her eyes narrowing. "Where are you going, Josephine?"

"Just out. To see a friend."

"Is this the same friend you went to see last night?"

"Yes." Joey ran her hand over the back of the faded sofa, thinking how worn and cheap it looked compared to the furniture in Blackie's house.

"You're not running off to see that Kincaid boy, are you?"

Joey hesitated, debating whether to tell a lie or the truth. The truth won. She wasn't ashamed of Blackie, and she wouldn't degrade their love by lying. "Yes, I am."

"I don't like it, Josephine. I don't like it one bit, you getting all gussied up to go see that boy. No good will come of it, mark my words."

"I might be home late," Joey said.

Maureen shook her head. "First that brother of yours goes missing," she muttered, "and now you're carousing with that half-breed. You'll both come to a bad end, you mark my words."

Joey took a firm hold on her temper. "Can I get you anything before I go?"

Her grandmother made a shooing motion with her hand. "Go on, get. But don't come crying to me when that boy gets you in trouble."

With a shake of her head, Joey left the house, yearning for the day when she and Blackie would have a place of their own. As she saddled her horse, she couldn't help wondering and worrying about her brother. Where was Charlie staying? They had no kin for him to stay with. Had he gone to Steel's

Crossing to hide out? Or maybe lit out for Dead-wood?

It was dark when she turned onto the trail that led to Blackie's. It wasn't really a trail at all, but a deer path she had discovered by accident, a route that saved her a good twenty minutes. She wasn't particularly afraid of the dark, but she felt a shiver as she rode between the tall trees that lined the path. Once, she glanced over her shoulder, certain she had heard hoofbeats behind her, and then, fueled by a sudden panic, she urged her horse into a gallop.

She breathed a sigh of relief when the lights of the Kincaid house came into view.

She was feeling foolish by the time she dismounted. Smoothing her hair and her skirt, she climbed the porch steps, her eagerness to see Blackie pushing everything else to the back of her mind.

Blackie opened the door before she could knock. "Hello, darlin'," he said, and swept her into his arms as soon as she stepped inside.

"Hello." Joey looked up at him, her brow furrowed. "What did your mother say when you told her I was coming over again?"

"Not much. I think she knows more than she's saying."

Her eyes widened. "She doesn't know that we're . . . ?"

"No," Blackie said, grinning, "I don't think she knows we're engaged. But I'm pretty sure she knows what was going on out in the lodge last night."

Joey felt a rush of heat warm her cheeks. She

never should have come here. How would she ever face Blackie's mother again?

"Come on," he said. "Dinner's ready."

She followed him into the dining room, murmured, "Oh, my" when she saw the balloons and the flowers and the hand-lettered sign that read *"Happy Birthday, Joey."*

Hannah appeared in the doorway between the kitchen and the dining room. "Hello, Joey," she said, smiling. "Happy birthday."

"Thank you, Mrs. Kincaid, but how did you know?"

"Oh, I overheard Big Mike mention it one day. Sit down, you two," she said. "Dinner's ready."

Joey felt the sting of tears in her eyes. Her own grandmother hadn't remembered that it was her birthday.

Blackie held Joey's chair for her, then bent down and kissed her cheek. "I love you," he whispered.

She lifted one hand to caress his cheek. "I love you too."

She quickly put her hand in her lap as Hannah entered the room carrying a large covered platter.

"Here, *nahkoa*," Blackie said, taking the platter from her, "let me help you."

Hannah smiled at him, then went back into the kitchen, returning with a pair of covered serving dishes, which she placed on the table. "Joey, I hope you like pot roast and mashed potatoes."

Joey nodded. "Yes, ma'am, very much."

Blackie held his mother's chair for her, then took his own seat.

Hannah bowed her head and said grace, as she had the night before, but Joey hardly heard the words. All she could think about was what Blackie had said. Did Mrs. Kincaid know that she had let Blackie kiss her, caress her? Did his mother know how close they had come to making love? Joey consoled herself with the knowledge that Mrs. Kincaid couldn't know, not for certain.

When the meal was over, Hannah brought in a birthday cake, complete with candles. Joey blinked tears from her eyes as she looked at the candles. It was the first birthday cake she'd had since she was a little girl. It reminded her of all she had lost.

"Blow out the candles," Hannah said.

"And don't forget to make a wish," Blackie added.

Joey looked at Blackie as she blew out the candles. He was her every wish for the future.

There were presents too. A white shirtwaist and a pretty blue-flowered skirt and a delicate white lace shawl from Hannah. A camera from Blackie, the same one she had admired in the Sears, Roebuck catalog.

Joey stared at it in disbelief. "You remembered," she whispered tremulously.

"Honey, I ordered it the day you told me you wanted one," he said, and then he grinned sheepishly. "But I'm afraid I forgot to order film."

"Oh, that doesn't matter." She threw her arms around him. "Thank you for remembering." Then, feeling suddenly self-conscious, she backed away, her cheeks hot.

Hannah patted Joey on the shoulder. "There's a full moon out tonight," she said. "Why don't you and Blackie go out on the porch and enjoy it? I'll clean up in here."

"I'll help you," Joey said.

"Next time," Hannah said. "Today's your birthday. Enjoy it."

Blackie smiled at his mother, then took Joey's hand in his. "Come on," he said. "*Nahkoa's* right. We don't want to let that moon go to waste."

On the porch, Blackie drew Joey into his embrace. "Happy birthday, darlin'."

"Thank you for making it wonderful. I'll never forget it."

They stood there a moment, their arms wrapped around each other. Blackie was about to kiss her when he heard Blue Hawk calling for his mother, and Hannah's reply.

"Come on," Blackie said and, taking her by the hand, he led her around back to the lodge.

Inside, he lit the fire in the pit. Joey sat down on the buffalo robe, and he sat beside her.

"Here," he said. "I have one more present for you." He handed her an odd-shaped package wrapped in white tissue paper.

Joey opened it slowly, revealing a round hoop that had been wrapped with a strip of rawhide. The inside of the hoop looked like a spider's web made of thread. There was a hole in the middle. Several small brown feathers hung from the bottom.

"What is it?" she asked, holding it up.

"It's a dream catcher."

"Where did it come from?"

"I made it for you today."

"You did? It's lovely." She kissed his cheek. "Thank you, Blackie. I'll hang it in my bedroom."

"That's the place for it. My father's people believe that the night air is filled with dreams. Dream catch-ers catch those dreams, both good and bad. Good dreams find the hole in the web and slip down the feathers, but bad dreams are tangled in the web, and when dawn lights the sky, the bad dreams perish. Infants and newlyweds should always have a dream catcher nearby so that only good dreams survive the night."

"I love you," she murmured. "I don't care if my grandmother disowns me, if Charlie never speaks to me again, so long as you love me."

"Joey!" He hugged her tight, felt her tears wet the front of his shirt. "It'll be all right, darlin'."

She looked up at him, her expression troubled. "How can it be? Everyone is against us."

"I don't know, but we'll work it out somehow." Taking the dream catcher from her hands, he hung it from the lodgepole. Sitting down again, he drew her into his arms.

She leaned into him, her arms wrapping around his neck, her lips seeking his. She slid her hand under his shirt, felt a tingle of excitement as her fingertips explored the hot bare skin of his back and shoulders.

He kissed her then, a long, slow, tantalizing kiss that sent waves of heat flowing through her, a deep, sensual kiss that made her forget everything but the fact that she loved him, wanted him. Needed him.

"Blackie." She slipped both hands under the front of his shirt and ran her fingernails lightly over his chest. She looked up at him, her gaze searching his. "Have you ever . . . you know, been with a woman?"

"No."

She couldn't hide her surprise. "Never?"

He shook his head. "I came close a time or two

when I was away at school, but—" He shrugged. "I guess I was waiting for you."

"I guess I was waiting for you too." She drew his head down and kissed him. "I don't want to wait anymore."

"Joey!"

Taking hold of his shirt, she drew it over his head and tossed it aside. His skin looked like smooth copper in the firelight. He sucked in a breath as her fingertips made lazy circles over his stomach, gradually moving down, down, until she reached the waistband of his trousers. And stopped.

He looked up at her, a smile hovering over the corners of his lips. "Did you run out of nerve?" he asked. "Or curiosity?"

"Both," she said. "Neither."

He reached for his belt buckle, slowly unfastened it and tossed his belt aside. He tugged off his boots and socks, then stood up and reached for the top button on his fly.

She watched his every move. The heavy material whispered softly as he drew his jeans down his long legs. Stepping out of them, he tossed them in the direction of his boots, then sat down beside her again, clad in nothing but his underwear.

"Your turn."

Her eyes widened as he reached behind her and began to unbutton her dress, slowly drawing it down over her shoulders until it pooled at her waist. He unfastened her undergarments as well, until her breasts were bared to his gaze.

"Beautiful," he murmured. "So beautiful." Leaning forward, he kissed her cheek. "Are you sure about this?"

She nodded, not trusting herself to speak.

His gaze remained on her face as he removed her dress and undergarments and threw them on top of his jeans. He removed her shoes and stockings, swallowing hard as she tugged his underwear over his hips and down his legs until, at last, they lay on the furry robe with nothing between them but desire.

She explored his body, shy at first and then with increasing boldness. Her hands moved restlessly over him, loving the feel of his skin, the way his muscles quivered at her touch. She loved the taste of him, the touch of him, the hot sexy smell of him.

And when he felt like he would explode with wanting her, he turned the tables on her, his hands and lips moving over her, learning what made her smile with pleasure, what made her cry out with delight.

She was more than ready for him when he rose over her, his dark eyes blazing with desire. There was a brief stab of pain and then there was only pleasure as his body became a part of hers. Complete. For the first time in her life she felt whole.

She closed her eyes, her fingers digging into his shoulders as she sought for something that seemed to elude her at every turn and then, in a single shattering moment, the world exploded in a burst of liquid pleasure the likes of which she had never imagined.

She heard Blackie cry her name, felt him convulse deep within her. She held him close, wanting to imprint the moment, the feeling, the sheer wonder of it, on her mind.

This, she thought, this was what love was. Now,

more than ever, she was glad she had waited, glad that she had shared this once-in-a-lifetime moment, this wondrous, earth-shattering moment, with Blackie and no one else.

She sighed and closed her eyes, deeply content. It had been worth the wait.

Later, wrapped in Blackie's arms, Joey traced the line of his jaw with the tip of her finger. "I never knew I could feel like this, that love would be like this. I wish we could stay here forever, just the two of us."

"I think you'd get tired of me pretty quick," Blackie said.

"No, never!"

She ran her fingertip over his lips; opening his mouth, he sucked it gently. "Sweet," he murmured.

"You are."

"Me?" He grinned at her. "Well, don't tell anyone."

She grinned back at him, and then her smile faded. "Do you think they've found Charlie yet?"

"I don't know, darlin'."

"They won't hurt him, will they?"

"That's up to Charlie. He never should have run away."

"He's just a boy."

Blackie lifted a hand to his left eye. "He didn't hit like a boy."

Leaning forward, Joey gently pushed his hand away and kissed him. "I'm sorry he hurt you."

"I guess it can't be easy on him, living with your grandmother. A boy needs a father."

"Grams spoils him something awful. Charlie looks just like my grandpa. She's always saying having Charlie in the house is just like having Grandpa back again." She signed heavily. "I feel like this is all my fault, too. He's my little brother. I should have taken better care of him."

"Don't blame yourself. You're not much older than he is."

"I hope he's all right."

He kissed her shoulder, the curve of her neck, nibbled on her earlobe. "It'll be all right," he said reassuringly. "There's nothing we can do to help him now."

She turned into his arms, everything else fading into the background as Blackie began to caress her. He was right; there was nothing she could do for Charlie now.

Blackie slipped his shirt over his head, pulled on his boots. "I'll see you home," he said.

Joey smoothed a hand over her dress. "I don't think you should leave your mother alone."

He didn't like the idea either, not with Caffrey and the others on the loose again, but his mother had more experience in looking out for herself than Joey did. "I don't want you riding home alone in the dark."

"I'll be fine. It's not that far. Besides, no one's after me."

He held the door flap open for her, then followed her outside. "As soon as my father gets back, we're going to tell everyone we're engaged," he said, drawing her into his arms, "so start looking for a dress and making plans. I don't believe in long engagements."

"Grams won't like it. I don't think your folks will, either."

"They'll get used to the idea, and if they don't—" He shrugged.

"Where will we live?"

"I don't know. We can live in my office if we have to." He winked at her. "I know the landlady."

Joey laughed softly. "If you treat her right, she might just give you the building for free."

Blackie tapped a finger on the tip of her nose. "Treating her right is my plan. Are you sure you'll be all right getting home?"

"I'm sure. Stop worrying."

Slipping his arm around her shoulders, he walked her to the front of the house, where she'd left her horse. He kissed her deeply before lifting her into the saddle. "Be careful."

"Don't worry about me. I'm a big girl. I can take care of myself."

He grinned at her. "I'd feel better if you had your frying pan with you."

She leaned down and kissed him. "I love you."

"I love you more." He gave her thigh an affectionate squeeze. "See you tomorrow, darlin'."

Joey smiled at him, then clucked to her horse. She turned once and waved, and then she was swallowed up in the darkness.

Chapter Twenty-six

I was sitting on the sofa in the parlor, waiting for Blackie, when he came in. "Where's Joey?"

"She went home."

"Alone?" I laid aside the shirt I had been mending. "You should have gone with her. It's late."

"I wanted to, but she didn't want me to leave you and Blue Hawk alone."

"We'd have been all right." I studied my son's face, noting that he didn't quite meet my eyes. I knew he had taken Joey into the lodge last night, and when I couldn't find them earlier, I'd assumed they had gone out there again. I told myself they were just looking for a quiet place to be alone. Anyone looking at them could see they were in love. Still I didn't want them to do anything they might regret later.

Blackie sat down across from me, his gaze not quite meeting mine. "Thanks for tonight, *nahkoa*. It meant a lot to Joey, the presents and the cake and all."

"I was happy to do it." I took a deep, calming breath, wishing Shadow was there beside me. "Is there anything you want to tell me, *naha*?"

Still not meeting my eyes, Blackie scrubbed his hands over his face.

I leaned forward, afraid that my worst fears had been realized. "You and Joey haven't . . ." The words died in my throat. How did a mother ask her son if he had stolen a young girl's innocence? And did I really have the right to ask? I had seduced Shadow when I was younger than Joey. Who was I to judge what my son did? "Blackie, talk to me."

He looked up at me. "We're engaged, *nahkoa*."

I sat there feeling stunned but not really surprised.

Blackie sat up straighter. He lifted his chin in a show of defiance much like his father's and met my gaze. "You don't approve?"

My shoulders slumped. What was it about our family, I wondered, that made each of us fall in love with the most unlikely person? Shadow and I had faced disapproval on all sides. Hawk had fallen in love with Victoria and her parents had disowned her for marrying him. Our daughter had been another man's wife when she fell in love with Cloud Walker. And now Blackie wanted to marry Joey McBride. I knew her grandmother and her brother would never approve. To tell the truth, I wasn't sure how I felt about having Joey in the family. I knew Joey wasn't responsible for what Charlie had done to Blackie. And if it turned out that Charlie had burned down our barn . . . well, I knew Joey wasn't responsible for that either. And yet, right or wrong, a small part of me held her accountable anyway.

"*Nahkoa?* Will she be welcome here as my wife?"

I thought of my mother and how she had taken Shadow under her wing and made him feel at home. My father had not been so quick to accept him, but I couldn't fault Pa for that. His parents, his sister, and two brothers had been killed by a tribe of Blackfoot Indians when Pa was a little boy. I knew if my mother was still alive, she would have welcomed Joey into the family without a qualm.

How could I subject my own son to the prejudices that his father and I had endured? No matter what Blackie had done, whether I approved or not, he was still my son and I loved him. Nothing could change that. I had always longed to be like my mother. So I took a deep breath and answered the way I knew my mother would have.

"She's going to marry my son," I said, taking his hand in mine. "That makes her my daughter. Of course she'll be welcome."

I saw the gratitude in Blackie's eyes. And then he leaned forward and hugged me tight. And in my heart, I repeated the words I had spoken to my son. From this day forward, Joey McBride would be my daughter.

Chapter Twenty-seven

Shadow reached for the battered coffee pot and refilled his cup. Trailing Charlie McBride had proven to be harder than he would have guessed. He didn't know if it was skill or just dumb luck that had finally put him on the boy's tracks after several days of fruitless effort. They had followed his trail all that day and found his camp just before dusk.

Scouting around, they had picked up three sets of footprints besides Charlie's. It had been late afternoon when they found Charlie McBride's body at the bottom of a narrow rocky ravine. Hawk had climbed down to tie a rope around the body and Shadow had hauled it up. McBride had been shot in the back, once, at close range.

"I don't look forward to breaking the news to

Joey," Hawk remarked, hunkering down beside his father.

"I do not envy you the task."

"Who do you suppose gunned McBride down?" Hawk wondered aloud. "And why? The kid didn't have anything worth stealing."

"Except your horse," Shadow remarked. "For some men, that would be enough."

Hawk nodded. "Reckon so."

Shadow gazed into the distance. After retrieving McBride's body, they had wrapped it in a blanket and then continued, following the tracks of the three men until they lost them in the rocks.

They had spent the rest of the day trying to pick up the trail but without any luck. Finally, Hawk had decided to give up the chase and take McBride's body back to town.

Shadow tossed the dregs of his coffee into the fire. If it had been up to him, he would have continued the search for the three men, but Hawk was the sheriff. The decision was his.

Chapter Twenty-eight

Blackie rode into town the next afternoon, ostensibly to pick up the mail and some supplies for his mother, though he was pretty sure she was just giving him an excuse to go to town and see Joey. He still couldn't believe how well his mother had taken the news of his engagement. He had been prepared for her to object; he wouldn't have been surprised if she had tried to talk him out of it. Instead, she had promised to welcome Joey into the family. He only hoped his father and Joey's family would be as understanding.

Blue Hawk had made a remarkable improvement in the last couple of days. He was sitting up in bed and that morning, to *nahkoa*'s happy surprise, he had walked into the kitchen, sat down at the table, and demanded a big breakfast.

Seeing his little brother up and around had improved Blackie's spirit too. Barns could be rebuilt, but it would have broken his mother's heart if Blue Hawk had died of his injuries.

Blackie's first stop was the post office. They didn't get much mail, but there was a new mailorder catalog from Montgomery Ward and a letter for his mother from Rebecca.

He was leaving the post office when he saw Cloud Walker coming down the street toward him.

"Ho, brother," Cloud Walker called.

Blackie nodded and they clasped forearms.

"How is Blue Hawk?"

"He's doing good," Blackie said, smiling. "He's starting to get restless, you know? Wants to go outside and see his horse."

Cloud Walker smiled. "A good sign."

"How are Mary and the kids doing?"

"The two little ones have runny noses and coughs, but they are getting better." He looked pensive a moment. "I worry for Shadow and Hawk."

"Me too. I should have gone with them. I hate not knowing what's going on."

Cloud Walker gave Blackie's shoulder a squeeze. "Waiting is always the hardest part. Tell your mother we will see her Sunday if the little ones are well."

"I will. Say hello to Mary and the kids for me."

With a nod, Cloud Walker went up the stairs into the post office.

Blackie stashed the mail in his saddlebag, then rode on down the street to Feehan's thinking that, while Joey was filling his mother's grocery list, he might be able to steal a kiss or two when Feehan's back was turned. He'd see about picking up a new book for Blue Hawk too.

The bell above the door peeled cheerfully when he stepped inside. His gaze quickly swept the room. There was no sign of Joey. Perhaps she was in the back.

He walked over to the counter, where Big Mike Feehan was wrapping up a package for Helen Sprague. The Spragues were longtime residents of Bear Valley. Years ago, Porter Sprague had tried to get Shadow run out of town, but then Shadow had saved their daughter's life, and since then nothing had been too good for Shadow and his family. Nelda had grown up and married Henry Smythe, and they had moved to San Francisco.

Mrs. Sprague nodded at Blackie as he approached. She was a tall woman. Her once curly red hair was mostly gray now. She had always been quite a talker, and that hadn't changed. "Good morning, young man. I heard you were back in town. You don't look none the worse for that trip back east. How's your mother doing?"

"She's fine."

"And how's your little brother getting along? We heard about the fire, of course. Terrible, just terrible. Land sakes, who would do such a thing?"

"Blue Hawk's doing much better, thank you, ma'am."

"Praise the Lord!" She patted his arm. "You tell your mother that Blue Hawk's been in our prayers and that we hope to see her soon. And young Blue Hawk, too."

"Thank you, Mrs. Sprague, I'll do that."

With a smile and a nod, Helen Sprague turned away from the counter.

Big Mike wiped his hands on his apron, then rolled up his shirtsleeves. "So," he said, "what can I do for you?"

Blackie handed Big Mike his mother's list. "Where's Joey?" he asked, glancing around the room.

"I don't know. She didn't come in today."

Blackie stared at Feehan, a sudden coldness settling in the pit of his stomach.

"What's this here say?" Big Mike asked, pointing at one of the items on Hannah's list.

"What?" Blackie squinted at the list, trying to make out his mother's handwriting. "Oh. Baking powder. Fill that for me, will you, Mr. Feehan?"

Without waiting for an answer, Blackie hurried out of the store. Outside, he swung into the saddle and urged his horse into a gallop. There were a couple of reasons why Joey might miss work. Her grandmother could be ill. Charlie might have come home. Joey might be feeling a little under the weather. But even as he searched his mind for excuses, he knew in his heart that something was wrong.

He was out of the saddle and running up the steps to her house before his horse came to a halt.

"Joey?" He knocked on the front door, and when there was no answer, he knocked again, harder this time. "Joey, you in there?"

After what seemed like an interminable wait, the door opened. Maureen McBride sat in her wheelchair, a black shawl around her shoulders, her legs covered by a tattered blue blanket. She stared up at him. "What do you want?"

"Is Joey here?"

"No, she ain't. She didn't come home last night, and I ain't seen her today." Maureen's eyes narrowed maliciously. "I thought she was probably shacked up with you."

He didn't bother with a reply. He took the steps two at a time and vaulted onto his horse's back. And all the while he cursed himself for not seeing her safely home the night before. If anything had happened to her . . . he couldn't finish the thought, couldn't bear to think he might never see her again. He told himself he was overreacting, but he knew with gut-deep certainty that something was terribly wrong.

He turned his horse toward home, then retraced Joey's route back toward town. Her tracks were easy to find. They were the only ones that led to the deer path near the back of the house. Joey's tracks were overlaid with fresh deer tracks leading down to the river. He had gone about half a mile when he saw a new set of tracks that emerged from the trees.

Blackie swore under his breath. If only his father were here! Shadow read trail sign far better than he did.

He followed the hoofprints a little farther. Though he wasn't the tracker his father was, he could see there were signs of a scuffle. He saw Joey's footprints in the dirt and larger, deeper prints made by heavy boots. It looked to Blackie like someone had grabbed hold of Joey's horse. She had dismounted, or perhaps fallen off her horse.

She had tried to run away on foot. He could see where her pursuer had caught up with her. The man had put her on her horse, then mounted his own. The tracks of the horses veered off the trail into the woods, leading away from town.

Pivoting on his heel, Blackie headed back for the house. Who did the second horse belong to? Had someone been lying in wait for Joey? Who? And why? He recalled Victoria saying that the three men who had been arrested with McBride had escaped from jail in Steel's Crossing. Blackie swore under his breath. Did they want revenge against his family so badly that they would take a chance on coming back here? Had they burned the barn in an effort to draw Shadow and Hawk away from home? He slammed his hand against the porch rail. Had his father and Hawk ridden into a trap? Or was he, himself, the target? If so, what better bait could there be than Joey? Even as the thought crossed his mind, he knew that was the answer. Someone had taken Joey to get at him.

And it had worked.

I stared at Blackie, a dozen thoughts and emotions running through my mind.

"No," I said. "No, you can't go, not alone. I won't hear of it."

"I've got to go," he said. "Pack your things. I'll take you to Mary's. You can stay there until I get back, or until *neyho* gets home."

I wanted to argue with him, but he didn't give me a chance. In minutes, he had packed a change of clothes for himself, taken a rifle and ammunition from the gun cabinet, tossed some food in his saddlebag.

"At least take Cloud Walker with you," I urged.

"No, someone has to stay here to look after you and the rest of the family. And I need someone to come out and look after the stock. Cloud Walker's the only one I trust."

Feeling numb, I packed two bags, one for myself and one for Blue Hawk. Blackie hitched the team to the wagon, then tied his horse to the back. I gathered up several blankets and pillows and made a pallet in the bed of the wagon for Blue Hawk. Blackie carried his brother outside. I closed the door behind them and walked down the steps. Blackie handed me into the wagon.

I looked back at our house as Blackie clicked to the team, wondering if I would ever see my family safe at home again.

Mary was surprised to see us but welcomed us in. I hugged my grandchildren, my spirits lifting as I felt their arms around me and saw their happy smiles. We quickly settled Blue Hawk in Adam's bed, and soon Adam and Blue Hawk were playing checkers while Joel and Linus looked on.

Cloud Walker assured Blackie that he would insist that Victoria and her kids spend the nights with him and Mary until Hawk got back.

I hugged Blackie. "Be careful," I said, my throat thick with unshed tears.

He nodded. "Pray for her, *nahkoa*."

"I will," I said. "And for you, as well."

He raked a hand through his hair. "I forgot to pick up the supplies from Feehan's. I'm sorry."

"Don't worry about that now. I'll send Cloud Walker to pick them up later."

I walked Blackie to the door, remembering what a sweet little boy he had been. He had always been a peacemaker, always wanted to make things better. He was a grown man now, but in my heart, he would always be my little boy.

I knew he would not want to see my tears, so I smiled and waved until he was out of sight, and then I put my arms around my daughter and wept.

Chapter Twenty-nine

"Over here," Shadow called. Dismounting, he hunkered down on his heels, his gaze skimming over the ground. There it was again, a hoofprint with a peculiar indentation in the shoe.

Hawk rode up beside him. "You find something?"

Shadow gestured at the print. "Caffrey's horse throws a print like that."

"Caffrey?" Hawk shook his head. "He's in jail."

"Is he?"

Hawk frowned as Joey's words came into his mind. She had told him that her brother claimed to have lost his watch in a card game while he was locked up with Caffrey and his cronies. What if McBride had lost it to Bob Caffrey? Maybe it hadn't been Charlie McBride who'd set the fire after all, but Caffrey and his pals. He had no proof, and yet it felt right. Caffrey's horse had been among those stolen from Crockers the night of the Fourth. He hadn't given it much thought at the time.

"Let's go," Hawk said grimly.

With a nod, Shadow gained his feet and swung onto Red Wind's back.

Hawk urged his horse into a gallop, troubled by a sudden foreboding.

An hour later, the trail was still clear.

A short time after that, Shadow drew his horse to a halt and gestured at the trail.

"What's wrong?" Hawk said, riding up alongside him.

Shadow's gaze met his. "They are heading back to town."

"You don't think . . . ?"

Shadow nodded.

Hawk considered a moment, then dismounted. Having an extra horse in tow would only slow them down.

Guessing what his son intended, Shadow dismounted and helped Hawk bury Charlie McBride's body.

Soon they were riding hard for home.

Chapter Thirty

Joey rode between two men. The third man trailed behind. They were men she recognized, the same men who had been arrested with Charlie for the attack on Blackie. How had they managed to escape from jail? What did they want with her? And where was Charlie?

She tugged against the rope that bound her wrists, but it only cut deeper into her skin, making her more uncomfortable.

She had never before known what fear was. She had been saddened at the loss of her parents. She had worried endlessly about Charlie since their father died. But she had never been afraid like this until now. She was afraid for her own life. She was afraid that Blackie wouldn't come after her. And more afraid that he would, and that these men would kill him.

She glanced at the surrounding countryside, wondering where they were and where they were going. And what would happen to her when they got there? The way the men looked at her made her skin crawl. If only she had let Blackie see her safely home last night!

From the remarks she overheard, she knew Blackie's life was in danger. The men were bent on revenge, especially the one called Caffrey. He had it in for Blackie, not only because Blackie had pressed charges against him and the other men, but because Blackie was part Indian, and Caffrey's father had been killed by Indians in a war that had ended over thirty years ago. Blackie hadn't even been born then.

At dark, the men made camp in the hollow of a hill. Joey huddled into herself, shivering, though not from the cold. Fear was a hard lump in her belly, a bitter taste in her mouth, each time one of the men looked at her.

Caffrey and Hackett lit a fire and set about fixing something to eat while Trijo looked after the horses. The men spoke in low tones, making it difficult to hear what they were saying. She felt her heart skip a beat when she overheard one of them mention Charlie's name.

She squeezed her eyes shut, determined not to cry as she wondered if she would ever see her brother, or Blackie, again.

Blackie reined his horse to a halt. Dismounting, he loosened the cinch and let the horse blow. The trail he was following was clear and easy to follow. Perhaps too easy. The thought that he could be riding into a trap had not been lost on him, and he wished again that his father and Hawk were there. Both of them had far more experience in this kind of thing than he did.

He stood there for several moments, one hand idly scratching Raven's ears. He wasn't a warrior like his father, he had no vision to guide him as did Hawk, but if the men who had taken Joey harmed her in any way, he would see them dead.

Looking up at the sky, he sent a silent prayer to *Maheo*, asking that the Great Spirit give him the strength and courage to do what he had to do. He prayed that the Great Spirit would protect Joey and keep her safe. He offered the same prayer to the God of his mother's faith, and then he tightened the cinch and stepped carefully into the saddle.

Joey rode slumped forward in the saddle, her eyes closed, her hands clinging to the saddle horn. They had been riding for three days. Thus far, except for their lustful glances, the men had paid her little attention, and for that she was grateful. They offered her food and water, and allowed her a few minutes privacy morning and evening.

She lifted her head when her horse came to a halt. The men had dismounted. Caffrey was leading the horses into a peeled pole corral. Hackett was striding toward a small shack made of rough logs. He drew his gun, opened the door, poked his head inside, and then disappeared into the building. He emerged a few minutes later, holstering his gun.

"All clear," he called to Caffrey.

Trijo yanked on Joey's arm. "Come on, you," he said, "get down."

She slid off her horse's back and stumbled up against him.

He caught her with a leer, whispered, "Maybe later," and pushed her away. "Can you cook?"

She nodded sullenly.

"There's some grub inside," he said, giving her a shove toward the cabin. "Go fix us something to eat."

She did as she was told, eager to be away from them.

The inside of the shack was as dreary as the outside. The floor was made of hard-packed earth. There were cobwebs hanging in every corner. Two rough-hewn wooden chairs and a table were the shack's only furnishings save for a single iron cot and a dusty bear rug in front of the fireplace. A wooden crate held an assortment of canned food.

She heard a gunshot from outside. It rattled the shack's single window. She ran toward the door and looked out, her heart in her throat. Blackie! She felt a quick rush of relief when she saw that Caffrey had killed a rabbit.

He burst into the shack a short time later and thrust the carcass at her. "Cook it," he said.

She held up her bound hands. Muttering an oath, he raised his knife, still wet with blood from skinning the rabbit, and cut the rope.

There was a burning, tingling sensation in her hands as she took the rabbit. She waited until Caffrey left the shack, then went to the fireplace. There was kindling in it. She lit the twigs with a match she found in a box on the narrow mantel, added some wood, then put the rabbit on the spit in the hearth.

She went through the canned goods, picking out potatoes and peaches.

She wandered around the small room while the rabbit cooked, looking out the window from time to time to keep an eye on the men, who were hunkered down in the shade, smoking.

She glanced at the oil lamp on the mantel. It would be getting dark soon. Crossing the floor, she picked up the lamp and shook it a little to see if there was any oil in the base. It was then that she saw the knife, partially concealed beneath a dirty rag. The knife looked old; the blade was a little rusty but the edge was still sharp. Taking it, she lifted her skirt and slid the blade inside her boot.

Having the knife gave her a measure of comfort. She had to get out of here, had to get away from these men. After listening to their conversation, she knew they were using her as a decoy in hope of catching Blackie. They wanted revenge against Blackie and his family for sending them to jail. She knew now that it hadn't been Charlie who'd burned down the Kincaids' barn. Caffrey and his cronies had done it in an act of revenge. And then they had kidnapped her, knowing that Blackie would come after her.

Where was Charlie? She hoped and prayed he was safe at home, but she had a horrible feeling that he had gotten mixed up with Caffrey and his men again.

Hawk and Shadow split up when they reached town. They had abandoned the trail and ridden hard for Bear Valley, afraid that Caffrey and his men were bent on more destruction.

It was dark by the time Shadow got home. Unsaddling his horse, he turned it loose in one of the corrals. He dropped the saddle over the top rail, spreading the blanket out beside it. His gaze moved over the house, the corrals, the other outbuildings. It was a quiet, peaceful scene. Cattle dotted the hillsides. A cat lay curled on the porch railing. A couple of dogs crawled out from under the porch. Tails wagging, they trotted up to him, lifting their heads to be scratched.

Shadow spoke softly to the dogs and they followed him as he moved toward the charred remains of the barn. A warm anger filled him when he looked at the carnage. Moving closer, he could see that Blackie had already started cleaning up. As soon as they disposed of the wreckage, they could start rebuilding.

He started for the house, then stopped and looked at the stock in the corrals again. Blackie's horse was missing, and so were the matched pair of grays they used to pull the buggy.

Feeling the first stirring of unease, he walked around the house, the dogs trailing at his heels. The little filly that had been burned was locked in a small corral in the back.

Opening the back door, Shadow stepped into the kitchen. A heavy silence filled his ears.

"Hannah? Blue Hawk? Blackie?"

Calling their names, he moved through the house. There was no sign of forced entry, no sign of trouble. Going out front, he checked the ground for sign. Fresh wagon tracks led out of the yard.

Moments later, he was riding hard toward town.

His first stop was Mary's house. Hannah came running out to meet him, something she had done every time he'd returned from a journey for as long as he could remember. He held her close, felt the tension drain out of him as he breathed in the scent of her hair, her skin.

"Did you find him?" she asked.

Shadow slipped his arm around her shoulders and they walked away from the house. "We found Charlie McBride up in the mountains. Dead. He had been shot in the back."

"Oh, no," Hannah murmured.

Shadow grunted softly. "I do not think he set the fire. Where is Blackie? Why are you here instead of at home?"

"Oh! I was so happy to see you, I almost forgot. Joey's missing. He went looking for her."

Shadow didn't swear often, but he swore now, a short pithy oath. "When did he leave?"

"Late Thursday afternoon. Wait, there's more . . ."

"Tell me."

"Blackie asked Joey to marry him."

He grunted softly. The news didn't really surprise him. It had ever been that way with Blackie. Even as a child, when he saw something he wanted, he went after it. And it had been easy to see that he wanted Joey McBride. And that she wanted him.

"You're going after him, aren't you?" Hannah asked. "You and Hawk?"

Shadow nodded. Blackie was a good man, but he'd had little experience with hunting men of Caffrey's ilk, men who killed because they enjoyed it, because it filled up the emptiness of their souls.

Shadow had known men like that in the past. Men who lived for violence and vengeance because they had nothing else to live for.

"How soon will you be leaving?"

"First thing in the morning."

Blackie had a three-day head start. If their son was in trouble, there was little chance he would get there in time. But he didn't mention that to Hannah.

Hawk took a deep breath, then knocked on the front door of the McBride house. Of all the rotten duties inherent in being a lawman, notifying the families of the deceased had to be the worst.

He glanced around while he waited for someone to answer the door. The place was in need of repair, he thought. One of the boards on the porch had a hole in it; the front window was broken and had been covered with a board. Both the house and the porch were in need of a good coat of paint. The top rail was missing on the corral beside the house. A skinny gray cat was stretched out on the porch rocker. It stared at him, unblinking, its tail twitching.

After a long pause, Maureen McBride opened the door. She looked him over from head to foot, her gaze narrowing suspiciously. "What do you want?"

Hawk removed his hat. "Afternoon, ma'am. I need to talk to you for a few minutes."

"About what?"

"About Charlie."

"Well, he ain't here."

"Yes, ma'am, I know that."

"Then why are you bothering me?" she asked plaintively, and then, as if she suddenly divined the reason for his visit, she wheeled her chair away from the door. "Come in."

Hawk followed her into the parlor.

"You might as well sit down," she said, pointing to a faded print sofa.

Hawk sat where she indicated, his hat balanced on his knee. "Is Joey here?"

"No, I don't know where that girl's gone off to. I ain't seen her in days. That brother of yours was here looking for her earlier. Land sakes, if Leona hadn't looked in on me now and then, I'd like to have starved to death."

Damn. He'd been hoping Joey would be here to comfort the old woman.

Hawk heard footsteps and a moment later Leona Bradshaw entered the room. She was a stern-faced woman with iron-gray hair and brown eyes that didn't miss a thing. She was rumored to be the biggest gossip in town, and Hawk believed it.

Leona glanced from Hawk to Maureen. "Is something wrong, dear?"

"I don't know," Maureen said.

Both women looked at Hawk, waiting.

"Well?" Maureen said. "What's that boy of mine done now?"

"I—" Hawk took a deep breath. There was no kind way to say it. "I'm afraid Charlie's dead, Mrs. McBride."

Maureen McBride stared at him for a full minute, and then her face sort of crumpled in on itself. Silent tears streamed down her cheeks and she seemed to age ten years.

"I'm right sorry, ma'am," Hawk said.

She nodded again. Tears continued to rain down

her cheeks. She made no move to wipe them away. "He was a good boy. A little wild, like his grandfather, but a good boy."

Hawk looked up at Leona Bradshaw. "Can you stay here with her?"

"Find Josephine," Maureen McBride said plaintively. "I want Josephine."

Hawk stood up. He looked down at Mrs. McBride for a moment, then put his hand on her shoulder and gave it a squeeze. "I'll find her."

Gesturing for Leona Bradshaw to follow him, Hawk stepped outside. Leona followed him a moment later.

Hawk settled his hat on his head. "Can you stay here with her for a few days?"

"Of course. I always knew that boy would end up bad," she said. "He always was a wild one. Poor Maureen. First Ira and now Charlie. Don't you worry, Sheriff, I'll get in touch with Amelia and Ester and the three of us will take turns staying with Maureen for as long as she needs us. Poor dear."

"Thank you, ma'am, I appreciate it."

Going down the stairs, Hawk swung onto the back of his horse and headed for the jail. He went through his mail, listened while Finch filled him in on the doings of the last few days. Things had been quiet, Finch said. There had been a fistfight over at O'Toole's. Mrs. Crowley had reported that one of her hens had been stolen. And a couple of boys had dragged Mrs. Olson's laundry through the mud. But mostly, things had been quiet.

"I'm beat," Hawk said. "I'm going home to get a good night's sleep. I'll be in early to relieve you."

All thought of spending a pleasant evening with

Victoria and the kids and getting a good night's sleep fled Hawk's mind when he reached home and saw one of his father's horses tied to the hitching post.

Chapter Thirty-one

Joey stared up at the ceiling of the shack. A big black spider was spinning a new web in the corner. She was like that web, she thought bleakly. Caffrey, Hackett, and Trijo were like the spider. And Blackie was the unwary fly.

She tugged on the ropes that bound her hands to the frame of the cot, rolled her head back and forth in an effort to loosen the gag that was tightly tied over her mouth. Three days had passed since Caffrey and his men had abducted her. Three days of living in constant fear of what they planned to do with her, of what they would do to Blackie should he show up.

Caffrey and the other two were waiting outside, hiding in the shadows, certain that Blackie's arrival was imminent. She had to warn him, but how? She couldn't move, couldn't cry out, could only lie there in the growing darkness, her heart pounding, her wrists aching from the chafing of the ropes that bound her.

She tugged on the ropes again, heedless of the pain. Why were these men doing this? It wasn't Blackie's fault they had been arrested, any more than it was Blackie's fault that Caffrey's father had been killed at the Little Big Horn. Caffrey and his cronies had attacked Blackie in the saloon because he was part Indian and for no other reason. They might have killed him . . . and they would certainly kill him now if she didn't warn him.

She glanced at the window, trying to judge the time. It was going on dusk. Tonight, she thought. He would come tonight. She knew it in the deepest part of her heart and soul, knew it with a certainty she couldn't explain.

The thought drove her to try harder to escape her bonds. Blood, she thought, blood might make the ropes slippery enough so she could pull one hand free. She tugged on the rope that bound her right hand, tugged until the pain brought tears to her eyes. She had to get free! The rough hemp abraded her skin. She felt the warm sticky wetness of blood trickle down her wrist and worked her hand back and forth in a frantic effort to slip free.

She glanced at the window. It was full dark now. Maybe he wouldn't come tonight. If she could just get free, maybe she could sneak away, unseen.

A muffled cry of pain was trapped inside the gag when, at last, she managed to free her hand.

She had just managed to undo the knot on her other wrist when she heard the sound of footsteps.

Not knowing who it was, she lay back on the cot, her hands gripping the ropes in the hope that her captors wouldn't notice she was free.

The door swung open and a man stood silhouetted in a pool of moonlight. He turned his head to the side, revealing a profile she recognized instantly.

Tearing the gag from from her mouth, she screamed, "Blackie! Look out! It's a trap!" but the words were lost in a hail of gunfire.

Blackie fell forward, the gun in his hand skittering across the hard-packed earth. With a wild cry, Joey scrambled off the bed and snatched up the gun. Hiding in the shadows, she held the weapon in hands that trembled.

"I got him!" Caffrey's exultant cry pierced the darkness.

"Hold on!" Hackett shouted. "Best wait and be—"

But Caffrey didn't wait. He bounded out of his hiding place, gun in hand, and ran up to the shack.

Time seemed to slow. Joey looked down at Blackie, who was sprawled on his stomach just inside the doorway. He didn't move. Didn't seem to be breathing.

"I got him!" Caffrey said again.

The satisfaction in his voice tore through Joey's heart like a knife.

It was dark in the shack. So dark that Caffrey didn't see her raise the gun. It wasn't until he'd stepped up to the doorway and heard the snick of the weapon being cocked that he realized he was in danger, but it was too late.

Joey aimed the gun at his chest like a finger of

accusation and squeezed the trigger. Blue flame spurted from the muzzle of the Colt.

The gunshot was very loud in the close confines of the shack.

Caffrey stood there for stretched seconds before he dropped his gun, then reeled backward.

With a strength she didn't know she possessed, Joey dragged Blackie out of the doorway. Slamming the door shut, she dropped the crossbar in place, then ran to the window and closed and barred the heavy wooden shutters.

Heart pounding, she dropped to her knees beside Blackie and shook his shoulder gently. "Blackie? Blackie, please wake up!"

She shook his shoulder harder, panic rising up within her when he remained motionless. She ran her hands over his body, searching for a wound, frowned when she couldn't find one. She slid her hands over his face, gasped when she felt wetness on her palms.

Blood! It was leaking from the side of his head, dripping down his cheek. With hands that trembled, she ripped a piece of material from the hem of her skirt and wrapped it around his head.

He moaned softly as she tied it off.

"Blackie! Oh, Blackie, thank the Lord, you're alive."

"Am I?" He lifted a hand to his head. "Damn, that hurts."

"Do you think they're gone?"

"I don't know. Where's my gun?"

"Here." She thrust it into his hand, felt the bile rise in her throat as she murmured, "I think . . . Oh, Blackie, I think I killed Caffrey!"

Sitting up slowly, he holstered his Colt, then slid his arm around her shoulders and drew her up against him. "It's all right. He had it coming. Are you okay? They didn't hurt you, did they?"

She was shivering now. "N . . . no. I . . . I think I'm gonna be sick."

Rolling away from him, she began to retch violently.

Murmuring softly, Blackie stroked her back. Pulling a kerchief from his back pocket, he handed it to her. "You okay now?"

"I k . . . killed him."

He cupped her cheek in his hand. "Would you rather I was the one who was dead?"

"No! Can we . . . can't we have some light?"

"I'm not sure that's a good idea. Hackett and Trijo might still be prowling around out there."

She nodded and huddled against him. He felt solid. Safe. A moment later, they heard the sound of retreating hoofbeats, and then silence.

"Do you think they're gone?" Joey asked again, hopefully.

"Wait here." Rising, Blackie made his way to the window. Lifting the bar, he opened one of the shutters and peered into the darkness. He couldn't see much, but three things were clear: His horse was gone, Joey's horse was gone, and so was Caffrey's body.

Muttering an oath, he closed and barred the window. "Looks like they lit out."

Taking Joey by the hand, he pulled her to her feet and led her over to the cot. Sitting on the edge of the thin mattress, he drew her down beside him. She was still shivering, whether from the cold or nerves or both he couldn't say. Dammit, she had killed a man because of him. He had come charging in to save her like a hero out of one of Blue Hawk's books when he should have been more careful. He should have waited until daylight. He should have scouted the area before he made his presence known. But he hadn't been able to wait. He had known Joey was in the shack. She might have been hurt, bleeding, dying. And now, because he had been careless, she had killed a man.

His arm tightened around her. "I'm sorry," he murmured. "Joey, dammit, I'm sorry."

She shifted against him, and he knew she was looking at him even though he couldn't see her face in the darkness. "For what?"

"If it wasn't for me, you wouldn't have killed that bastard."

"It's all right, Blackie. To save you, I'd do it again."

He laughed bitterly. "I was supposed to be rescuing you."

Her hand caressed his cheek. "You did."

"Why don't you get some sleep?" he suggested.

"I don't think I can."

"Try." He eased her down on the mattress and covered her with the blanket, then sat beside her, his back against the wall, her hand in his.

Ten minutes later, her quiet, even breathing told him she was asleep.

His head throbbed dully and he swore under his breath. Some hero he'd turned out to be.

He woke with a start, wincing as pain lanced through the side of his head. Beside him, Joey was still asleep. He watched her for several minutes. She was the most wonderful woman he had ever known and he had almost lost her. Closing his eyes, he offered a quiet prayer of thanks that she was safe, that Caffrey and his men hadn't put their filthy hands on her.

Slipping quietly from the bed, he filled the coffeepot with water and dumped a handful of coffee in the strainer. After stirring the embers in the fireplace, he set the pot at the edge of the fire. There didn't seem to be any food in the shack except some canned goods.

Joey stirred as the scent of coffee filled the air. And then, all too clearly, the memory of the previous night came rushing back. She had killed a man. The thought sickened her, and yet she couldn't be sorry it was Caffrey who was dead and not Blackie.

Blackie! She sat up, her gaze sweeping the shack. Relief washed through her when she saw him standing in front of the hearth, a tin cup in his hand.

He turned slowly, the expression in his eyes softening when he saw her. " 'Morning."

" 'Morning." She slid her legs over the side of the cot and padded toward him. "How's your head feeling?"

He shrugged. "A little sore. Don't worry about me; I'm all right."

With a nod, she wrapped her arms around his waist. He was here. He was alive. Nothing else mattered.

"Want some coffee?" he asked.

"Thanks." She took a sip from his cup. It was hot and bitter.

"Finish it if you want. I've already had one cup."

She drank what was left, then put the cup on the mantel. "Blackie, what's wrong?"

"Nothing."

"Yes, there is. Tell me."

He shook his head.

"You're upset about last night, aren't you?"

"Shouldn't I be? I came here to rescue you and almost got myself killed instead."

"It doesn't matter. It was a brave thing for you to do."

"It was a stupid thing to do. I should have scouted around. I should have known better. Dammit, my father would never have blundered in here like that."

"Your father has had a lot more experience than you."

"Stay here. I'm going outside to have a look around."

She started to tell him to be careful but thought better of it.

He gave her a hug and a kiss, then drew his Colt and moved toward the door. Lifting the bar, he opened it slowly and peered outside. Nothing moved. There was no sound save for birdsong and the whisper of the morning wind sighing through the trees.

"Bar the door behind me," he said, and stepped out into the open. He circled the cabin, noting the hoofprints that led away from the shack. He recognized the tracks of his horse among the others.

Returning to the front of the shack, he rapped lightly on the door. "Open up, it's me."

Joey opened the door a crack and then stepped back so he could enter. "They're gone?"

"Yeah. We'd better go, too. It's a long walk home."

They had nothing to pack and little to carry. Blackie wrapped the coffeepot and the can of coffee in the blanket he pulled off the bed, closed the door, and they were on their way.

His head throbbed with every step. Maybe he should have stayed back east, he mused. He seemed to be everybody's target since he'd returned to Bear Valley.

They walked for several miles before they paused at a narrow stream to rest and quench their thirst. A few handfuls of late summer berries provided something to eat.

Blackie lay back on the grass, his hands folded behind his head, and closed his eyes. Joey was safe and that was all that mattered. They would be home in a few days. Together, they would go and break the news of their engagement to her grandmother, and then they could settle down. If he could make a go of being a vet, Joey could quit working at Feehan's, stay home, and raise some babies.

"What are you smiling about?" Joey asked.

He cracked one eye in her direction. "I was just imagining you surrounded by a dozen little ones."

"A dozen?"

He rolled onto his side and smiled up at her. "Too many?"

She stretched out beside him, her head propped on her hand. "I don't know." Her eyes widened suddenly. "Oh, my gosh! I could already be pregnant!"

"Would you mind?"

"Oh, no! I hope I am. Oh, Blackie, won't it be

wonderful when we're married with a place of our own?"

He curled one hand around her nape and drew her toward him. "Wonderful," he murmured, and kissed her.

At the first touch of his lips on hers, tremors of excitement rippled through her. It was all still so new—the wonder of his kisses, the thrill of his caresses, the soul-shattering ecstasy she experienced when he made love to her. He rolled her over until she lay on top of him, her breasts flattened against his chest.

Like a flame to kindling, desire sprang to life between them. She felt the swell of his desire, heard it in the quickening of his breath, and her own.

His hands moved up and down her back, then settled on her buttocks, pressing down so she could more fully feel his erection.

"Joey . . ."

"Are you sure?" she asked. "Your head . . ."

"It doesn't ache near as bad as some other places," he replied with a wry grin.

She laughed softly, happiness welling up inside her like bubbles in a bottle of soda pop.

They undressed each other, then fell back on the thick sod. She ran her hands over him, touching, teasing, until he turned the tables on her. His gaze was hot as his eyes moved over her, his hands playing over her body with a sure knowledge that quickly carried her to the brink of fulfillment. She was ready for him when he entered her. A soft sigh escaped her lips, and then she clutched his shoulders, her fingernails digging into his flesh. Closing her eyes, she gave herself over to the sheer magic of her beloved's touch.

Later, when she lay breathless and sated in his arms, she could scarcely believe they had made love out in the open.

"What if someone had come by?" she asked, mortified.

"We would have asked them for a ride back to town," he replied, grinning.

"Oh, you!" She smacked him on the shoulder. "How long will it take us to get home?"

"Well, it took three days of riding to get here. I reckon about six days on foot."

"Six days! We'll starve!"

He laughed softly. "*Neyho* taught me a few things. I reckon we'll get by."

She smiled at him. "That's right. Indians know how to live off the land, don't they?"

"I'm not near the expert my father is, but I think I can manage to find enough game to keep us from starving."

"Oh, Blackie, I love you so much."

"Why? Because I won't let you starve?"

She laughed. "Well, partly."

"Partly?"

"I also love your mouth." She kissed him. "And your nose." She kissed that too. "And your stubborn chin."

"Stubborn? Me?"

She kissed his chin. "And the color of your skin." She ran her tongue over his chest. "Your broad shoulders." She kissed each one.

"So," he drawled, "you just love me for my body."

She laughed merrily. "I love you because you

love me. Because you make me happy, so happy."
She gazed into his eyes. "Will we always feel this
way?"

"I don't know. I hope so."

"I've heard some of the women in town talking,"
Joey said, serious now. "Some of them don't sound
very happy. They make it sound like . . . like being
with their husbands in bed is a chore. And some of
them sleep in separate beds. I don't want that to
happen to us. I don't want our love to grow old and
die."

"It doesn't have to be that way. Look at my folks.
They're more in love now than they ever were."

"I know." She snuggled closer to him. "I want us
to be that way. I want you to look at me the way
your father looks at your mother. Even if he doesn't
say anything, you can tell he loves her more than
anything in the world."

"That's how I love you, Joey. More than anything
else in the world."

"And I love you. Promise me, Blackie, promise
you'll never leave me."

"I promise." He hugged her close, one hand
stroking her hair. "I promise, Joey, nothing but
death will part us."

They walked all that day. At dusk, Blackie found a
place in a shallow draw to spend the night. He left
Joey there while he went in search of game and
returned a short time later carrying a rabbit.

Joey watched, grimacing, as he skinned and gut-
ted the carcass, then fashioned a spit out of a couple of pieces of wood and a slender branch.
Together, they gathered wood for the fire that

Blackie lit with a match from the box he carried in his pocket. Soon, the smell of roasting meat filled the air.

When it was done, Blackie lifted the spit from the fire. When the meat was cool, he tore off a piece and offered it to Joey.

"Is this how the Indians eat it?" she asked.

"Close enough, I guess. How is it?"

"Why do I have to eat it first? You cooked it!"

With a shake of his head, Blackie tore off another chunk, blew on it, and took a bite. "Go on, try it," he said. "It's good."

And it was. Between them, they finished it all; then Blackie tossed the bones in the brush. "For the coyotes."

"Coyotes?" Joey looked around, as if expecting to find one lurking over her shoulder.

"They won't come near the fire," he assured her. She didn't look convinced.

"Come here," he said. She scooted closer and he draped his arm around her shoulders. "Just pretend we're at home."

"I don't remember sitting on the ground at home," she muttered.

Blackie laughed, then kissed her on the cheek. "What would you think about building a house when we get home?"

"A house? Of our own? Do you mean it?"

"Sure. Where did you think we were going to live?"

"Well . . ." She shrugged. "I don't know. Everything's happened so fast. But a house of our own . . . what about Grams? She can't live by herself."

"You want us to live with your grandmother? I

don't know, Joey. I don't think she'll let me in the house. Maybe we can build a place between my folks and yours. That way you can check on your grandmother every day to make sure she's all right. And we'll be close if she needs you."

Joey kissed him soundly on the cheek. "That's sweet of you."

"I just want you to be happy, darlin'."

"I am happy."

"We'd best get some sleep," Blackie suggested. "We've got a long walk ahead of us."

Blackie woke abruptly, every instinct he possessed screaming that they were in danger. He lay there, his senses alert. And then he heard it again, the scrape of a footstep over damp grass.

He turned slowly toward the sound, his eyes narrowing, focusing on a dark shape crouched in the shadows.

Moonlight glinted on metal.

What happened next happened very fast. Blackie shoved Joey away from him, then rolled to his right, grabbing for his Colt as he did so.

He heard the snick of a gun being cocked, the sound like thunder in the still of the night.

Joey called his name and he hollered for her to get the hell out of there.

He felt the hot breath of a bullet brush his cheek and lifted his gun and fired in the direction of the muzzle flash.

A hoarse cry of pain rose from the shadows, could still be heard when another gunshot rent the air. Blackie fired again, and then everything went still.

He moved away from the campsite and circled around to where the unseen attackers had fired from. He approached cautiously, the way his father had taught him, every sense alert, attuned to the nuances of the night.

The bodies lay facedown in a patch of dappled moonlight. He kicked their weapons out of reach and then turned the bodies over. A dark stain spread across Trijo's shirtfront; blood oozed from a hole in Hackett's forehead.

Blackie stared at the two men, his heart pounding so loudly he almost missed the faint dry creak of a branch breaking behind him.

Whirling around, he dropped to one knee, aimed his Colt like a finger pointing, and fired at the tall man barely visible in the darkness.

With a low groan, Bob Caffrey staggered out of the shadows clutching his chest.

Chapter Thirty-two

Without hesitation, Blackie fired again, and Caffrey dropped to his knees, then toppled sideways and lay still.

Weapon at the ready, Blackie moved forward cautiously. He kicked Caffrey's gun out of reach, then knelt down and checked the man's pulse. There was none.

Blackie stood slowly, his Colt heavy in his hand. He had killed three men. If he had been a warrior in the old days, he would have lifted his voice in a shout of victory. He would have given thanks to the Great Spirit of the Cheyenne for helping him to defeat his enemies. He would have counted coup on their bodies. He would have taken their scalps. He knew how it was done. His father, Two Hawks Flying of the Cheyenne, had taught him. It was a skill he had never thought to have a use for. Though Blackie had never taken a scalp, he was surprised to find that the urge to do so was strong within him now.

He holstered his gun.

He dropped to his knees.

He drew his knife. Lifted a hank of Caffrey's hair . . .

"Blackie! What are you doing?"

He looked up, startled to find Joey staring down at him, her eyes wide with revulsion.

Blackie stared down at Caffrey for a long moment; then, with a shake of his head, he gained his feet and sheathed the blade.

Joey glanced at the body, her eyes growing even wider. "That . . . that's Caffrey . . . but . . . how can it be?" She looked up at Blackie. "I killed him."

"Apparently you didn't."

She glanced around. "What about Hackett? And Trijo?"

Blackie jerked a thumb over his shoulder. "Over there."

"You killed them too?"

Blackie nodded.

"Are you all right?"

"Yeah, I'm fine." He had never killed anyone before. As long as he could remember, he had wanted to save life and ease suffering. Now he had killed three men and come damn close to scalping one of them. In his heart, he knew he would have killed them all again, and a dozen more, to protect Joey.

She moved up close to him and slid her arms around his waist. Her hair brushed his chin, her nearness warmed the dark cold places within him. With a wordless cry, he held her close, his face buried in the wealth of her hair.

They stood that way for a long time. He had always wondered how his father had endured the hardships of the war trail, how he had survived the days and months when he had been hunted like a wild animal. Now he knew. Knew he could endure any hardship as long as Joey was there to comfort him at the end of the day.

He sent Joey back to their campsite while he went in search of the dead men's horses. He found the mounts tethered to a tree about a quarter of a mile away. Raven whinnied softly as he approached.

Blackie scratched the stud's ears for a few minutes, then led the horses back to where Joey was waiting for him. Lifting her onto the back of one of the horses, he swung onto Raven's back and rode away from their campsite.

About two miles later, he drew rein. Dismounting, he lifted Joey from the back of her horse. Tying the horses to a bush, he unsaddled them, then went through the dead men's gear. Among other things, he found spare shirts, ammunition, hardtack, and jerky. Blackie took the food, two of the bedrolls, and the ammunition, and left the rest.

He looked over at Joey, who was sitting on a log, watching him through troubled eyes.

"Are you hungry?" he asked.

She shook her head.

He let out a sigh. He didn't have much of an appetite either.

He spread one of the bedrolls on the ground and

dropped another one on top of it. "Come on," he said, "let's get some sleep."

Joey slid under the blanket beside him and snuggled against his side. It was a long time before she fell asleep.

He was still awake when dawn stretched her curtain across the sky.

In the morning, they ate a quick breakfast. After cleaning up their campsite, Blackie saddled Raven and then saddled one of the other horses for Joey. He lifted her onto the mare's back, adjusted the stirrups, and handed her the reins.

They had been riding about an hour when Joey asked, "What did you do with the bodies?"

"I left them where they fell."

"You didn't bury them?"

He shook his head. "Let the coyotes have 'em."

She looked at him sharply, her eyes reflecting her horror.

"You disapprove?"

"Yes . . . no; I don't know. It just seems so—" She lifted her hand and let it fall. "I don't know."

"Barbaric? Savage?"

"I didn't say that."

"But you were thinking it."

"Would you have scalped Caffrey if I hadn't been there?"

"I don't know."

His answer unsettled her. One of the reasons she had fallen in love with Blackie was that he seemed so gentle, so kindhearted. Her father had been a good man, but he had been a harsh taskmaster. He had put a roof over their heads, made sure they had food to eat, clothes to wear, but he had been a cold man, not given to physical displays of affection.

The image of Blackie, knife in hand as he knelt in a pool of moonlight beside Caffrey's body, was burned into her memory. There had been a feral look in his eyes when he looked up at her. It had frightened her more than she cared to admit. In that moment, he had reminded her of his father. It occurred to her that if they had lived in the old days, Blackie would have been a Cheyenne warrior. Her people would have been his enemies.

She slid a glance at Blackie. She had thought him warm, gentle, tender, and kind. Had she been wrong about him?

He looked over and caught her gaze. His eyes narrowed, as if he knew what she was thinking. He clucked to his horse and Raven broke into a trot, leaving her behind with her troubled thoughts.

Shadow looked at Hawk across Caffrey's body. The scavengers had already been gnawing at it. "They have not been dead long. Less than a day."

"You think Blackie did this?"

"Who else? See there? Those are his tracks. And those are Joey's."

"I never thought he had it in him, you know, to kill a man. Let alone three."

Shadow nodded. Blackie had never been aggressive, never cruel, but there was an underlying strength in him that had never been tapped. He would have been a warrior of power in the old days.

Shadow rose. Had the kills been his, he would

have taken Caffrey's scalp, and those of the others too.

"I should probably take the bodies back to town," Hawk remarked without much enthusiasm. "They might have kin hereabouts."

Shadow grunted softly. "Leave them."

"I don't know . . ."

"I am not packing any of them on my horse. If you wish to take them back to town, you will have to walk."

Hawk grinned. "All right, you talked me out of it. How far ahead of us do you think Blackie is?"

"Not far. We will catch up with them tomorrow morning. There is a stream a few miles ahead. Let us camp there tonight. The horses could use a rest."

"Maybe life will settle down again," Hawk muttered as he swung onto the back of his horse. "I haven't had a decent night's sleep since these guys broke out of jail."

Joey stared into the heart of the fire, wondering how to bridge the gulf that lay between herself and Blackie. Would he accept her apology? What, exactly, should she apologize for? She felt a deep sense of purely feminine satisfaction that the man she had chosen for her husband was capable of protecting her, and yet, at the same time, she had been frightened by the rage she had seen in his eyes. She was repelled by the fact that he had wanted to take Caffrey's scalp. Would he have taken it if she hadn't been there to stop him? She covered her mouth with her hand as a new thought occurred to her. Good Lord, had he done such a thing before?

The mere thought made her stomach churn. Her grandfather had been scalped. She wasn't supposed to know that, but she had overheard her grandmother talking about it with Mrs. Jackson. The thought of such a thing happening to someone she had known and loved had made Joey's stomach clench in horror and she had been violently ill.

She slid a glance in Blackie's direction. He was sitting on the opposite side of the fire, also staring at the flames. What was he thinking? If she went to him and said she was sorry, would he forgive her? She wondered how she could explain her conflicting emotions, and then wondered if it would even be necessary. She had a feeling he understood what was bothering her far better than she did.

If only they were back home. She knew instinctively that Hannah would understand how she was feeling. Perhaps she could even explain it so Joey could understand.

The tension remained between them that night when they went to bed. Tears burned Joey's eyes and dripped down her cheeks, but she didn't wipe them away because she didn't want Blackie to know she was crying. He was no more than half an arm's length away, and yet it seemed as if the gulf between them was as wide and deep as the Grand Canyon—and just as impossible to cross.

He stirred beside her and her heart skipped a beat. If only he would take her in his arms and make everything right between them again. But he didn't reach for her, just turned on his side, putting his back toward her.

Pain filled her heart and knifed through her soul. Her tears came harder and faster, and try as she

319

might, she couldn't stifle the sob that rose in her throat.

Blackie immediately rolled over to face her. "Joey, what's wrong?"

"N . . . nothing," she said, sniffling.

He put his hand on her shoulder. "Honey, what's wrong?"

She was sobbing too hard to speak.

"Dammit, Joey . . ." Sitting up, he drew her into his arms. He smoothed back her hair, wiped the tears from her cheeks. "Honey, please don't cry."

"You hate me!"

"Hate you? What are talking about?"

"You've been angry with me ever since . . . since you . . . you killed Caffrey and . . . and the other men."

"Joey, honey, I'm not angry with you. Why would you think that?"

"Because . . . oh, Blackie, you looked so . . . so fierce, and I was so afraid. And I know you wanted to"—she swallowed the bile that rose in her throat—"to scalp him, and you couldn't because I was there . . ."

"Shh." He covered her mouth with his hand. "I'm sorry if I frightened you. As for scalping Caffrey, it's true, I thought about it. Maybe I would have if I'd been alone; I don't know. Dammit, Joey, those men kidnapped you. They might have . . ." He took a deep breath. "They might have killed you, or worse. I'm just sorry I could only kill them once. But, honey, I was never mad at you. I thought—hell, I thought you were having second thoughts about marrying me."

"No." All her doubts and fears seemed foolish

now. Blackie loved her. How could she ever have doubted it? He had put his life in danger to rescue her.

"I'm sorry I frightened you."

"It was silly of me."

He hugged her close, his lips moving in her hair. "I love you, Joey, more than my own life."

"Oh, Blackie, I love you so much!"

He kissed her then. He had meant it to be no more than a sign of his affection, but one taste of her lips brought his desire to full flame. The uncertainty of the last few days, the fear that he had lost her forever, the knowledge that it could have been he lying in the dirt instead of Caffrey made him cling to Joey with a fierce possessiveness he had never known before.

He lowered her to the ground, worshiping her with his hands and his lips, whispering that he loved her, would always love her. And every kiss, every caress, was an affirmation of life.

They slept late and made love again upon waking. Joey was hesitant at first. After all, it was daylight and they were out in the open, but Blackie quickly kissed away her doubts. There was something deeply primal about making love outside, with the sun shining brightly overhead and the sound of birds singing in the trees.

Had Eve felt like this in the Garden of Eden? Had Adam been as handsome as Blackie, as gentle, as tender? Had the grass smelled as sweet, the sky been as blue?

She moaned with pleasure as Blackie caressed her, arousing her until she was beyond caring, beyond thinking of anything but this moment, this man.

She cried his name as satisfaction exploded through her like rays of summer sunshine, warming her from the inside out.

Later, after washing up in the stream, Joey prepared something to eat while Blackie looked after the horses.

They had just sat down to breakfast when Shadow and Hawk rode into view.

Joey stared at Blackie's father and brother, then looked at Blackie as a wave of heat flooded her cheeks. Thirty minutes earlier and his family would have gotten an eyeful!

"*Hau naha*," Shadow said, dismounting.

"*Neyho*, Hawk, what are you doing here?"

Hawk swung down from his horse. "We thought you might need some help, but it looks like we could have stayed home." He sat down next to Blackie. "Got any coffee left?"

"Yeah, I think so." Lifting the pot from the coals, Blackie refilled his cup and passed it to Hawk.

Shadow hunkered down next to Hawk.

Joey felt her cheeks flame anew under Shadow's regard. She ran a hand over her hair, smoothed a wrinkle in her badly rumpled skirt. She told herself he couldn't possibly know what she and Blackie had been doing just a short time ago, but she had a feeling that he knew only too well.

Shadow reached out and touched the side of Blackie's head with his fingertips.

Blackie flinched and pulled away. "Hey, that hurts."

"Who did this?"

"Caffrey. If it wasn't for Joey, I'd likely be dead."

Shadow and Hawk both looked over at Joey and then back at Blackie.

"She thought she'd killed him. So did I. Turned out we were wrong. They came up on us night before last and I got in a couple of lucky shots."

"We saw the bodies," Hawk said. "That was some good shootin'."

Blackie shook his head. "Just luck," he said again. "And a lot of it."

"And a good woman," Shadow remarked.

Blackie took a deep breath. "She is that. I've asked her to marry me."

"And she said yes."

Blackie stared at his father. "How do you know that?"

"Your mother told me."

Of course, Blackie thought. His parents had no secrets from one another.

"Have you set the date yet?" Hawk asked.

Blackie looked at Joey. "Not yet. But it'll be soon, I can tell you that."

A rare smile curved Shadow's mouth as he leaned forward and took both of Joey's hands in his. "Welcome, *na-htona*. From this day forward, you will be blood of our blood. Anyone who harms you, harms us all."

"Thank you."

Hawk leaned over and kissed her soundly on the cheek. "I hope you'll be happy, Joey. If Blackie gives you a bad time, you let me know. I can still box his ears."

"You can try!" Blackie retorted, grinning.

Shadow snorted. "If you need help, *na-htona*,

come and see me. I can still whip them both."

She didn't doubt it for a minute. "Thank you, Mister . . . ah, Shadow."

"*Neyho*," he said.

"*Neyho*," she repeated. "What does *na-htona* mean?"

"It means 'my daughter' in Cheyenne," Blackie explained.

Love and acceptance filled Joey's heart and spilled over in the tears that trickled down her cheeks. And then she looked at Hawk. "Did you find Charlie?"

Hawk glanced at his father. "Yeah, we found him."

"Is he all right?" She glanced at Shadow, then looked back at Hawk. "He's not hurt, is he?"

Hawk cleared his throat. "No, he's not hurt."

"You didn't arrest him?"

"No."

"Where is he?"

Hawk hesitated a moment, but there was no way to soften the blow. "He's dead, Joey. Caffrey killed him. We found his body up in the mountains."

"No." She shook her head. "No. No—" She stared at Hawk, tears of grief stinging her eyes. "I don't believe you."

"I'm sorry," Hawk said.

"No." She stumbled toward Blackie. He caught her in his arms and held her while she cried. Sobs wracked her body. He would have given his right arm to bring her brother back, would have done anything in his power to ease her pain. But there was nothing he could say or do now, nothing but hold her.

It wasn't enough.

Chapter Thirty-three

I was sitting on the front porch of Mary's house, watching Adam and Joel playing kick the can in the yard. As much as I enjoyed staying with Mary and my grandchildren, there hadn't been an hour when worry for my men wasn't uppermost in my mind.

Victoria had stopped by the day before, and the three of us had spent a pleasant afternoon together. We had sat under a tree in the backyard, watching the children play, careful not to say anything that would upset the kids who were old enough to understand that Shadow, Hawk, and Blackie were in danger. But I had seen the knowledge reflected in Mary's eyes, and in Victoria's as well.

The one bright spot was that Blue Hawk was recovering rapidly. I knew he would have been bored at home, being forced to stay in bed for so long, but here, in Mary's house, he never had time to be bored. One or another of Mary's boys was always there to keep him company.

Still, as much as I enjoyed spending time with Mary and Cloud Walker and their children, I missed my own home. And I missed Shadow.

I closed my eyes, praying he would return soon, and when I opened them again, he was turning down the tree-lined path that led up to the house. Joy and thanksgiving welled within my heart. He was home. He was safe.

I fairly flew out of the chair and down the porch steps. And then he was stepping out of the saddle and running to meet me, sweeping me into his arms, swinging me round and round. There had been many changes in our lives over the years— wars had been won and lost, loved ones had been taken from us, our children had grown, married, and had children of their own. But two things had not changed, and that was my love for this man and the way my heart leapt within my breast whenever he was near.

He hugged me to him, and for that one moment, nothing else mattered except that he was home again, where he belonged. Gradually, I became aware that Blackie and Joey were watching us. Blackie looked faintly amused, the way our kids always did when they saw their mother and father embracing. I couldn't help thinking they should have been used to it by now. There was a deep sadness in Joey's eyes that told me that she knew her brother was dead. I knew what it was like to lose a loved one and my heart went out to her. Only time would ease the pain.

"Where's Hawk?" I asked.

"He went back for Charlie's body. Come," Shadow said. "Let us go home."

"All right," I said. "Why don't you hitch the team to the wagon while I get Blue Hawk and tell Mary we're leaving?"

It was good to be home again. I took Blue Hawk and Joey into the house while Shadow and Blackie put the horses away, and took a look around to make sure everything was all right. On the ride home, Shadow had told me about Caffrey and his men, and how Blackie had killed them. I could summon little regret that Caffrey and the others were dead and my son alive. Still, it was hard for me to imagine Blackie taking a life, any life. He had always been a healer.

I settled Blue Hawk on the sofa with a tablet and a pencil and then went into the kitchen to put some coffee on. Joey trailed behind me like a lost lamb, the haunting sadness in her eyes tugging at my heart.

"Is there anything I can do?" she asked.

"The cups are in that cupboard," I said, thinking that having something to do, however mundane, might take her mind off Charlie, at least momentarily.

I put on the coffeepot. The milk in the icebox had spoiled in our absence. I wondered if we would ever get electricity here in the valley. I had seen the wonders of electricity when we visited Blackie in the East and longed for the day when I could get rid of our old icebox and buy a refrigerator like the one I had seen in the Sears, Roebuck catalog. And an electric Singer sewing machine. It would be wonderful to have electric lights in the house, and out in the barn on those cold winter nights. With electricity, we would be like any other modern city, I thought, with streetlights and telephones. It would be nice to have those things and yet, in a way, I hated to think of the changes they would bring to our way of life.

"Sit down, Joey," I said. "Make yourself at home."

"Home," she said dully. "I should have had Blackie take me home. Grams must be worried sick." She picked up a fork and turned it over in her hand, staring at it as if she had never seen one before. "Charlie was a good boy. He was going to settle down. He asked me to talk to Mr. Feehan about giving him a job—" She dropped the fork back on the table. "My job," she said. "I forgot all about it."

"Don't worry about it, Joey. I'm sure Mike will understand when you tell him what happened."

"It doesn't matter now." The words, *nothing matters now*, hung unspoken in the air. I couldn't blame her for feeling that way, but it would pass. She was young and strong and would get past the despair that was weighing her down.

Blackie and Shadow came in a few minutes later. Joey rose and went straight into Blackie's arms. "I need to go home." Her gaze searched his. "Does Grams know about . . . about Charlie?"

"Yes. Hawk asked Mrs. Bradshaw to stay with her."

"Can we go now?"

"Sure, darlin'."

Blackie cast a worried glance at Joey as he drove her to her grandmother's house. She hadn't stopped crying since they'd left the house. How could such a small girl hold so many tears? He tried to think of something he could say to her, some comfort he could offer, but nothing came to mind. In lieu of words, he slid closer to her, put his arm around her shoulders, and gave her a squeeze.

"It's all my fault," she murmured. "I should have been firmer with him. I should have . . ."

"Done what? He was old enough to know what he was doing."

"He was only seventeen."

"Joey, I know you loved him, but you can't keep blaming yourself for what he did."

"You don't understand—"

"I understand that he was old enough to know right from wrong. He let you work while he spent his time hanging around in saloons with men who were no better than they ought to be, and—" He took a deep breath. What the devil was he doing? She was grieving for her brother. Instead of comforting her, his verbal attack on Charlie was only making her feel worse. "I'm sorry, Joey."

"No," she said in a small voice. "You're right. About everything. But he was going to change; I know it. He wanted me to ask Mr. Feehan about a job." She sniffed. "I know—" She put her hand over her heart. "I know in here that he was going to try to do better. I know it."

They arrived at the McBride house a short time

later. Blackie reined the team to a halt. "Do you want me to come in with you?"

Joey hesitated and then nodded.

Somewhat surprised, Blackie wrapped the reins around the brake, then swung down to help Joey to the ground. Taking her hand in his, he gave it a squeeze, and then they went up the stairs.

Joey took a deep breath, then opened the door.

Blackie followed her inside. The first thing he noticed was that all the blinds were drawn and that the house smelled musty.

"Grams must be in her room," Joey said.

"I'll wait for you out here," Blackie said.

"All right. Why don't you raise the blinds and open the windows? The place could use a good airing out."

Squaring her shoulders, Joey walked down the hall to her grandmother's room. The door was open. The blinds were drawn in this room too.

"Grams?"

"She's asleep, dear."

"Oh, Mrs. Bradshaw, I didn't see you there. Thank you for staying with her."

"I was glad to do it. Amelia and Ester and I have been taking turns."

Joey walked closer to her grandmother's bed and looked down at her. Grams looked old, Joey thought, old and worn-out.

"I was sorry to hear about your brother," Mrs. Bradshaw remarked.

"Thank you."

"Maureen took it hard. Where've you been, dear? Your grandmother's been worried sick about you."

"It's a long story. I really don't feel like going into it now."

Mrs. Bradshaw nodded, a speculative look in her eyes. "I understand," she said, but Joey could tell by the tone of her voice that she was eager to know more.

"Well, I'd best be going," Leona Bradshaw said, rising. "Mr. Macklin at the pharmacy sent a tonic over for your grandmother. She's to take it twice a day. It makes her sleep quite a lot, but he said that would be good for her right now. I'll look in on her tomorrow. If you need anything, just let me know."

"Thank you, I will."

Joey followed Mrs. Bradshaw down the hall to the front door.

Blackie had raised the blinds and opened all the windows. Mrs. Bradshaw paused when she saw him standing near the fireplace.

"Mr. Kincaid."

"Ma'am."

Mrs. Bradshaw looked at Joey, her eyebrows raised in silent speculation, and then left the house.

Joey grimaced. "By tonight, it'll be all over town that I brought you home."

"Do you want me to leave?"

"No." She walked around the room, straightening a limp doily on the arm of a faded, overstuffed chair, fluffing a pillow on the sofa. "This place looks like a dump compared to your house."

Blackie shrugged. "We can buy some new furniture if you like."

She looked at him askance.

He sat down on the sofa and patted the cushion beside him. "Come here."

331

She did as he asked.

He leaned back against the couch, one arm stretched over the back, the other loosely draped around her shoulders. "I've been doing some thinking. I know I asked you if you wanted to build a place of our own, but on second thought, it doesn't seem practical right now. I figure we have four choices. We can live with my folks. We can live in the lodge out back. We can stay at my office—"

He shrugged when she made a face at him.

"Or we can stay here so you can look after your grandmother. I'm not sure she'll be happy about having me here, but—" He shrugged. "What do you think?"

"I think you're the sweetest, most wonderful man in the whole world."

He frowned at her. "What brought that on?"

She made a broad gesture that encompassed the house. "I don't know any other man who would be willing to move in here."

"Darlin', I don't care where we live as long as we're together. Your grandmother needs you, and so do I. Staying here seems like the easiest way for you to keep the two of us happy."

She nodded, her eyes filling with a sudden sadness. He knew she was thinking about Charlie again. Time, he thought, time was the only thing that could heal the hurt.

He tightened his arm around her, hoping his nearness would comfort her.

Joey closed her eyes and leaned into Blackie, finding solace in his presence. All the tears in the world wouldn't bring Charlie back, but she couldn't seem to stop crying. First her mother had run off, then her father had died, and now Charlie. Was she wrong to love Blackie? Would she lose him too?

She was half-asleep when the sound of a bell ringing roused her.

"I'd better go see what she wants," Joey said, rising.

"Call if you need me."

Nodding, she left the room.

Blackie sat there a moment, then stood and walked around the room. The throw rugs on the floor were faded and frayed, the sofa and chair were badly worn, the curtains at the window were faded, but everything was clean. The tables, though scratched and scarred, shone with a coat of wax.

Moving into the kitchen, he went through the cupboards. As he'd suspected, there wasn't much in the way of food: a couple of cans of vegetables, a container of flour that was almost empty, a box of crackers, half a loaf of bread, a jar of strawberry jam.

Walking down the hall, he found Mrs. McBride's bedroom. The old lady was sitting up in bed, bolstered by a couple of pillows. She frowned when she saw him in the doorway.

" 'Afternoon, Mrs. McBride," he said.

She glared at him in reply.

Blackie looked at Joey, wondering how she had managed to live with her grandmother for so long. He didn't think he had ever seen the old lady smile.

"I'm going into town," he said. "Do you need anything?"

Joey shook her head.

He hesitated, wondering if he dared kiss her

good-bye in front of the old woman, and decided against it. "I won't be long."

He left the room, aware of Maureen McBride's gaze burning into his back.

He went to Feehan's for supplies. He found Mike in the back room.

"Blackie!" the big man said. "We heard you'd had some trouble. Hell of a thing, Charlie getting hisself killed like that. How's Joey taking it?"

"About as well as can be expected."

"Why would anyone want to kill Charlie?"

"He was mixed up with a rough bunch. They're the ones who kidnaped Joey."

"Bastards." Big Mike shook his head. "But that doesn't explain why they kidnaped Joey."

"It's a long story, but it's over now. I need to buy some groceries."

"Sure, sure." Big Mike gestured for him to go out into the other room. "What can I get for you?"

Blackie reeled off a list of fresh and canned goods.

"Want me to put these on your father's account?"

"No, put them on mine."

"Yours?" Big Mike lifted a skeptical brow.

"Joey and I are engaged. I'll be looking out for her and her grandmother from now on."

"Engaged!" Big Mike exclaimed, and then he chuckled. "Well, congratulations, son. She's a fine girl. I guess that means she won't be working here anymore."

"That'll be up to her, I reckon, but she won't be coming back right away. Her grandmother's feeling a little under the weather."

334

"Bad luck seems to dog that family," Big Mike remarked. He totaled the supplies and put them in a couple of string bags. "Need any help with those?"

"No, thanks, I can manage."

"Give Joey my best. Tell her that her job's here waiting for her if she wants it."

"Thanks, Mr. Feehan."

Taking a bag in each hand, Blackie left the store. He hung the bags over the saddle horn, made quick stops at the meat market and the candy shop, then swung onto his horse's back and rode to Joey's house.

Joey stared at the groceries spread out on the table. It was the most food she had ever seen in the house at one time. Fresh apples, carrots, lettuce, potatoes, onions, flour, sugar, a package of steaks and another of pork chops, a good quantity of canned stuffs. And a sack of saltwater taffy.

"Blackie, you shouldn't have . . ."

"Why not?" He stood with one hip braced against the kitchen counter. "I've got a big appetite."

She held up the sack of candy. "And a sweet tooth?"

"That too."

Blackie sat at the table, watching her put the groceries away. When she was finished, he took her by the hand. "Come on, let's go for a walk."

She didn't argue, but let him lead her outside.

They walked along a narrow dirt path that wove in and out of a stand of young cottonwoods. Beyond the town, the land spread out in gently rolling hills peppered by stands of timber. Overhead, the sky seemed to stretch away into forever. He loved this land, he thought. It was one of the things he had missed the most when he had been away, the sense of openness, of space, that surrounded them now.

He glanced at Joey, worried by the hollows in her cheeks, the shadows under her eyes.

They walked for about half an hour before Joey turned back toward home. "I need to fix dinner," she said. "Grams is used to eating at six. You must be hungry too."

"I could eat something. It'll give me a chance to find out if you can cook anything besides fried chicken."

She smiled faintly.

"We should probably tell your grandmother we're engaged."

Joey nodded. Putting it off wouldn't make it any easier. But she wasn't looking forward to it, or the explosion that was sure to follow.

Chapter Thirty-four

To say Maureen McBride was unhappy when she found out that her granddaughter planned to marry one of the Kincaid men had to be the understatement of the century. For a minute there, Blackie had been afraid the old lady was going to have a fit of apoplexy. And when she learned that Blackie was planning to stay in her house for a few days, he was sure of it. The old lady's face turned red with outrage at the thought of an Indian sleeping under her roof. In the end, Joey had had to give the old woman something to calm her. Once her grandmother was asleep, Joey went into the parlor to sit with Blackie.

"Well," he said with a wry grin, "that went well."

"She'll get used to the idea."

"I doubt it." He slipped his arm around her shoulders. "You really are a good cook."

She blushed prettily. "Thank you, but it wasn't anything special. Just steak and fried potatoes."

"My favorite."

"I'll remember that. What else do you like?"

"Ham and eggs. Flapjacks smothered in butter and syrup. Fresh baked bread. Roast beef." He ran his fingertips up and down her arm. "Your kisses for dessert."

She looked at him and smiled, a soft sultry smile. "Are you ready for dessert?"

The throaty sound of her voice, the look in her eyes, sent a flood of heat to his groin. "Oh, yeah," he said, his own voice husky. "I'm more than ready, darlin'."

Her smile widened. "Do you want to eat in bed?"

"You must be readin' my mind." Rising, he scooped her up into his arms. "Which way?"

"Across from Grams's room."

He carried her down the hall and into the room on the right. After nudging the door closed with his foot, he let her slide down his body to stand on her own two feet.

"I'll get the light," she said.

He heard her move across the floor. A moment later, there was the smell of sulfur, and then a soft golden glow lit the room.

Blackie glanced around. It was a small room. A narrow bed was situated against one wall. A plain white bowl and pitcher stood atop a four-drawer chest. There were a couple of hooks for her clothes. A sheet hung over a rope, dividing the room. Crossing the floor, Blackie peered over the top of the flimsy makeshift wall and saw another narrow bed and chest of drawers.

"Charlie sleeps . . . slept there."

Blackie turned around to face her. "Joey—"

"Don't," she said, her voice thick. "Don't say anything." She looked at him through tormented eyes. "How could I have forgotten?"

She was on the verge of tears. Murmuring her name, he gathered her into his arms.

He wanted to apologize to her. He couldn't shake off the feeling that it was his fault that her brother was dead. Charlie would still be alive if Blackie hadn't gone into O'Toole's that day. He wanted to tell her that he was sorry, and yet, dammit, it wasn't his fault. It was Charlie's fault for hanging around with a bunch of no-account drifters.

Walking backward, Blackie sat down on the edge of the bed and pulled Joey onto his lap. She curled up in his arms, weeping softly.

Blackie searched his mind for something to say, but nothing came to mind, and in the end, he just held her close, lightly stroking her back and her hair, until, with a sigh, she fell asleep.

And still he held her. She felt good in his arms, soft and warm. And trusting.

He lost track of time as he sat there, holding her. He would have been content to hold her until morning if Maureen's bell hadn't called him away.

Joey didn't stir as he tucked her under the covers. Bending down, he brushed a kiss across her cheek.

Then, steeling himself to face the old woman, he went across the hall to see what she wanted.

Maureen McBride's eyes widened in astonishment when he entered the room, then narrowed with hatred.

"You!" she hissed. "How dare you come into my room! Where's Joey? What have you done to her?"

"She's getting some much-needed sleep. What do you want?"

"I need some water to take my medicine."

Blackie glanced at the pitcher on the table beside her bed.

"It's empty," she said plaintively.

"I'll fill it for you."

"I want Joey . . ."

"I told you, Joey's asleep."

"I don't want you in my house," Maureen said, her hands worrying the bedclothes.

"And I don't want to be here, but if I go, I'm taking Joey with me. It's up to you." He picked up the pitcher. "I'll be right back with your water."

He could feel Maureen's gaze burning into his back as he left the room. With a shake of his head, he went into the kitchen. His staying here was never going to work. The old woman had been nursing her hatred for Indians for more than thirty years. He doubted if there was anything he could do to change her opinion, either of him or of Indians in general.

He filled the pitcher, took a clean glass from the cupboard, and returned to her room.

She looked suspicious when he offered her a glass of water. "Probably poisoned," she muttered.

With a shake of his head, Blackie put the glass and the pitcher on the table. "Then don't drink it," he retorted, and left the room.

Joey was sleeping soundly. After removing his

boots, trousers, and shirt, he slid into the narrow bed. She made a soft sound in her throat as he drew her into his arms.

Blackie kissed the top of her head. He could put up with the old woman, he thought, as long as he could end each day with Joey in his arms.

They held Charlie's funeral two days after Hawk returned with the body. Not surprisingly, there was quite a crowd at the church. Of course, by then the story of how Charlie had been killed had spread throughout town, along with how Joey had been kidnaped and Blackie had gone off to rescue her. The women in town looked at him as if he was some kind of knight in shining armor; men slapped him on the back and offered to buy him drinks. Old Oscar Tewksbury gave him a free shave and a haircut and doused him with some of his special sandalwood cologne.

The next couple of days passed peacefully. Blackie opened his office and was pleased and a little surprised when the townspeople and the ranchers sought his help. He treated Joe Dawson's milk cow for a swollen udder, helped Ned Donnelly's hunting dog with a difficult birth.

A week after the funeral, Joey asked Blackie to take her out to the cemetery.

It was a pretty place, located about two miles east of town and surrounded by a white picket fence.

Blackie parked the buggy near the gate, wrapped the lines around the brake handle, and swung down to the ground. He lifted Joey from the seat and then, hand in hand, they went inside.

A plain white headstone marked Charlie's final

resting place. Maureen hadn't skimped on the stone, or the engraving.

Charles Ira McBride
Beloved Son and Brother
Born March 3, 1891
Died July 7, 1908
He Will Be Missed in This Life
And Welcomed in the Next

Kneeling beside the grave, Joey removed the wilted bouquet of yellow daisies from the container and replaced it with the flowers she had brought.

Blackie stood across from her, his heart aching for the pain he saw in her eyes.

She sat there for a long time, her head bowed.

Blackie waited patiently. In the old days, his people had slashed their flesh to show their grief. He knew the whites thought such a practice barbaric, but he understood it. It was an outward sign of an inward grief, causing pain to the flesh in the hope of easing the pain of the heart.

After a time, she wiped away her tears, and Blackie helped her to her feet.

"We'd better get home," Joey said. "I should probably go talk to Mr. Feehan."

"Do you want to go back to work?" He held open the gate for her and followed her out.

She glanced at him over her shoulder. "What choice do I have? I have to take care of Grams."

Blackie lifted her into the buggy, then swung up beside her. "I think you should stay home." Taking up the reins, he clucked to the horse. "Your grandmother needs someone there to look after her."

"But . . . how can I afford that?"

"I think we can manage. I know you're still mourning your brother, but I can't go on living at your place, unless you're my wife. People are starting to talk. What would you think about getting married right away?"

If they got married so soon, she knew people would talk about that too, but she didn't care. Waiting wouldn't bring Charlie back. Marrying Blackie now didn't mean she hadn't loved her brother, or that she mourned him any the less.

She hesitated only a moment before saying, "I think it's a wonderful idea."

Chapter Thirty-five

My son was getting married. They had set the date for August 25. After all the worries and sadness of the past few weeks, it was good to have something pleasant and life-affirming to look forward to. I had to admit I was surprised that Joey was ready to move forward so soon. I knew it wasn't easy for her, and yet, in spite of the fact that her brother had passed away so recently, I thought the marriage would do both of our families a world of good.

I was pleased beyond measure when Joey asked me to help her pick out her gown. We took the train to Steel's Crossing and spent the day shopping. The dress she decided on was simple yet elegant. Mary and Victoria offered to pitch in and help with the food. Hawk and Shadow spent a couple of days over at the McBrides', helping Blackie make some much-needed repairs and generally sprucing up the place, even going so far as to give the place a fresh coat of paint and putting in a new front window.

Instead of being grateful, Shadow told me that Maureen McBride complained about the inconvenience and noise the whole time they were there. She was a stubborn, argumentative, bitter woman. I had to admire my son for agreeing to live there after the wedding so that Joey could care for her grandmother. I wasn't sure I could have put up with that vindictive old woman.

Joey came to dinner almost every night, and as I got to know her better, I grew to love her. She was a sweet girl, eager to help, eager to please. And so eager to be a part of our family. I was proud of my children and my grandchildren as they opened their arms to Joey and made her welcome.

It did my heart good to see Blackie and Joey together. Any qualms I might have had about the two of them were quickly laid to rest. Though they hadn't known each other very long, it was easy to see that the love they shared ran deep, that they would be good for one another in the years to come.

Blackie's practice was going well. Any fears he'd had about making a go of it proved to be unfounded. Most everyone in town kept animals of one kind or another: cattle, horses, sheep, goats, pigs, and chickens. And, of course, everyone had at least one dog and a couple of cats.

And now it was Sunday night. Our children had come for dinner and I had immersed myself in their presence, rejoicing in the merry laughter of my grandchildren, delighting in their hugs and kisses.

Joey and Blackie were never far apart, and I felt an aching tenderness as I watched them. New love was such a wondrous, fragile thing, filled with the joy of discovery, the excitement that was reserved for those who were newly and truly in love. Sometimes I missed the newness of it all, and yet I wouldn't change a minute of the time Shadow and I had spent together. The love we shared had grown and deepened into something far more lasting, far more satisfying. And far more rare.

After kissing my grandchildren one more time and bidding everyone good-night, I stood on the front porch, enjoying the beauty of the night as I counted my blessings. My children all lived nearby. Now that Blue Hawk was on the mend, we were all healthy. We had a comfortable home filled with peace and love.

Shadow found me there a few minutes later. His arm slipping around my shoulders was a welcome weight and I leaned against him, glad of his nearness.

After a while, I said, "They'll do well together, don't you think?"

Shadow nodded but said nothing.

I looked up at him. "Is something wrong?"

"No. Blackie has asked me to arrange for a medicine lodge before his marriage."

Even though I'd known that this was something our son yearned for, the fact that he had mentioned it to his father still caught me by surprise. "What did you say?"

"I told him I would do so."

"Do you think . . . ?" I bit off my words.

"Yes," Shadow said. "I think he is strong enough

to endure it. Tomorrow I will go to the reservation and find a shaman."

"Does Joey know?"

"He will tell her tonight."

Chapter Thirty-six

"I'll be glad when we're married," Blackie said. "I'm getting tired of having to go home after I kiss you good night."

Joey smiled up at him. "Just as long as you don't get tired of kissing me."

"That will never happen."

They were sitting on the new swing on Joey's front porch. With the help of his brother and father, the McBride place was no longer a rundown hovel. There was new glass in the windows. The front door had been replaced, the sagging steps repaired. They had torn down the old corral and built a new one.

Blackie had mentioned to his father that he was thinking of building a barn and the next thing he knew, his father, Hawk, Cloud Walker, Jed and Jed

Junior, Big Mike Fechan, Joe Finch, and Bobby Evans had the frame up. Tomorrow, they'd put the roof on.

The house sported a fresh coat of paint—white with bright yellow shutters. They had painted the inside of the house as well. His mother and sisters had made new curtains for the windows, scrubbed the floors, scoured the stove. It had taken a lot of hours and a lot of hard work, but it had been worth it. Blackie had the feeling that, in spite of all her complaining, Maureen was pleased with what had been done. And if she wasn't—well, that was too damn bad. As soon as he got a little money saved, he was going to buy a new sofa and a new table for the kitchen.

"You're awfully quiet tonight," Joey remarked.

"There's something I need to tell you."

"Oh? Is it good news?"

"I guess that depends."

"On what?" She poked him in the ribs. "Tell me."

"You remember I told you about the medicine lodge?"

"Yeah."

He took a deep breath. "I asked *neyho* to arrange one for me."

"Did he say he would?"

"Yes." He slid a glance at her, waiting for her reaction. Would she be shocked? Disapproving?

"Would you mind if . . . are women allowed to be there?"

"You want to watch?"

"If it's all right."

He hugged her close. "I'd like you to be there. And if it's too much for you, you don't have to stay."

She smiled up at him. "If you can endure the pain, I guess I can watch."

Two weeks later, all was in readiness. Shadow had found a shaman who was willing to do a modified version of the medicine lodge, as well as two men to beat the drum. In the old days, the medicine lodge had lasted eight days as the Cheyenne came together to celebrate and renew their acquaintances with the members of other bands. In the old days, for reasons I had never understood, the Cheyenne had moved their camp on each of the first four days.

The shaman, Rain Falcon, was an aged warrior with long gray braids. He was a man who remembered the old days and still practiced the old customs. In spite of his age, he stood straight and tall. Holding to ancient tradition, Blackie offered Rain Falcon a pipe filled with tobacco and then requested the old man's help. Rain Falcon accepted the pipe and smoked it, thus agreeing to instruct Blackie.

Rain Falcon then took up residence in our lodge out back, along with the other two warriors, and Blackie spent the next two days being instructed in how to behave and what to expect.

I knew, from talking to Shadow, that Rain Falcon would warn Blackie that what he was about to do held great significance, and that he should not undertake it without serious and careful consideration. He would also tell Blackie that to fail was no disgrace, and that he should not be ashamed if he lacked the strength to break free or the endurance to carry out the ordeal to the end.

350

The days that followed reminded me of the days we had spent preparing Hawk to participate in the medicine lodge. As we had then, we told no one of what we were planning. The medicine lodge was a sacred ritual, one few whites had ever been allowed to attend, one that few of them could understand or appreciate.

At the proper time, Shadow, who had been chosen as the scout, went in search of a cottonwood tree tall enough and straight enough to be used for the medicine lodge pole. He returned to tell us that the tree had been found, much as scouts in the old days had returned to camp to announce they had come upon an enemy.

The following day, the shaman painted the medicine lodge pole, and when that was done, cutouts of a male buffalo and an Indian warrior, both depicted with exaggerated male genitals, were placed in the fork of the tree.

Then Shadow, Cloud Dancer, Hawk, and Rain Falcon did a war dance around the medicine lodge pole.

I sat between Blue Hawk and Joey, with Mary and Victoria flanking us. The four of them were wide eyed as they watched. I saw the admiration in Blue Hawk's eyes, the looks of wonder on the faces of my daughters. I knew what they were feeling. Clad in clouts and moccasins, with feathers tied in their long black hair and paint on their chests and faces, the men in our family had shed the trappings and demeanor of civilization.

I watched Shadow dance, his muscles rippling in the sunlight, his dark eyes glowing and alive as he lost himself in the ancient steps of the dance. His movements were supple, intricate, and he was again Two Hawks Flying, warrior of the Cheyenne.

The next day, a little before dawn, we gathered at the medicine lodge pole again. Puffs of snow-white cloud drifted across the sky. The forest was quiet, subdued, as if all living things knew something special was about to take place.

Blackie stood near the medicine lodge pole, surrounded by Shadow, Hawk, and Cloud Walker. The men were clad in nothing but loincloths and moccasins. Eight long strips of rawhide hung from the top of the pole.

Rain Falcon stood a little apart. Lifting his arms overhead, he began to chant softly. He had a deep rich voice and as he sang, my mind filled with images of days gone by. Inside, I wept for all that had been forever lost. I grieved because my grandchildren would never see the great herds of buffalo that had once covered the prairie. They would never live inside a hide lodge, never know the wonder of riding across the plains in the midst of hundreds of Cheyenne men and women as they moved to a new camp.

Using red and black paint, Rain Falcon painted the face, chest, arms, and legs of each of the men. Each man had one distinctive drawing—Rain Falcon painted a red-tailed hawk on Shadow's left shoulder, a streak of yellow lightning on Cloud Walker's chest, a blue dragonfly on Hawk's right biceps, and a black otter on Blackie's right shoulder.

Each man was given an eagle bone whistle to blow on when the pain grew intense.

And then it was time for the piercing.

A sudden stillness, like the quiet inside a church, fell over us.

First Shadow. Then Cloud Walker. Then Hawk. They were taking part in the dance to support Blackie, to give him courage, to lessen his pain by sharing it.

And then Rain Falcon moved in front of Blackie.

I saw my son take a deep breath as the medicine man stopped in front of him. Rain Falcon had done this many times in the past and he moved quickly, efficiently. Pinching the flesh over Blackie's left breast, the shaman ran a knife through the skin and then inserted a thin wooden skewer into the opening. He repeated the procedure on the right side and then fastened the rawhide thongs to the skewers.

Joey looked over at me once, her eyes wide, her face pale, and then she stared at Blackie, her hands tightly clenched in her lap.

I wondered if Blackie had explained the meaning of the medicine lodge to her. I knew it was something only another Indian could fully understand. I knew warriors endured the pain for a number of reasons. Some danced to ensure the prosperity of their tribe, some in hope of obtaining a vision, some to obtain victory in battle.

My gaze moved to Shadow as the medicine man moved away from Blackie and the drumming began. Until then, I didn't realize how much I had missed that sound. Its beat was steady and strong, like the heartbeats of the men now dancing around the pole.

Forward and back, forward and back they danced, their bodies straining against the rawhide that connected them to the pole. Faces lifted to the sun, which drifted in and out of the clouds, they danced, and when the pain grew unbearable, they blew on the eagle bone whistles. The sound rose in the air, the notes high-pitched and plaintive, begging for strength, for courage.

As the morning wore on, the sun climbed higher in the sky. Sweat poured from the faces and bodies of the men as they shuffled back and forth. Blood trickled from the wounds in their chests, mingling with their sweat.

Blue Hawk clutched my hand. "Is it almost over, *nahkoa?*"

"Soon," I said, and hoped I was right.

The hours passed slowly. The dancers grew hungry, weary, and still they danced. And still they prayed.

Shadow's eyes met mine. I knew he was offering his pain to the Great Spirit on behalf of our family, that he was praying to *Maheo* to bless us, his loved ones, with health and happiness and wisdom, and I loved him all the more.

With a mighty lunge, Shadow broke free. He fell back, exhausted. Rain Falcon went to him, chanting softly as he washed the wounds in Shadow's flesh, then sprinkled them with sacred pollen and healing herbs. When that was done, he led Shadow over to a buffalo robe. Shadow sat down, and Rain Falcon offered him a drink of cool water.

Cloud Walker and Hawk broke free within moments of each other, and each was treated by Rain Falcon, then led over to the buffalo robe for nourishment and rest.

And then only Blackie remained. Head thrown

back, his body glistening with sweat, he danced around the pole until, at last, his flesh gave way and he was free. He staggered backward and might have fallen, but Shadow was there, one arm circling our son's shoulders, his dark eyes filled with love and pride.

Rain Falcon had erected a brush arbor, and now he took the men inside so that they could get cleaned up and dressed.

The drummers dismantled the medicine lodge pole and swept the area clean so that no one would know what we had done there.

We stayed where we were and waited for the men. Our voices were hushed when we spoke to one another.

I knew none of us would ever be the same again.

Blackie stood at the corral, idly scratching Raven's ears. It was almost dawn. He had been exhausted after the ordeal of the medicine lodge. He had slept for hours afterward and awakened famished.

Hawk, Victoria, Cloud Walker, and Mary had returned to their own homes. Hawk had dropped Joey off at her house. Blackie hadn't had a chance to talk to Joey. She had come up to him after the ceremony and kissed him, had sat beside him in the wagon on the way home, but they had said very little. What did she think of him now? He had felt her gaze on him while he danced. Her presence had made him strong, buoyed his courage when he faltered, eased his pain. She had watched him, her eyes wide, her hands clenched in her lap.

He stared into the distance, reliving every moment. The way his muscles had tensed when Rain

Falcon stood before him, knife in hand. The quick, painful thrust of the blade. The sense of unreality as he stood facing the medicine lodge pole, a long strip of rawhide, like an umbilical cord, connecting him to it.

At first, he had been aware of his father at his left, of Hawk at his right, but gradually, everything else had faded into the red haze of pain that had settled over him as he danced back and forth. Now and then he had rocked back hard on his heels, testing his strength, gritting his teeth as pain lanced through him. And when the pain was unbearable, he had blown on the eagle bone whistle, the high-pitched notes mirroring the pain in his body.

He had stared up at the sun, felt its heat engulf him, lost himself in its brilliant light. Sometimes he felt as if he were floating, weightless, mindless; sometimes his body felt alien, heavy, a shell he would gladly have shed, along with the pain that had accompanied every breath, every beat of his heart . . . every beat of the drum. The sound had risen up through the soles of his feet as he danced, surrounded him, engulfed him. His father had told him that the beat of the drum was the heartbeat of the people. He had believed it then; he knew it now.

"Pave-voona'o, naha." Good morning, my son.

Blackie glanced over his shoulder to see his father walking toward him.

" 'Morning, *neyho*."

"It is good to watch the rising of the sun."

Blackie nodded. In the east, the sky was turning light as a new day chased the night from the sky.

Shadow moved up beside his son. "Was it everything you hoped it would be?"

"Yes. And more."

Shadow rested his arms on the top rail of the corral. And waited.

"Did Rain Falcon tell you of my vision?"

"Only that you had one."

Blackie nodded. "I saw a mountain lion in my vision. He told me that I had the heart of a Cheyenne warrior."

"I have always known that," Shadow said quietly.

"He said that I was bound to the old ways by blood and by choice, and that I would know the same happiness as my father, so long as I followed the Life Path of the People."

"*E-peva'e.*" Shadow said. It is good.

Blackie drew a deep breath, let it out in a long sigh. It was good, he thought. And that said it all.

Chapter Thirty-seven

Joey woke with butterflies in her stomach. Today was her wedding day.

So much had happened in the last three weeks, but nothing had been as horrible, or as beautiful, as watching Blackie dance. She had known he was half Cheyenne, but that day, as she watched him stand there while the medicine man inserted skewers in his flesh, and later, as she watched him dance, his being Indian had taken on a whole new meaning.

That day, he had been wholly Indian, and though he spoke her language and dressed like the other men in town, he was not like other men and she would never think so again. She had watched him in awe, her stomach churning with horror and pride, as he danced back and forth trying to free himself from the medicine lodge pole.

She had been aware of his father and Hawk and Cloud Walker too, but it had been Blackie who'd held her gaze and her heart. The pain she had seen in his eyes and on his face had been her pain. She had listened to the voice of the drum, felt it creep into her very soul. It had spoken to something primal deep within her being, something she had never felt before.

And now she was going to be his wife.

She stood before the mirror in her bedroom. It was a new mirror, one Blackie had bought for her. He had given her a new home, a new life. And after today, she would be a part of him, a part of his life forever. She pressed a hand to her stomach, a smile hovering on her lips. She would tell their child about the medicine lodge when he was old enough to understand. She would tell him how she had sat with his Grandmother Kincaid and his Aunt Mary and Aunt Victoria and Blue Hawk. She would tell him how bravely his father had endured the medicine lodge, and how proud of him she had been.

She pinned her veil in place, then took a last look at her reflection in the mirror, wondering what Blackie would think when he saw her. The dress was made of white silk, with a modest neckline, long fitted sleeves, and a full skirt. It made her feel beautiful. Would Blackie think so too? Taking a deep breath, she left the room.

Hawk had come by earlier to take Grams to the church. He had kissed Joey's cheek and wished her well. Now, as she waited for Shadow to come and pick her up, she thought of her brother. If only Charlie could have been there to give her away.

Shadow arrived a few minutes later. Joey stared at Blackie's father, unable to believe her eyes. She had never seen him in anything but jeans and cowboy shirts; now he wore a crisp white shirt, a black suit, and a dark gray tie. And moccasins.

"Ready, *na-htona*?" he asked.

She nodded, pleased that he thought of her as his daughter.

"Then let us go. Blackie is waiting."

Joey's breath caught in her throat when she peeked into the chapel from the vestibule. The altar was decorated with bouquets of fresh flowers. Large white bows adorned the pews; a long white runner ran down the center aisle. Several large white wicker baskets filled with ferns and flowers had been placed on either side of the altar.

A moment later, Mary and Victoria entered the church, along with Amanda Marie, who was the flower girl, and Adam, who was the ring bearer. Mary's dress was pale blue, Victoria's lavender. They both wore flowers in their hair. Amanda wore a pink dress with a ruffled skirt and a white sash that tied in back with a big bow. She wore a white ribbon in her hair, and new patent leather shoes. Adam wore a blue suit, a white shirt, and a pair of new boots.

"Joey, you look beautiful," Mary said. "Just beautiful. I love that dress. And your veil . . . it's perfect."

"Are you ready?" Victoria asked. "Do you have everything? Something old?"

"My grandmother's comb," Joey said, lifting a hand to the tortoiseshell comb in her hair.

"Something new?" Mary asked.

Joey grinned. "Everything I'm wearing."

Mary and Victoria grinned at each other.

"Something borrowed?" Victoria went on.

"My hanky."

"Something blue?" Mary asked.

"My garter."

"Guess you're all set, then," Mary said. She gave Joey a hug. "I'm so happy you're going to be my sister."

"Thank you."

"Yes, indeed," Victoria said, kissing her on the cheek. "We needed another woman in the family."

"Amanda, come here," Mary said. "Your bow's coming undone. Remember to walk slowly. And don't giggle."

"Have you seen Blackie?" Joey asked.

"He's a nervous wreck," Mary said, grinning.

Joey could sympathize with that. Her stomach was in knots, her palms damp.

"But, oh, my," Mary said, rolling her eyes, "does that boy look handsome."

"Well," Victoria said as the organ began to play, "time to go." She smoothed a hand over her hair and straightened Adam's tie. "Remember, now," she warned, "don't run down the aisle."

"Are you sure you want to marry Blackie?" Mary asked with a teasing grin.

"Oh, yes, I'm sure," Joey said.

"Do not listen to her," Shadow said as he stepped into the vestibule. He looked at Mary, his dark eyes dancing. "She was always a naughty child."

Mary kissed her father on the cheek, then gave Joey's shoulder a squeeze as she went to stand behind Adam. "Here we go," she said cheerfully. "But don't say I didn't warn you."

Shadow placed Joey's hand on his arm and gave it a pat. "Soon you will truly be my daughter."

Joey smiled up at him, pleased beyond words that Blackie's family had made her feel welcomed, loved. Accepted.

The doors to the chapel opened.

Amanda went first, scattering rose petals.

Adam followed her.

Then Mary and Victoria.

The wedding guests rose to their feet as Joey started down the aisle. She saw Blackie's mother sitting in the front pew, surrounded by her grandchildren. Hannah smiled at her, a warm, friendly smile, so unlike the stern look of disapproval on Maureen's face. Joey glimpsed other familiar faces looking at her, smiling at her. Big Mike Feehan, Mr. and Mrs. Clancy, Jeremy Brown, Jed Crowley and his brood. Mary held the new baby in her arms.

But Joey had eyes only for Blackie. Clad in a black suit, white shirt, and black vest, a white flower in his lapel, he stood at the altar with Hawk, Cloud Walker, and Blue Hawk.

His gaze met and held hers as she walked down the aisle toward him, and then her hand was in his and they were facing the Reverend Dunford.

Blackie was certain she had never looked more lovely. She wore her hair down around her shoulders because he preferred it that way. Her hand trembled in his. Blackie was hardly aware of the words that were spoken until the reverend said, "Do you, Samuel Black Owl Kincaid, take Josephine Marie McBride, here present, to be your wedded wife . . ."

The rest passed in a blur as they exchanged their vows. He slipped his ring on her finger and then, at last, came the words, "You may kiss your bride."

His hands shook a little as he lifted her veil, and then he took her in his arms and kissed her. Both Hawk and Cloud Walker had warned him to keep it short, but once he had her in his arms, he didn't want to let go.

With her lips on his and her arms around him, he forgot about everything else until the sound of applause filled the chapel.

Feeling somewhat sheepish, Blackie stepped back.

Joey was blushing furiously, but she was smiling ear to ear.

"And now," the reverend said, "I present Bear Valley's newest couple, Mr. and Mrs. Blackie Kincaid. May God bless you and make you fruitful. Amen."

There was a party afterward, with music and dancing and enough food to feed the whole town.

Joey was overwhelmed by the attention, by the hugs and good wishes of people she hardly knew. A table near the door was piled high with presents.

She danced with Blackie, and with Hawk and Cloud Walker, with Shadow and even with Blue Hawk.

And then Blackie was leading her away from the others. When they were out of sight, he drew her into his arms and kissed her. "Are you ready to go?" he asked.

She nodded, eager to be alone with him.

"Good. Come on," he said, taking her hand. "The buggy's waiting out back."

*   *   *

They spent their wedding night in the bridal suite at the Cosmopolitan Hotel.

Joey had never been in a hotel before, and she looked around in awe as Blackie carried her over the threshold. The room was large, with an enormous brass bed. The walls were a muted shade of blue. A thick carpet muffled Blackie's footsteps as he carried her into the room and placed her on her feet.

Joey stood there, suddenly nervous. Everything had happened so fast. She had only known Blackie for a short time, but in some ways she felt as though she had known him her whole life.

He closed the door. She heard the click of the lock, and then he came up behind her, his arms slipping around her waist, his hands sliding up to cup her breasts as he leaned forward and kissed her cheek.

She turned in his arms, her hands pressed against his chest as she rose up on her tiptoes and kissed him. Excitement thrummed through her as the heat of his body penetrated her clothing. She could touch him, she thought, kiss him all night long, fall asleep in his arms.

His gaze moved over her, warm with love and desire. "You're beautiful," he murmured.

She flushed with pleasure. "So are you."

"Me?" He grinned at her. "Well, I'm glad you think so."

He bent his head, feathering kisses over her cheeks, her neck. Lifting her into his arms, he carried her to the bed and enfolded her in his embrace.

"I love you," he said. "I promise I'll do everything I can to make you happy."

"And I love you," she replied fervently, "with all my heart and soul."

"Show me," he whispered huskily.

They undressed each other with trembling, eager hands.

Blackie rained heated kisses over her back and shoulders, along her neck, behind her ear, and each kiss sent little frissons of pleasure rippling through her. In moments, she had no thought for anything except Blackie, the touch of his hands exploring her willing flesh, the heat of his mouth on hers, the quivering excitement in her belly as he rose over her.

Her body welcomed the weight of his, the sweet invasion of his flesh making her feel wonderfully whole, blissfully complete. Would it ever be so? she wondered. Would every time he made love to her be better than the last?

She reveled in his possession, exulted in being able to touch and stroke him in return, to fondle and caress him to her heart's delight. His body held endless fascination for her. It was so like her own and yet so very different. She delighted in learning the taste and the texture of him, in learning what made him laugh and what made him groan with pleasure. She had never imagined that making love could be like this, wild and wonderful, filled with magic and mystery and laughter. No wonder people wrote stories and poetry and songs about falling in love.

Her heart was singing now.

Epilogue

I sat on the front porch, watching Blue Hawk put the little Appaloosa filly through her paces. Both the filly and my son had recovered from the fire with only a few scars to show for what they had been through.

They were both strong, I thought, and they both owed that strength to good sires and good bloodlines.

Life had returned to normal. A new barn stood in place of the old one. Cattle grazed on the hillside. Our dog Storm lay stretched out in the shade whining softly, his back legs twitching in his sleep. A new litter of kittens scampered across the yard, while the mother cat lay in the sun, lazily cleaning her whiskers. Chickens scratched in the dirt near the barn. Somewhere in the distance, a calf bawled for its mother. A faint breeze stirred the tall grass.

My gaze moved to Shadow, who was sitting on the top rail of the corral, a broad smile on his face as he watched our son.

Tomorrow was Sunday, and I was looking forward to having my children to dinner. I was especially anxious to see the newest addition to our family. Little Sam was already two months old. Black-haired and brown-eyed, he had a dimple in his cheek and a smile to melt the heart of any grandmother. It made my heart swell to bursting whenever I saw Blackie playing with his son. Whatever doubts I'd had about Blackie and Joey had proven unfounded. They were blissfully happy together. Blackie's practice was going well, so well that some of the big ranchers from Steel's Crossing came to seek his advice and expertise.

Maureen McBride remained opposed to the marriage, but I had noticed signs that she was softening ever since Little Sam was born. She had even come out to the house to celebrate Blackie's birthday. I had bet Shadow five dollars that she would break down and buy Blackie a present next year. It was a bet I felt sure I would win.

Rising, I walked across the yard to the corral and climbed up on the rail beside Shadow.

He looked over at me and smiled. "No one rides like the Cheyenne," he said, an unmistakable note of pride in his voice.

"Yes," I said dryly. "I know."

Shadow put his arm around me and gave my shoulders a squeeze. "Perhaps we could go riding later."

He grinned at me, a wicked gleam in his dark

eyes, and I knew he wasn't talking about horseback riding.

I pretended to be shocked, but inwardly I felt a quick curl of desire unfold deep within me.

"It has been a good life, *na-htse'eme*," Shadow said, and then he pointed overhead. "Look!"

Shading my eyes against the sun, I followed Shadow's gaze and there, soaring with effortless grace, I saw two red-tailed hawks.

Shadow smiled as he watched his old friends drifting on the air currents. "A long life together and happiness for our children, Hannah," he murmured. "That was what they promised us."

And in my heart I knew it would always be so.

Hi—

I've been wanting to write another *Reckless* book for a long time, mainly so I could visit with Hannah and Shadow again (but mainly with Shadow). Of course, I love ALL my heroes, but some of them just seem to stay with me longer than others, and Shadow is one of them. Along the way, I fell in love with Blackie, and I hope you will too.

It was such fun, going back to Bear Valley and renewing old acquaintances. I hope you enjoyed the trip as much as I did.

One of the reasons I love being a writer is because of all the wonderfully supportive and creative people I've met along the way. Special thanks to Kim Ivora, who made the trip with me, to my critique group, who loved what they got to hear of the story before I turned it in, and to Mike, who made sense out of my nonsense and went crazy trying to figure out the time line.

God Bless America.

Madeline
DarkWritr@aol.com
www.amandaashley.net

RECKLESS HEART

MADELINE BAKER

They play together as children—the Indian lad and little Hannah Kincaid. Then Shadow and his people go away, and when he returns, it is as a handsome young Cheyenne brave. Hannah, now a beautiful young woman, has never forgotten her childhood friend—but the man who sweeps her into his powerful arms is no longer a child. He awakens in her a wild, erotic passion she has never known. But war is about to erupt in the Dakota Territory, a war that will pit the settlers against the Indians. Both Hannah and Shadow know that the time is coming when they will have to choose between happiness and hatred, between passion and duty, in a conflict that will test to the limit the steadfastness of their love. . . .

___4527-3 $5.99 US/$6.99 CAN

Dorchester Publishing Co., Inc.
P.O. Box 6640
Wayne, PA 19087-8640

Please add $1.75 for shipping and handling for the first book and $.50 for each book thereafter. NY, NYC, and PA residents, please add appropriate sales tax. No cash, stamps, or C.O.D.s. All orders shipped within 6 weeks via postal service book rate. Canadian orders require $2.00 extra postage and must be paid in U.S. dollars through a U.S. banking facility.

Name_____
Address_____
City_____State_____Zip_____
I have enclosed $_____ in payment for the checked book(s).
Payment <u>must</u> accompany all orders. ❑ Please send a free catalog.
CHECK OUT OUR WEBSITE! www.dorchesterpub.com

RECKLESS LOVE

MADELINE BAKER

RECKLESS DESIRE

MADELINE BAKER

**Winner Of The *Romantic Times*
Reviewers' Choice Award For Best Indian Series!**

Cloud Walker knows he has no right to love Mary, the daughter of the great Cheyenne warrior, Two Hawks Flying. Serenely beautiful, sweetly tempting, Mary is tied to a man who despises her for her Indian heritage. But that gives Cloud Walker no right to claim her soft lips, to brand her yearning body with his savage love. Yet try as he might, he finds it impossible to deny their passion, impossible to escape the scandal, the soaring ecstasy of their uncontrollable desire.

_3727-0 $4.99 US/$5.99 CAN

APACHE RUNAWAY

MADELINE BAKER

"Lovers of Indian romance have a special place on their bookshelves for Madeline Baker!"
—Romantic Times

Ruthless and cunning, Ryder Fallon can deal cards and death in the same breath. Yet when the Indians take him prisoner, he is in danger of being sent to the devil—until a green-eyed angel saves his life.

For two long years, Jenny Braedon has prayed for someone to rescue her from the heathen savages who enslaved her. And even if Ryder is a half-breed, she'll help him in exchange for her freedom. But unknown perils and desires await the determined beauty in his strong arms, sweeping them both from a world of tortured agony to love's sweet paradise.

___3742-4 $5.99 US/$6.99 CAN